"It sounds like one of our more powerful enemies," Wonder Woman mused.

Almost imperceptibly, Batman shook his head. "Not according to the computers. While individual events might point to particular supervillains, the overall pattern does not support that hypothesis."

"I'm sorry, but then, what hypothesis *does* it support?" Superman asked.

In reply, Batman nodded toward his own monitor, where the computer bank's conclusions were scrolling down the screen. *Unknown enemy. Unknown power source. Unknown motivation, though testing is indicated.*

"Testing?" Green Lantern frowned. "Testing *what*, exactly?"

"Us." Batman's tone seemed to drop even lower than normal. "Whatever our foe was, it targeted the five of us."

JUSTICE LEAGUE of AMERICA™
BATMAN®

THE STONE KING

ALAN GRANT

BATMAN CREATED BY BOB KANE

POCKET BOOKS
New York   London   Toronto   Sydney   Gotham City

This book is a work of fiction. Names, characters, places and incidents are products of the author's imagination or are used fictitiously. Any resemblance to actual events or locales or persons, living or dead, is entirely coincidental.

An *Original* Publication of POCKET BOOKS

POCKET BOOKS, a division of Simon & Schuster, Inc.
1230 Avenue of the Americas, New York, NY 10020

ISBN: 0-7434-1710-0

First Pocket Books printing March 2002

10 9 8 7 6 5

POCKET BOOKS and colophon are registered trademarks of Simon & Schuster, Inc.

For information regarding special discounts for bulk purchases, please contact Simon & Schuster Special Sales at 1-800-456-6798 or business@simonandschuster.com

www.dccomics.com
Keyword: DC Comics on AOL

Printed in the U.S.A.

for my granddaughter, Abby Rose

CHAPTER 1

The Mysterious Pyramid

Gotham County, September 23

"This is Anneka Marram, for GCTV, reporting live from the Gotham County Dam, where a disaster of unparalleled proportions is fast becoming reality!"

The television station's news helicopter circled in the evening air, as Chuck Gaines, the pilot, brought it another fifty feet closer to the top of the massive dam that lay below them.

Inside, the ride was remarkably smooth. Gaines was an Air Force veteran and had been piloting choppers for twenty-five years. He liked to keep his passengers happy.

Flicking a twist of her curly, honey-colored hair from her face, Anneka Marram craned to get a better view from the chopper's open observation window.

From their vantage point a hundred yards up, she could see the large crack that zigzagged down the concrete wall of the dam. Jets of water spurted through in a half dozen places, each one blasting a spray of fine debris out into the air with it. Surely it couldn't hold much longer. Two billion cubic yards of water were putting that crack under intolerable stress.

Anneka shook her head slightly, as if unwilling to entertain the thought of what might happen next. She leaned across the chopper's cramped cabin and touched Les Dowd, her cameraman, on the shoulder. He nodded without looking and started to pan his lens across the top of the dam.

Countless police cars and fire engines were parked at each end, looking like little more than toys from this height. Human figures stood in clusters close to the vehicles, monitoring the water that poured more forcibly from the dam's damaged area with every passing minute.

The mayor was at the scene, taking personal charge of the emergency. Commissioner James Gordon of the GCPD was on hand as well. There was little they could do but wait. All staff had already been evacuated. The relief sluices had been opened, carrying roaring torrents of water away from the eight-mile long lake that had been formed when the dam first closed off this stretch of the Gotham River.

But everyone who stood there—police officers, public officials, dam and hydroelectric personnel—all knew that it was futile. It might take an hour, it might be only a minute—but the dam *was* going to burst.

Dowd slowly raked his lens down the face of the massive concrete structure. On her monitor, Anneka saw the picture shift to follow the course of what had once been the mighty Gotham River. Its raging waters had flowed here for millennia, carving out a steep-sided gorge that was fifty feet deep and double that across. Now the river was little more than a stream meandering away from the dam, dwarfed by the bluffs on either side.

A quarter-mile downstream Anneka could see the hydroelectric station. A dozen figures straggled away from it, making for the high ground above the steep banks, abandoning the installation completely.

Anneka lifted her microphone closer to her lips to blot out the steady thrum of the rotors and began to speak: "The generating station is in the process of being evacuated now, and I'm informed by dam management that all personnel have been accounted for."

She paused as her monitor showed Dowd's camera panning down the valley toward distant Gotham City. "An estimated twenty thousand people live between the dam and the city. And although the authorities are doing their best to evacuate those at risk, there are serious fears that there are just too many people, and not enough time."

Pausing again, Anneka twisted her head to look back at the dam through the opposite window. The sun was starting to sink, casting a purple autumn glow over the wooded hills. But there was light enough for Anneka to see that the main crack had doubled in size, and several new, smaller ones in a spiderweb network were already gushing water.

A never-ending flood would wash away dozens of

farms and thousands of acres of fertile soil as it swept down to the ocean. Anneka shuddered to think what would happen when that wall of water and mud roared into Gotham City itself.

It's only a question of time, she thought, and, perversely, a surge of excitement coursed through her. She'd been junior reporter on the GCTV chopper for almost six years now, spending her life describing traffic jams and highway accidents. They'd been on their way to a three-vehicle pileup on the interstate this afternoon when the emergency call came in about the dam. Now she was reporting *real* news. And the station would be relaying her report not just across the state, but to the whole country. She'd be seen by a hundred million viewers. A billion, if it went global.

It might be a black day for Gotham City, but Anneka's career was going to skyrocket.

Anneka switched her mike off. "How does this sound, Les?" she asked the lensman. "We go down, hover in front of the dam for some close-up shots of those water jets. Then back up to five hundred feet, wait for the final collapse . . . and follow the wall of water all the way down the valley till it hits the city."

"Good thinking." The lanky cameraman nodded. Straight out of journalism school, he'd been with the station only a few months. But if they caught *this* on film, it would be Hollywood calling. "We better move it, though. Be dark in another half hour."

"Can we do it, Chuck?" Anneka called to the gruff, middle-aged pilot.

He shrugged his shoulders without turning to look

at her. "Strap in tight," he rasped, his voice hoarse
from a lifetime of cigarette smoking. "We're goin' for
the money shot!"

Chuck hit the controls and the chopper banked
steeply, turning back toward the dam, dropping as it
approached. Fifty feet from the valley floor, just level
with the top of the banks, Chuck leveled out, hovering
directly in front of the massive, cracking wall.

Les's camera raked up the face of the dam, visible only
through the thick curtain of water cascading from above.

Anneka felt another frisson of fear. Gazing up at the
rends in the dam, she could almost feel the relentless
pressure of countless tons of water that was fighting to
escape its confinement.

She switched her mike back on. "From above," she
began, "the debris that the torrents are tearing free
looked small and insignificant. From this vantage
point, however, we can see chunks of concrete the size
of cars! I'm no engineer, but I really don't see any way
the dam can hold much longer."

Somewhere above them the water tore a new hole in
the dam face, sending out a gusher that reached almost to the hovering chopper before it fell away.
Lumps of concrete and infill clattered off the fuselage.

"Goin' up," Chuck Gaines mouthed, pointing upward with one forefinger. Twenty-five years as a pilot
had thrown him into a whole host of dangerous situations, from blizzards to ice storms to rescues at sea. A
bursting dam was a new one for him—and not one he
chose to stay close to for too long. The helicopter
started to rise.

Fifty feet above, a section of dam the size of an SUV erupted under the force of the water behind. A fountain of broiling, muddy water shot out with all the power of a huge geyser. Almost instantly, the chopper was assailed by cascading water and concrete blocks. It pitched wildly from side to side as Chuck Gaines struggled for control, throwing Anneka and Les violently around the interior.

The cameraman's head hit an area of unpadded airframe, and he blanked out immediately. Anneka screamed, clinging onto her safety strap so tightly her knuckles were white.

"I can't hold her!" Chuck cried out, his voice barely audible over the chaos of the water. "Hang on! I'll try—"

He never finished the sentence. A rain of concrete chunks thudded into them from above. The windshield shattered, and there was a loud metallic shriek as one of the rotors snapped under the bombardment. The chopper pitched forward and started to plunge toward the growing maelstrom below.

Buffeted by the water pouring in, hardly able to breathe, Anneka Marram struggled in vain to undo the catch on the chopper door. The acrid smell of shorting electrical wiring stung her nostrils. Silently, she kissed her big break farewell. A hundred million people might well see her on the evening news that night, but it would be as a statistic on a long list of fatalities.

Abruptly, her panic ebbed away, and a strange sense of calm suffused her. Almost matter-of-factly, she contemplated her impending death.

But what, she wondered, was that red and blue blur streaking through the air?

Powering through the skies at more than a hundred miles an hour, Superman saw a flash as the setting sun reflected off the helicopter's fuselage. Instantly, his telescopic vision zoomed in on the plunging craft, revealing the three people inside.

Shifting the direction of his flight, he increased his speed until he was bulleting down toward the foot of the dam face. A two-hundred-pound concrete block struck him on the back, the debris splintering as it ricocheted off his near-invulnerable body.

At the last second Superman checked his forward motion, angling his body upward so he was directly under the tumbling helicopter. Ignoring the water and rubble that poured down around him, he reached up with both hands and braced himself to take the doomed chopper's weight.

Superman has the helicopter. J'onn J'onzz, the Martian Manhunter, watched from the riverbank as he relayed the telepathic message directly to the minds of the other Justice League members who were present. Telepathy was part of his Martian birthright, and now Manhunter used his amazing mental ability to coordinate and keep the team in touch while in action. *He's carrying it to safety now.*

The Justice League—the elite team of the Earth's mightiest super heroes—had been formed with the protection of the planet in mind. They sprang into action like a well-oiled machine whenever any disaster or superhuman villain was too much for one hero to handle alone.

Six of them had been in the Watchtower, their lunar headquarters, when the crisis broke. A message from the mysterious Oracle, who ran their vast computer network from her HQ in Gotham City, had filled their monitor screens. They hadn't needed Batman, Gotham's grim guardian, to urge them to teleport to the scene at once.

Now, perched atop a rocky crag overlooking the entire dam front, silhouetted against the September sky like some twilight demon, Batman took control.

He didn't particularly like using the telepathic link Manhunter established between the team members. A lifelong loner, Batman preferred to act with only one voice in his head: his own. But even he had to admit that the facility often came in useful.

Complete collapse could come at any second. Green Lantern, use your power ring to keep the dam standing. The thoughts blasted from Batman's mind with the speed and accuracy of bullets. *Manhunter, get those people on the dam edge to safety. Flash, go down the valley. Use your superspeed and warn everyone you can.*

Flash and Manhunter didn't pause to speak. One took to the air, the other started running, and both veered away to accomplish their tasks.

Protected by the force field generated by his power ring, Green Lantern hovered before the dam. With every second that passed, more of the concrete was disintegrating, allowing a deluge of water to escape. Lantern's right arm extended, the ring on his middle finger suddenly flaring bright green as he focused his willpower through it.

Instantaneously, a thin green beam emanated from the center of the ring, widening dramatically as it traveled toward the collapsing dam. It grew until it covered the entire dam face, shutting off the water spouts, holding back the collapsing concrete like a wall of shimmering, impenetrable green energy.

Green Lantern smiled wryly to himself. The ring had been the gift of an alien, the very last Guardian of the Universe. Kyle Rayner had never wanted to be a hero, never expected to be one—and would have run a mile if anyone had told him otherwise. But now he *was* a hero—and not just any hero, either. He was the Emerald Warrior, one of the most powerful super heroes of them all. The ring acted directly to achieve anything he willed. Kyle was sure it must have limitations, but he hadn't discovered them yet.

Gotta admit, Lantern thought, taking care to keep the sentiment to himself, *it's a kick I wouldn't change for the world.*

Superman deposited the chopper up on the lakeside, well away from the dam, staying only long enough to check that the occupants were safe before flying back to join his companions. *Wonder Woman and I will go in behind the energy wall.* His thoughts came through loud and clear to all of them. *We'll use high-speed friction and my heat vision to fuse the dam face.*

No! Batman's thought stabbed almost painfully into their minds. *We can't save the dam. Use your speed and strength to gouge out a channel deep enough to take the water all the way to Gotham harbor.*

Are you sure that's best? Superman queried.

Positive, Batman thought curtly. *Whatever we do, that dam is coming down—and time is running out.*

Batman blanked off his mind, shutting out any further protest Superman might make.

Of all the dozens of members of the Justice League, from the underwater monarch Aquaman to the mighty Steel, Batman was the least natural team player. His years of service as Gotham City's Dark Knight had turned him into the perfect lone hero. But often, in a team situation, he came across as arrogant and high-handed—especially when he insisted things be done exactly as he wanted, not caring if it rubbed his teammates the wrong way.

J'onn J'onzz glided down to join Batman on his crag, the red and green of the Martian's costume glinting in the fading sunlight. The whole dam had been cleared; Jim Gordon and the others now stood a good hundred yards back from any danger.

The two heroes watched in silence as Wonder Woman and Superman began their colossal task. Operating at superspeed, their movement so fast it was only a blur, they ripped into the valley bottom below the dam with their bare hands. Both possessed superstrength and invulnerability; their hands were superior to any tool.

Within seconds, the first fifty yards of a wide channel, thirty feet deep, had been scoured out, leaving massive piles of infill on the channel sides. It was like

watching a videotape in fast-forward, the duo working at such a rate that only the constantly growing lev-
ees were evidence of their presence.

And all the while, Green Lantern fixed his
willpower on the dam, vibrant green energy pouring
from his ring to hold back the waters of the man-made
lake.

At last, Manhunter spoke. "How do you know we
cannot save the dam?"

"Trust me," Batman replied, glad that his colleague
was using speech instead of telepathy. Though he
would never admit it to the others, hearing their
voices inside his head always unsettled him, made
him feel as if his mind was being probed—despite
knowing that Manhunter would never do such a
thing. "I've done the research."

They had a lot in common, these two, not least the
fact that both their backgrounds were shrouded in
grief and pain. As an eight-year-old child, Bruce
Wayne had watched his parents mercilessly gunned
down before his horrified eyes. That traumatic event
had changed his life forever, eventually leading him to
don the costume and mask of Gotham's most feared
crime fighter.

Similarly, J'onn J'onzz had watched helplessly as his
entire society died. An ancient way of life that had
lasted for millennia on the Red Planet had sunk into
terminal decay and decline. Nothing—and no one—
had survived except him. Like Batman, the pain of
what he had lost would be locked in his heart forever.

Manhunter threw his companion a sidelong glance.

"We all know you are not in the habit of making mistakes," he acknowledged. "But sometimes, we would appreciate being taken more fully into your confidence. After all, the Justice League *is* a team."

Batman nodded slightly to signify he understood. Having worked alone for so long, it was easy to forget how sensitive teamwork could be.

Evacuation complete! They heard the thought an instant before they saw the red streak that told them the Flash was returning from his duties.

Wally West had been doused in a mysterious chemical formula that changed the entire molecular structure of his body, giving him the ability to move thousands of times faster than normal. Only he could have covered the dozens of square miles in the valley in little more than minutes.

I even had time to move all the livestock! The very air seemed to ripple as Flash slowed from superspeed to zero, drawing to a halt alongside the duo on the crag.

"Don't stop now," Batman told him, though his eyes never lifted from Green Lantern. "Check that the hydroelectric plant employees are all clear. There's a complex of tunnels and offices under the turbine rooms—might still be people in there."

Flash was gone as silently as he'd arrived.

Manhunter threw Batman a quizzical glance. "How do you know—"

"I memorized the plans when the dam was built. You never know when information will be useful."

The Martian nodded to himself. He should have known, really. Batman was a perfectionist. He never left anything to chance. In his business, with no super-powers to protect him, Batman was in constant danger in a way few of the other Leaguers ever were. Super-man might have been vulnerable to the cosmic mineral kryptonite, and Manhunter was weakened by fire, but they didn't encounter those dangers very often. Batman walked with death at his shoulder every night of his life. For this reason alone, J'onn wouldn't have been surprised if Batman had committed to memory the ground plans for every building in Gotham.

"I will assist Flash," J'onn stated, and soared away from the crag.

Even across the distance that separated them, Batman could see the growing strain on Green Lantern's face. His alien ring seemed to possess almost infinite power, but the application of that power depended entirely on the will of the ring wearer. Lantern was holding back an unbelievable volume of water, and the effort was beginning to take its toll.

Batman slipped open a pouch on his Utility Belt and pulled out a pair of miniature binoculars. Taking his eyes off Green Lantern for the first time, he trained the 50X binoculars down the valley, tracking the massive spoil-pile that marked out Superman and Wonder Woman's progress. They had almost reached the out-skirts of the city, a feat of power akin to building the Great Wall of China in a morning.

Marveling at the sheer strength that allowed them to excavate this engineering wonder with their bare hands, Batman snapped the binoculars shut and replaced them in their pouch. *These beings can shift planets in their orbit*, he'd thought more than once in his many years as a League member. *What am I doing working with them?*

Manhunter and the Flash reappeared silently by his side. The site was clear. It was time.

This is it, Lantern, Batman thought. *Let the dam go!*

The energy field faded and vanished, and Green Lantern shot high into the air under the power of his ring.

For an endless second, nothing happened. No water spouted from the holes. The cracks in the dam face seemed frozen, checked in their relentless expansion.

Then, with a roar like some maddened behemoth, the waters broke free. There was a thunderous snap, like a giant whip cracking, and, almost in slow motion, the whole dam face crumbled into little more than a sandpile.

A mighty cataract of seething, roiling water poured from the collapsing dam, carrying thousands of tons of concrete with it. A wall of water fifty feet high swept into the craggy valley side, gouging out a half-mile section. The wave crashed over the hydroelectric plant with the intensity of a tsunami, smashing down walls and buildings as if they were toy bricks.

As Batman had realized, there was no way the tailrace and riverbed could cope with the sudden inundation. The angry waters churned as they plunged into the channel dug by Wonder Woman and Superman, spilling over the sides in massive waves, scouring away the earth and soil of the valley sides, ripping out century-old trees, carrying away rocks as big as houses.

But the channel held, funneling the waters until a ten-foot-high wave raced down it at almost a hundred miles an hour.

Minutes later, Superman and Wonder Woman hovered in the air over the city harbor, watching as the waters of Lake Gotham swept through and plunged headlong into the sea. If any ships were put in danger, they wanted to be on hand.

"Excellent." Wonder Woman nodded her satisfaction. The setting sun glinted off her tiara and the amulets she wore on her wrists, making her look every inch the Amazon Princess that she was. "There's no damage caused except the digging of the channel itself, and we can fill that in once the waters recede."

She soared higher in the air, beckoning for Superman to follow. "Let's join the others."

Seconds later, they stood with their companions on the crag, looking down on the scene of destruction. More than half the dam had disappeared, carried off by the raging flow. The surging waters had settled slightly, but it would take days for the man-made lake to drain off completely.

"So . . . why wouldn't you let us fuse the dam?" Superman asked Batman.

"There were suspicions when the dam was built," Batman told them all. "Substandard materials. For every rip you fused, a dozen others would have opened."

Batman turned away, then thought better of it as he

recollected J'onn J'onzz's subtle reminder that they were a team. "I wasn't withholding information from anyone," the vigilante continued. "There just wasn't time to explain. All in all, we did a good job."

"Maybe better than you think," the Flash grinned. "We might even be rewarded for services to archaeology. Look down there—"

He pointed to the valley side just below the dam, where the broiling water had swept away thousands of tons of soil and vegetation.

Revealed there, in the last bright rays of the setting sun, stood a hundred-foot-tall truncated stone pyramid. It seemed out of place—so alien and enigmatic. Shafts of mellow purple light played for a moment across its stonework. Then the sun was gone, and the pyramid remained shrouded in darkness.

CHAPTER 2

Descent into Darkness

Gotham County, October 19

"Incredible!"

Jenny Ayles stood on the top of the pyramid, a flat platform about thirty feet square, her head turning slowly to take in the panoramic views. Night was falling, and the surrounding Gotham Hills seemed to glow deep purple in the fading light. The planet Venus shone brightly just above the horizon, and the first stars were already twinkling softly in the rapidly darkening sky.

"This view can't have changed all that much since the pyramid was first built."

Beside her, Jenny's companion nodded agreement. "Nearly five thousand years," Peter Glaston murmured. "More than a hundred and fifty human generations." He glanced up, raising his right hand to point to the brightest star. "Of course, the land might be the same, but the night sky was very different. Polaris wasn't the Pole Star then. It was one of the stars in the constellation Taurus, I think."

"And tonight we'll find out if the ancients recorded what they saw in the architecture of their pyramid," a skeptical voice broke in from behind them. "Right, Peter?"

Jenny and Peter started. They hadn't realized Robert Mills, professor of archaeology at Gotham University and leader of their little expedition, was standing so close. Instantly, Peter became defensive at the faintly mocking tone in the older man's voice.

"You might find it far-fetched, Professor," Peter said evenly, his lanky frame turning to acknowledge Mills's presence, "but you can't deny it *is* a possibility. And you've always taught us to investigate *every* aspect of an artifact."

Mills didn't reply. Casting his eyes to the side, Peter could see the renowned archaeologist's handsome face as he appraised the night sky, now filled with a thousand glittering stars. The aquiline nose and prematurely silver-gray hair gave Mills a distinguished, almost aristocratic look that men envied and women admired.

"I mean, look what they discovered about Stonehenge," Peter went on, irritated with himself for being so sensitive to Mills's unspoken criticism.

It had been rumored for centuries that the massive stones that made up England's most famous neolithic monument were somehow connected to the night sky. But confirmation had to wait for the creation of computer software that could accurately plot the changes in the night sky due to Earth's tilt against the solar plane. Now, archaeologists were turning up established and potential stellar alignments at ancient sites all over the world.

"A possibility, yes. But not a probability," Professor Mills said smoothly. "We mustn't allow preconceptions to color anything we might find."

Peter took a deep breath. Sensing he had more to say, Jenny grasped his arm and squeezed it lightly, a gentle hint that he'd said enough already. Peter was the professor's star student, and they'd always argued in friendly, if heated, fashion. But their relationship had deteriorated seriously since the previous year.

Jenny sighed. Peter and Robert had good cause to dislike each other, and she had given them that cause. With increasing frequency, she found herself trying to act as a buffer between them. Somehow, it was easier than facing up to what had happened and sorting it out like intelligent adults.

"We should join the others," Jenny found herself saying. "They'll be cursing us for slacking while they do all the work."

She took a step away, tugging on Peter's arm for him to follow. Obstinately, he didn't budge, and Jenny's heart sank.

"One of the reasons our profession advances so slowly," Peter said, choosing his words carefully, "is that certain *older* archaeologists refuse to approach their work with an open mind."

Robert Mills smiled, his expression invisible to the others in the darkness that swathed the landscape.

"I'll check with Lorann and the guys," he said amicably, as if unaware of the accusation and insult in Peter's words. Flicking on the heavy-duty flashlight he held in one hand, the professor walked away across the pyramid's flattened top.

It was almost a month since the Gotham Dam had burst and its swirling waters divulged the mysterious structure. What the expedition had established was astonishing. Radiocarbon dating of vegetable fibers found in the structure's foundations pointed to its having been built approximately forty-five hundred years ago—the only such pyramid ever discovered in America. Unlike the Great Pyramids at Giza, this one had been built in steps, in the same fashion as the pyramids of Central and South America, or the ziggurats of ancient Babylon. Europe's largest Stone Age structure, Silbury Hill in England, had been similarly constructed. Ten feet of rock, ten feet of chalk with soil infill—the process repeated until the pyramid stood a hundred feet high, ending in a flat, rocky platform about thirty feet square.

Reconstruction of the dam was due to begin in another three or four months, after the structural engineers had finished their investigations. In the meantime, Robert Mills and his select team of top students had been asked to excavate and analyze as much of the site as they could in the brief time left.

They had found an enigma, wrapped in a mystery.

"We've all heard the legends surrounding Silbury," one of the other students, David Rymel, had said. "A giant king buried at the center, a hidden chamber filled with treasure. Any chance of that here, Professor Mills?"

They were digging a trench into the side of one of the chalk layers, their progress impossibly slow as every trowel of soil was painstakingly sifted for artifacts. They'd found a pea-sized bead of black jet, some charred animal bones, and a single broken deer antler with a crude spiral incised on it.

"Unlikely," Robert Mills replied. "Remember, nothing was ever found at Silbury. Still, it's not completely impossible," he admitted. "Only a full-site sonic scan would reveal if there's anything inside, and unfortunately, that's a resource we don't have this time around."

Under Mills, the same team had spent the previous summer on excavations at Sipán in northern Peru, working on vegetation-covered ruins that dated back more than two thousand years. It was a well-funded operation, meticulously planned, and it paid off in spectacular fashion. They'd found elaborate tombs buried deep inside the ruins, in several layers, and a rich profusion of priceless jade face masks and jewelry.

"The Gotham pyramid is much older than its counterparts at Sipán, and of completely different structure," Mills went on. "They were tombs, especially built to house the bones of the tribe's religious leaders. Our pyramid would appear to have been built for a different purpose entirely. Religious, perhaps."

"That's what they always say." There had been a sneer in Peter Glaston's voice, one that was often there these days, Jenny had reflected sadly. "When they don't know what something was for, they say it had 'religious' or 'ritual' significance."

"Then perhaps you could enlighten us, Peter," Mills said coldly, for the first time visibly stung by the younger man's criticisms. "Why do *you* think the pyramid was built?"

"I can't say for sure, of course." Peter rose to the challenge. "But I can make several suggestions. First, the chalk/granite makeup: alternate layers of organic and inorganic material. Almost like a gigantic storage battery. But what kind of energy would such a thing store?"

Peter's eyes were alight as he took off on one of his flights of fancy. Speculative archaeology, he called it.

He'd continued, the words falling over themselves to get out: "Well, science has recently shown that Earth energies *do* exist"—he cast a quick, knowing glance at his teacher—"despite most archaeologists having denied it for years. There's *piezoelectricity*, generated by the grinding of quartz rocks under the surface. On a small scale, Japanese scientists can now duplicate it in the lab, where it manifests as plasmoid light.

"Then there's *telluric* energy, the flow of natural energy from points of varying resistance on the earth's surface. Almost every sacred site ever found has stood on one of these flows—raising the possibility they might once have formed a worldwide grid. And the magma mantle, deep in the earth's crust, may have properties we can't even guess at."

Peter paused, noting the skepticism on the faces of his audience before plunging on with his theory. "It's suspected that at least some of these energies are capable of interacting with electromagnetic fields . . . such as those generated by the human brain."

"Phew, Peter!" Lorann Mutti, the youngest and prettiest of Mills's team, whistled. "That's some stretch of the imagination you're calling for. How exactly do you think it affected humans?"

"Who knows?" Peter shrugged. "But if things like this pyramid were built to store the energies, someone must have been able to *use* them. My guess is that the shamans, the tribal priests, somehow used it to cause hallucinations in their people.

"Imagine the degree of control they'd have if, for instance, they could make people see a giant representation of whatever gods they worshiped. Or maybe the shamans could directly access the energies—which would explain how supposedly primitive tribesmen could move stones that weigh tens, even hundreds, of tons."

"Interesting theories, Peter," Mills had observed, "but as you admit, not a shred of proof. And definitely not the sort of thing to be preserved in the archaeological record. So we've no way of ever knowing—"

"Yes, we have," Peter broke in. "If we can rediscover precisely *how* they harnessed the earth energies, we can replicate anything they did."

Lorann Mutti laughed. "We have super heroes," she pointed out. "Superman and Green Lantern. Do they count?"

"If you won't take me seriously, then what's the point?"

There was anger on Peter's face as he turned and
strode away. Jenny had hurried after him, trying to
soothe his ruffled feelings. She knew that it was more
than the jokes of his peers that was upsetting him.

Almost midnight, and the excavation team's patient
astronomical experiments had failed to pay off. Using
the surrounding hilltops as sighting beacons, they'd
been trying to extrapolate the straight lines into space,
to see if they aligned with any particular stars. But
there was nothing that could be attributed to anything
other than random chance.

Len Dors, the final member of the six-strong expedition, snapped the case shut on his theodolite. "Waste
of time," he said curtly. He blew out through his
mouth, making the hairs of his burgeoning mustache
quiver. "It's beginning to get cold, too."

A chill breeze had blown up not long after sunset,
and though it wasn't particularly strong, they'd been
exposed to it on the pyramid top for hours.

"I vote we go back to the SUV and head for home,"
David Rymel suggested. He swung the beam of his
flashlight, playing it over their equipment. "We can
leave this stuff till tomorrow, rather than try to carry it
down tonight."

"Oh, *very* adventurous." Scorn dripped from Peter
Glaston's reply. "Good thing Werner and Evans and a
thousand other archaeologists didn't say that—'Ooh,
I'm cold, I want to go home'—or we might still not
have discovered Troy, or the Tomb of Tutankhamen!"

Jenny saw Rymel bristle, and hastened to smoothe things over. "That's a little unfair, Peter. It's been a long day, and David's right, we haven't found anything interesting tonight. We should go home and get some sleep. We'll all feel better in the morning."

"I feel fine right now," Peter snapped. "If you want to go, I'll stay here alone. I have a feeling about this place. There's something important here, and I for one don't intend to give up until I find it!"

"We're not giving up, Peter," Robert Mills added, "just taking a much-needed rest."

"And we'll be back tomorrow—" Jenny began, but Peter cut her off.

"I might have known you'd side with *him*," he accused Jenny, and she flushed. "Well, enjoy each other's company." He picked up a flashlight, snapped it on, and started to follow its beam to the edge of the small plateau.

"Where are you going?" Jenny cried in alarm.

"Maybe there are no stellar alignments from the top," Peter muttered, "but that doesn't mean the ancients didn't use another part of the pyramid for their observations."

"Peter! Come back here!" Robert Mills insisted. The professor moved to follow him, but Jenny shook her head.

"Give him a few minutes to calm down," she said. "He's just a little overwrought."

They saw the beam of Peter's flashlight dip, and a faint motion as he clambered down the rope ladder they'd erected for access to the pyramid's lower courses. As the beam of light disappeared, Jenny felt a sudden chill that seemed to penetrate to her bones.

The breeze was picking up. It really was time to leave.

Peter Glaston's mind was buzzing as he lowered himself down the rope, picking out the rungs with his flashlight before trusting them with his weight. He didn't know what was wrong with him lately; he was always arguing, even with Jenny, picking fights for no reason at all.

A brief memory of the previous summer flashed through his mind. The long hot days in the Peruvian desert . . . the freezing nights under the brightest panoply of stars he'd ever seen . . . and Jenny, her blond hair burnished by moonlight, wrapped in the arms of . . .

Why couldn't he forget? Why couldn't he just accept the fact that what was done, was done, and get on with the rest of his life? He was an adult now. Why couldn't he control this constant frustration, these unwelcome bouts of rage?

He had just stepped off the ladder onto the fifth course, halfway down the pyramid's face, when it happened. His concentration wandered and he looked up into the star-strewn sky, idly wondering if perhaps it had been from here that the pyramid builders made their astronomical observations. Suddenly, his left foot slid on some gravel, and before Peter could recover his balance, he was wedged between two protruding boulders.

Cursing to himself at the pain that stabbed through his ankle, praying nothing was broken, Peter tried to ease his foot free. One of the football-sized boulders was slightly loose, and he trained the flashlight on it as he rocked it from side to side. Without warning, the stone dislodged, freeing his trapped foot and revealing a small hole in the rocky platform below it.

Peter wrinkled his brow, for a moment failing to appreciate just what he might have found here. Then, with mounting excitement, he angled the flashlight so it pointed down into the cavity, illuminating what appeared to be a buried chamber.

Struggling to contain the feelings that surged through him, working quietly with the flashlight, Peter started to clear away the rocks and boulders that obviously formed the chamber roof. All his dark, brooding thoughts of just a few minutes ago had dissipated, to be replaced by a strange sense of wonder. The Gotham pyramid was an unprecedented find, and now he was going to enter its subterranean chamber, hidden for hundreds, possibly thousands, of years.

It wasn't the lure of treasure that drove him on as he carefully removed the small, square-cut slabs that the builders had used to roof the structure. It wasn't the thought of the ancient artifacts, buried for nearly five thousand years, that might lie inside, or the fame and fortune they might bring him. It was the purest feeling known to any archaeologist—the rolling back of the unknown, the discovery of another piece of the mysterious jigsaw that had been the culture of our predecessors.

The roofing slabs fit perfectly into one another, and Peter couldn't help marveling at the craftsmanship and the knowledge these ancients must have possessed. Who knew—maybe this chamber was the stellar observatory that he suspected the site contained. Surely this would make Mills and the others sit up and take notice!

Peter worked for a full ten minutes before he'd achieved his goal—the clearing of a circular space, almost like a chimney, that gave him enough room to lower his lean frame inside. Requiring both hands for the task, he switched the flashlight off and jammed it in his pocket before he began his descent into the darkness.

Holding onto one of the slabs, its sharp edges threatening to slice his fingers, he lowered himself feetfirst through the hole he'd dug out. A momentary shiver of fear ran through him as his legs dangled in midair. What if the chamber had no floor? What if it dropped away for another fifty feet, right to the very base of the pyramid?

But then his outstretched, scrabbling feet found solid ground, and with a sigh of relief Peter lowered himself down onto the chamber's dusty floor.

The air inside the room was thick and oppressive, and the dust his excavations had kicked up made him cough heavily. Peter stood for a few seconds in the darkness, anticipation building inside him. For the first time in uncounted centuries, human eyes were about to view a long-concealed mystery.

Peter took a deep breath and flicked on his flashlight.

Meanwhile, on the pyramid's flat top, the others had packed up most of their gear and were ready to make the descent to the valley floor. The moon had risen now, its pale silver glow lighting up the sky and blotting out the stars.

"What about Peter?" Jenny asked.

"If the guy wants to act like a spoiled brat," Lorann Mutti replied, "we should just leave him to his tantrums. Let him find his own way back to Gotham."

David Rymel nodded his agreement, and Len Dors's mustache quivered as he growled, "Serve him right, too."

"It's not as straightforward as that," Jenny said quietly. "Peter has . . . good reason to be upset." Her voice tailed off; she had no desire to go into this, not now, not ever really. She threw the professor a sidelong glance and was glad when he came to her rescue.

"Peter's been under a lot of stress," Robert Mills said, "with his postgraduate thesis due, and all the work we've been putting in here." He went on, making sure Lorann heard his words. "But we can't just abandon him. We're a team. We have to look out for one another."

Mills snapped on his flash and walked over to the top of the rope ladder. "You guys finish up here. I'll go on ahead and coax Peter out of . . . whatever's bugging him."

Without waiting for their reply, Mills swung his body out over the edge and started to descend.

Peter Glaston played his flashlight over the chamber interior and marveled.

The stone walls and corbeled ceiling had been constructed without mortar, the stones cut and shaped to fit so precisely that Peter could hardly see where they adjoined. Two larger stones set into the chamber wall had been incised with spiral shapes, and Peter frowned. Almost all of the spirals that he'd seen in Stone Age art were drawn clockwise; the two here were their mirror images, spiraling tightly into their centers but in a counterclockwise direction.

The left-hand path . . . Unbidden, the phrase popped into Peter's consciousness. The left-hand path—the territory of witches and sorcerers. The path of black magic.

The chamber was completely empty, except for a large rectangular block of granite that stood against the west-facing wall. By the light of his flashlight, Peter could see a shallow runnel that ran the full length of the stone. He couldn't be sure, of course, but on other artifacts he'd seen, a carved runnel was to allow blood to drain off. The stone was an altar . . . and someone had used it to make blood sacrifices.

Peter's gaze was drawn to a spot on the floor just in front of the altar stone. It was hard to tell in the flickering shadows, but it seemed that the hard-packed earth floor had at some point been disturbed.

Eyes narrowing, Peter sank to his knees in front of

the altar block. He'd been extra careful not to touch anything in the chamber for fear of contamination—the bacteria on a normal human hand could be enough to do it, and once contaminated, it was near-impossible to get a proper radiocarbon dating fix. Peter and Mills might not get along, but Peter had never forgotten the first rule the professor had taught him: *Never do anything to disrupt an ancient site.*

But now Peter's head was pounding. He'd discovered something unknown, something no one else even suspected. His thoughts of Robert Mills, of careful assessment, of nonintrusion, were forgotten as he stared hard at the small patch of disturbed soil. Something had been buried there.

Balancing the flashlight on the floor to illuminate the spot, he leaned forward and began to scrabble at the surface with his bare hands. He knew that he shouldn't be doing this—that he should call the professor and arrange for a proper stone-by-stone excavation—but his mind was curiously detached, he felt driven, and he didn't even register the pain in his fingertips as they scraped at the stony earth.

The soil came away more easily than he'd expected, and his heart thudded as his right hand closed around something cold and hard. He tugged at it, twisting it slightly to ease it from the earth that held it. It came free with a jerk, sending an almost electric tingle shooting up his wrist and arm.

Peter picked up the flashlight in his other hand and focused its beam on his find.

It was a carved stone ax head, made from some kind

of heavy granite rock, four or five inches wide and double that in length. At each end it had been honed to a razor-sharp edge that seemed unaffected by its long years below ground. And on each side of the ax blade, a spiral was carved—a counterclockwise spiral.

In his excitement, Peter hadn't heard the noise behind him as Robert Mills lowered himself into the chamber. But the student heard him now, as a low, angry growl escaped from the professor's lips.

"Glaston! Glaston, what the hell do you think you're doing?"

Peter tried to answer him, but no words would come. His right hand and arm were still tingling, as if the ax head he held were sending out jolts of low-voltage current. His thoughts refused to focus. There was a buzzing in his ears, low and rhythmic and throbbing. It almost sounded like voices chanting.

Slowly, Peter rose from his knees to stand fully erect, swiveling to face the accusing gaze of his teacher.

"Heaven knows, I've tried to make excuses for you, but this is unforgivable!" Mills hissed through clenched teeth. "Who knows what damage you've done here? Come on—out! Now!"

Peter stood paralyzed, trying to figure out what was wrong with him. His mouth had gone dry and his tongue felt thick and swollen, preventing any attempt at speech. Images flashed deep in his mind, disturbing pictures that were gone before he could pin them down. The noise in his ears grew louder.

Yes, it was definitely chanting. But the words

sounded completely alien, in no language that he had ever heard.

"Are you deaf?" Mills barked. "I want you out of here before the room's completely contaminated!"

He reached to grasp Peter's arm, trying to tug him away from the altar, and found himself surprised by the student's strength as he resisted. "Stop acting like a spoiled brat, or—"

The professor broke off as Glaston's right hand, the one clutching the ax, rose above his head. In the light of his flash, Mills could see that the boy's face was blank and expressionless, but his eyes glinted in a way Mills had never seen before.

"Wh-what are you doing?" Mills felt suddenly afraid. Something was wrong here. Glaston hadn't spoken since Mills surprised him, and that look in his eyes was inhuman—even murderous!

He looked up at the ax head held high in Glaston's hand. As if refusing to accept the atrocity that he knew with awful certainty was about to be committed, he took note of the artifact. The dark, beautifully shaped stone. The curious left-hand spiral, like none he'd ever seen before. The impossibly sharp blade, honed to a razor edge, that was coming down fast toward his head. . . .

The others were descending. They were almost at the fifth course when they heard the scream.

Jenny froze. "That sounded like Rob . . . like Professor Mills!" she exclaimed.

"Maybe he's fallen." Lorann shone her flashlight

down the pyramid face till its beam was lost in the shadows. "Can anybody see anything?"

They scrabbled down the rope ladder till they stood on the ledge that was the pyramid's fifth step. Four flashlights shone as one, and for an instant the hole Peter had made seemed to blaze with reflected light.

"There's someone in there!" Len Dors handed his flash to Lorann and swiftly began to lower himself through the opening. "Keep your beams on me."

There was a dull thump as Len landed on the chamber floor.

"Catch," Lorann called down, dropping Len's flashlight.

There was a long, pregnant silence.

"Len?" Dors heard the anxiety in Jenny's voice as she craned her neck, vying for a better view of the chamber interior. "What have you found?"

But Len Dors couldn't answer. He stood rooted to the spot, the flashlight fixed on the chamber's altar stone. The body of Robert Mills was draped across it, lying on his back. An ugly wound in his head oozed blood, staining his silver hair before dripping to the ground, where the dry earth absorbed it greedily.

"Professor?"

There was no reaction, and Len's voice was hoarse with shock as he called up to the others. "It's the professor. He—he's lying here bleeding. It looks like he's been attacked!"

Quickly, the student knelt by the altar and grasped the professor's wrist, feeling for a pulse. There was none. "I—I think he's dead!"

Up above, Jenny felt suddenly faint. "Omigod!" she whispered. Then, louder, her voice strained. "And Peter?"

"Not here," came Len's muffled reply.

Jenny moved away from the aperture, one hand reaching to steady herself against the pyramid face. Above, the half-moon's light cast an eerie glow. "Peter!" she shouted. "Peter, where are you?"

But the only reply was the night wind soughing through the cottonwood trees on the far side of the valley.

In the chamber, Len Dors's brow furrowed as he saw the wide, dark stain on the left side of Mills's chest. He angled the flash beam to get a better view. The stain was blood. The professor's jacket and sweater had been torn away, and the flesh of his chest had been gouged open to expose his rib cage.

Len doubled over, vomiting painfully on the chamber floor, when he realized the professor's heart was missing.

CHAPTER 3

Fear Is a Gift

Gotham City, October 24

Seven P.M., and the streets of downtown Gotham were all but empty.

Most of the day people had gone, on the exodus of buses and cabs and trains and subways that every evening carried office workers and store assistants, city tycoons and street vendors, home to the suburbs. The city was theirs during daylight only.

When night fell, it was as if a new species ventured out from its hiding places to take over the streets.

Within an hour, downtown would be buzzing with life again. The bars and restaurants would fill up, crowds would stream toward the theaters and night-clubs. Malefactors would begin making their illicit plans, and the cops on patrol would check their guns and ammunition.

But not quite yet. The limbo would last for an hour

or so, as late workers straggled home, and the night people prepared themselves for the hours of darkness.

A hundred feet above Kane Avenue, Batman moved through the city like a wraith. Time and again a grapnel flew from his hand, anchoring itself on a flagpole, or the cornice of a building, or one of the thousands of grimacing gargoyles that adorned the rooftops. Then he would dive from his perch, swinging on the grapple's attached bat-line, reveling in the chill night air as he headed inexorably for his next landing.

He stopped for a minute every now and then, balancing deftly on some precarious ledge, raising his night binoculars to the slits in his mask, scanning the quiet roads below for signs of trouble. He didn't expect to find much—it was still too early—but he went through the routine anyway. In a city like Gotham, it was virtually impossible to predict where trouble would erupt next.

Movement drew his gaze to the fringes of the Clock District. In contrast to most of downtown, here there were hundreds of people out and about. Of course, Batman concluded, there was a major All-Faith religious meeting tonight at the Gotham Cathedral. At a similar meet a couple of weeks earlier, the worshipers had witnessed what the newspapers later called a "spontaneous miracle." Listening to the praises and prayers offered up by John Consody, the charismatic preacher, a blind man found that his sight had returned.

"Faith is the key," Consody told his congregation. "Just have faith, and you too can move mountains!"

Maybe he's not so wrong, Batman thought. *The human mind is an amazing thing.*

But ultimately, the only thing Batman had faith in was himself.

After the dam burst, Batman had reported his suspicions about the substandard materials to one of the few people he called a friend—Jim Gordon, commissioner of the Gotham Police Department. Two high-flying executives from the company that had built the dam a decade ago were under arrest, with charges pending. Several more employees were being interrogated as to their role in the scandal that had so nearly caused disaster. It might take a long time, but eventually justice would be done.

And justice was something that Batman pursued with every fiber of his being.

Batman replaced the infrared binoculars in their pouch in the Utility Belt that circled his waist. There was nothing here that required his services. At least, not above ground.

He swung himself up over the parapet of a building and dropped lightly to his feet beside the small array of lights that acted as a guidance beacon for aircraft heading to Gotham Field. Quickly, he popped the catch on another of his belt's pouches and pulled out a sheet of paper. Unfolding it, he bent to study the map of the Gotham City sewer system.

He'd memorized it years earlier, but this was the latest version. It showed all the new tunnels, constructed as part of the city's rolling program to replace the original nineteenth-century sewer system. Although a

technical marvel in its time, it had long since passed
its use-by date. The brick-lined tunnels were crumbling, the old iron pipework was rusted and leaking,
and the budget for emergency repairs marched
steadily upward every year.

The map also showed those old tunnels that had either collapsed or been closed down and were no
longer viable. There was a whole network of them underneath Gotham Cathedral, and that was where Batman was headed.

Otis Flannegan was down there somewhere, hidden
in that maze of tunnels, with the loot he'd stolen in a
series of daring robberies during the past few weeks.

Otis Flannegan: the Ratcatcher.

Where he found Flannegan, Batman knew he'd also
find his "pets." Rats. Tens of thousands of them.

Batman folded the map into a small square and
stashed it away. He readjusted his bat-line, then kicked
off backward over the parapet and dropped quickly
down the side of the building, his cape billowing around
him like the wings of some hell-spawned demon.

He landed in a dingy alley. Teenage vandals had
smashed the streetlights, and the local restaurants
used the alley as a convenient—if illegal—dump.
Black plastic trash bags were piled five feet high, the
stench of their rotting contents filling the narrow area.
There was no one around.

Batman smoothly levered up the manhole cover at
the side of the alley. He went in feetfirst, then replaced
the cover behind him before scrambling down the
rusting iron rungs set in the wall of the access shaft.

Within seconds, he had left the city behind and disappeared into the shadowed world below its streets.

"The sign outside says you do tarot card readings. I want to know my future."

Raymond Marcus sat in the small consultation room, fighting to still the involuntary twitch that threatened the entire left side of his face. His cheek was puffed up and swollen, half closing his left eye. He should have taken his dose of painkillers an hour ago. But they clouded his mind, and tonight—for once—he wanted to be able to think straight. No matter how much it hurt.

Across the table from him, Madame Cassandra pursed her lips. "That's a tall order. The future doesn't give up its secrets easily," she said quietly. "There are so many possibilities, most of them intertwined. It's easier—and usually more accurate—if you can focus on one particular problem."

"Oh, I can do that all right," Marcus said bitterly. "Problem: facial neuralgia. Result: constant pain verging on agony. Treatment: painkillers so strong they're destroying my mind."

Cassandra looked directly at him, and in the light of the small art nouveau lamp on the polished tabletop, Marcus noticed her eyes for the first time. They were the deepest blue he'd ever seen, set off perfectly by the cluster of platinum curls that fringed her pretty face.

"And what exactly do you want to know, Mr. Marcus?" Cassandra asked.

"I've tried everything for this condition. The doctors

are fed up seeing me, but nothing they prescribe seems to work. I just can't stand the pain any longer." Marcus hesitated for a moment, a little embarrassed, before going on. "I'm thinking of attending an All-Faith meeting tonight. The guy on television said they can do miracles. There was a blind guy who had his sight restored." Marcus hesitated again, as if fearing ridicule, before finishing. "I want to know— Do they have a miracle for *me?*"

"I'm a clairvoyant, Mr Marcus." Cassandra gestured with one hand, taking in the whole room. Marcus had already noted the bookshelves filled with arcane literature, and the idols and artifacts from a dozen cultures that stood everywhere. "I don't count many religious people among my clients."

The pain in Marcus's cheek was mounting. A serious attack was about to come on. "I'm not religious," he snapped. "I'm desperate!"

Cassandra didn't reply. All her life, she'd been inordinately sensitive to other people's feelings. "Empathy," her mother used to tell her. "It's a gift, girl. My own mother had it. You must use your empathy to help people."

For a long time after her mother's death, Cassandra had done anything *but* help people. She didn't want to feel the pain of others, didn't want to empathize with them, didn't want to be burdened with the problems of total strangers. So she'd dropped out of her university art classes and set off to find the world. Or, perhaps, to lose herself in it.

She went to Egypt, and to the Rose City of Petra

carved out of the sandstone rocks of Jordan. She spent a year in an Indian ashram, fasting and meditating. Only when the Chinese soldiers turned her back as she tried to enter Tibet over the mountain passes did she realize her long journey was over.

She'd seen a lot in those years, but the most important thing she'd learned was, you can never run or hide from yourself and what you are.

Now, twenty-five years old, Cassandra was back in Gotham City, back in the apartment she grew up in, doing exactly what her mother had told her was her duty—helping other people.

Cassandra took a small black silk bag from a shelf behind her, loosened the drawstring, and slid out the pack of worn tarot cards it held. Slowly, deliberately, she began to shuffle the well-thumbed cards, at the same time striving to relax and let her mind go blank. Foretelling the future—or even reading a person's character—never seemed to work properly when her ego was involved.

Finally, she held out the pack to Marcus, facedown. "Select a card," she told him. "Lay it on the table, picture side up."

Tarot cards had been used for centuries to pierce the veil of the future. Cassandra had read a library of books on the subject, from medieval texts to modern psychologists' treatises on universal archetypes and their interactions. But, as with all divination, it was her own subjective interpretations that would count the most.

" 'The tower,' " Marcus read aloud from the card as

he laid it face up. The image on the card was of a medieval siege tower, starting to disintegrate as lightning bolts from the clouds struck it. "Is that a good sign . . . or bad?"

"The cards themselves are neutral," Cassandra told him, almost automatically. "They merely reflect the situation. It is the human reaction to the situation that is significant."

"Yeah, yeah," Marcus muttered. A stab of pain raged through the left side of his face, all the way from his mouth to his forehead. "Spare me the details. Is it good or bad?"

Cassandra gazed steadily at the upturned card, striving to understand how it might apply to this man's pain-wracked life. Although it had its positive aspects, the tower card often signified death, or outright destruction. But how did that tie in with Marcus's hope for a miracle cure?

She frowned suddenly. There was something in the image on the card she'd never seen before. How could that be? She'd used this deck for a thousand readings, practiced with it for a thousand more. She knew every card, every detail of every illustration, back to front and inside out.

Narrowing her eyes, Cassandra stared harder. She could swear something in the picture was *moving*—something hidden behind the tower was making its presence known. Fighting down a little knot of panic, she forced herself to stay calm. When you're dealing with the unknown, she reminded herself, you should always expect the unknown!

The image on the card seemed to expand until it filled her consciousness, sucking her into it like a visual whirlpool. Marcus, and the whole consultation room, could have gone up in flames and she wouldn't have noticed. Her entire attention was fixed on that hidden figure.

Suddenly, it revealed itself to her. It was a man—or at least the semblance of a man. It stood on two bare human legs, but from the waist up it had the body of a beast. Thick, matted hair covered its torso, darkened here and there by black stains that she somehow knew were blood. Its head was that of a bull, red eyes glinting dangerously from a deep-shadowed face surmounted by two golden horns. The figure was chanting, a singsong noise that made no sense to her at all. She looked at the ground beneath the beast and saw the twisted, broken body of Raymond Marcus lying there, drenched in his own bright red blood.

"No!"

Marcus started as Cassandra jerked from her reverie. Her breathing was fast and shallow, and though she tried to hide it, her deep blue eyes showed terror.

"What is it?" he demanded anxiously. "What's wrong?"

"Nothing," Cassandra lied. She shook her head, as if to clear it of the final traces of that hellish vision. "If I were you, Mr. Marcus," she told him, doing her best to keep her voice even, "I would go home now. I would not go to the Gotham Cathedral tonight."

"And that's it?" Marcus's disappointment was so

profound that, for a moment, it made him forget his pain.

Cassandra nodded in silence. It was obvious she wasn't going to say any more. Marcus got to his feet, pushing back his chair.

"Twenty bucks, right?" He started to dig in his jacket pocket for his wallet, but Cassandra quickly shook her head. She always hated taking the money; despite all the readings she'd done, it never seemed to get any easier to accept people's payment. But this was different.

"I failed to give you what you wanted, Mr. Marcus. There will be no charge."

"Wish my doctors had the same attitude," Marcus riposted. "I'd be a rich man."

The heavy bead curtain across the doorway clacked as he walked through it, and out of the apartment.

For a long time after his departure, Cassandra sat at the table, trying to understand what she'd seen. She'd never had a hallucination in her life before, let alone a full-blown vision. It just didn't seem to make any sense. What were the cards trying to tell her? Why would this bull-headed creature want to slaughter Raymond Marcus?

She couldn't help wishing he'd never come.

Twenty feet under the surface of Forty-first Street, Batman moved cautiously along a wide, red-brick sewage tunnel.

Gotham's underground services had been laid down during the late nineteenth-century boom the city had enjoyed. No expense had been spared on hiring the best engineers and a skilled workforce, and buying top-grade materials. The result had almost been a work of art, solidly built brick tunnels that curved gracefully as they converged toward the massive treatment plant discreetly tucked out of the way near Gotham Docks.

But the sewers had deteriorated badly since those first halcyon days. Successive city administrations had ducked the issue of repairs and maintenance. "Out of sight, out of mind," as one mayor had memorably put it, shortly before he was arrested for embezzlement. Now the elegant brickwork was crumbling away in hundreds of locations, and backed-up sewers were a common problem in several districts.

Batman ran as fast as he dared on the slippery surface underfoot. He wore noseplugs, with filters specially designed to keep out both infection and the sewer's noxious stench. A powerful penlight lit his way through the stygian darkness. Just outside the focus of its beam, he could hear the squeaks and grunts of the sewer's inhabitants. Rats.

Suddenly, he pulled up short. Something had changed. Batman flicked off his flashlight and strained his ears, listening intently.

From several places, he could hear the steady drip-drip of falling water. A distant rumble echoed hollowly—a subway train on the nearby downtown line. Apart from that, there was only silence . . . and it filled him with sudden suspicion. Why had the rats gone quiet? What were they *doing*?

He could picture them—ten thousand rats seething with disease, yellowed teeth bared, waiting like predators just beyond the range of his vision. Waiting for Otis Flannegan, their human leader, to give them the order to attack.

An ordinary person might have panicked then, gone running blindly in search of an exit from the awful darkness of this claustrophobic place. But Batman had lived with fear all of his life, and had come to treat it almost like an old friend. He never tried to quiet it, never ignored it.

Batman knew fear for what it really was: a gift. A message from his unconscious mind, warning him to be alert to danger he might not consciously be aware of. Fear was a feeling to be listened to, heeded, and acted upon.

Batman's hand slipped to his Utility Belt and popped open a pouch. Fortunately, he'd come prepared. Rats had extremely sensitive hearing in the high-frequency range; the sonic gadget he'd spent most of the daylight hours preparing in the Batcave should be enough to scare them off.

He held the small metal box gingerly, unwilling to switch it on until absolutely necessary in case it scared Flannegan himself away, and began to move stealthily forward in the darkness.

There was a sudden, high-pitched whistle, and Batman knew his fear had served him well. Flannegan used a whistle to control his rodent army. But even as Batman's gloved finger hovered over the sonic emitter's trigger, the rats attacked.

There were several on a narrow ledge just above his head, which he'd failed to see in the pitch-black shadows. They launched themselves at him like tiny dervishes, eyes glowing red, their angry squeals filling his ears. One landed on his wrist, and the sonic emitter went spinning from his hand, splashing into the stream of muck and effluent at his feet.

Batman wasted no time cursing his bad luck. He brushed two rats off his shoulder, and lashed out with a foot to scatter the small band nipping at his ankles. His costume was Kevlar-lined, impervious to inflictions such as rat bites. His cowl and mask protected his face, and gauntlets covered his hands. But the rats were present in such numbers, it would be only a matter of time before they bore him to the ground and found their way through his defenses.

He squeezed the touch-sensitive barrel of the penlight he still carried in his other hand, and saw for the first time the peril that he faced. Thousands of rats were streaming down the tunnel-side ledges toward him, a living river with murderous intent. And there, directing them in their charge, was the surreal figure of the Ratcatcher.

Otis Flannegan's head and face were covered by a gas mask, its rubber hose snaking down to the oxygen canister fixed to his belt. He wore fisherman's rubber wading boots that came up to his thighs, and a gun butt jutted from the holster around his waist. In his left hand he carried a powerful work lamp; as he switched it on, the sewer was flooded with bright light.

"This is my domain, Batman," the Ratcatcher exclaimed, and Batman could hear the mania that lay beneath the man's words. "And my little friends do not like intruders."

As Ratcatcher's eerie whistle sounded again, Batman pulled his bola from a pouch in one long-practiced gesture. Holding it in the center, where its three leather cords were joined, he whirled it at full speed in front of him, careful to keep it low. The trio of half-pound lead weights at the end of the leather rope sang in the foul sewer air.

Rat after rat dropped like stones as the spinning weights thudded into them, breaking bones and crushing skulls. But still the others came on, oblivious to pain and death as they strove to obey their master's orders.

Batman knew he couldn't keep this up for long. Spinning the bola in front of him, he inched his way toward his sonic emitter that lay in the muck.

Once, Otis Flannegan had been the official Gotham City ratcatcher, employed by the Sanitation Department. For years he had more or less lived in the sewers, punctuating his mass poisonings of rats with bizarre attempts to turn them into his pets.

It was during one of his rare outings aboveground that Flannegan had run into trouble. Not used to alcohol, he'd gotten drunk and somehow found himself involved in a street brawl. A man had died, and Flannegan exchanged one dark home for another when the judge sentenced him to fifteen years in Blackgate Island penitentiary.

After a short while, his "pets" helped him escape

from prison. Consumed with thoughts of vengeance, Flannegan had kidnapped several of the people responsible for his incarceration: the policeman who'd arrested him, the witnesses against him in court, even the judge who'd handed down the sentence.

For months Flannegan kept them locked up in a subterranean cell, feeding them scraps, constantly taunting them, making them pay for the indignities they'd heaped upon him. He'd have kept them there until they rotted and died, had it not been for Batman's intervention.

The vigilante found Ratcatcher's secret jail, freed the prisoners, and sent the miscreant back to Blackgate. Ever since, Ratcatcher hated Batman with a passion that dwarfed everything else in his life, except love of his rats.

He'd last escaped during the Cataclysm, when Gotham was hit by an earthquake measuring 7.5 on the Richter scale. Half of downtown had collapsed, whole blocks had sunk into the ground, and the map of the city changed forever.

Flannegan had managed to stay on the loose ever since, an uncatchable fugitive in the subterranean domain he had made his own.

"That's right, boys!" Ratcatcher laughed as his rat packs threw themselves at Batman and his whirling bola. "You'll have him in a minute. Bite him! Rip him! Kill him!"

The high-pitched whistle sounded again, and Batman risked a glance behind him. Hundreds more rats were scuttling from their holes and hideouts, scampering over the pitted surface of the brickwork, running along the narrow walkway to attack from the rear.

No way I can hold them all back, Batman realized. *Phosphor grenades might blind them, but I'd need hundreds to be rid of them all. There's only one thing to do . . .*

Without warning, Batman dived full-length onto the walkway. For an instant, the surprised rats drew back—and that was all the time the Dark Knight needed. Even as the rodents surged forward again, Batman's hand closed around the sonic emitter in the stream, and his thumb pressed down hard on the trigger.

The sound was so high-pitched, Batman himself couldn't hear it. But he could see its effect on the rats as it assaulted their sensitive hearing: many of them screamed, a high, keening noise that grated on Batman's senses. Then they broke formation, turned, and ran as fast as they could to put distance between themselves and the source of their pain.

Like some modern-day Pied Piper of Hamelin, Ratcatcher blew desperately on his whistle. But his rodent friends could no longer hear him over the high-frequency cacophony that was jangling their nervous systems.

Batman rolled to his feet, leaving the sonic emitter where it lay, still dispensing its inaudible whine. He knew the real problem wasn't the rats. It was Ratcatcher.

Knowing that his scheme was foiled, Flannegan had turned tail and was about to flee into the maze of tunnels. The bola whirled in Batman's hand for a final time. He sent it spinning through the air, its weights wrapping themselves around Flannegan's ankles and bringing him down heavily to the sewer floor.

Ratcatcher sprawled in the muck, jabbering frantically, his voice muffled by his sinister gas mask. "Boys! Boys, don't leave me now!"

"Too late," Batman growled. "Your 'boys' are long gone."

Ratcatcher tried to scramble to his feet, but Batman's foot sent him face first into the disgusting slurry that ran down the center of the sewer. Batman grabbed the villain's hands and roped them behind his back with a small length of bat-line.

"Where's the loot, Flannegan?" the vigilante rasped. "Or do we have to do this the hard way?"

A low rumbling noise echoed along the tunnel.

At first, Batman dismissed it as a subway train on the downtown line. But the noise grew louder and closer, and Batman was puzzled to realize it was coming from underground—almost directly beneath his feet. Suddenly the sewer floor began to shake and quiver, as if the earth below were buckling.

Another earthquake? Batman wondered. *It can't be. We lined the whole city with seismic detectors after the last one.*

Batman grabbed Ratcatcher by his cuffed hands and dragged him hurriedly aside, throwing them both against the sewer wall. Just in time . . .

The ledge was vibrating violently, and small sparks of blue light seemed to seep up through the cracks between the bricks. Then, with a deafening roar, a patch of floor the size of a manhole cover erupted as a solid column of blue light burst up from below.

"Look out!" Batman yelled a warning to his prisoner as the column of energy powered its way up and smashed through the ceiling a couple of yards above them. Debris rained down, and Batman did his best to shield them both.

Raymond Marcus sat on one of the hard wooden pews in the main body of Gotham Cathedral. For the first time in many weeks, there was a smile on his face—a smile that didn't hurt. John Consody, the main speaker at the night's event, was in top oratorical form. He was so inspiring, Marcus was glad he'd ignored Madame Cassandra's warning and come to the All-Faith meeting anyway.

"Faith is the rock on which we must build our lives," Consody pontificated. He stood in the ornately carved wooden pulpit, addressing the thousand citizens who'd turned up to hear him speak. Many were obviously sick; a dozen pairs of crutches leaned against the pews, and several people in wheelchairs sat in the aisles off to the side. "The works of Man last only awhile, then crumble into sand. But faith endures forever."

Everyone's attention was fixed intently on Consody as the congregants waited for what he'd say next. Waiting to see if the miracle would come.

"If we have faith, all will one day be well. Faith can move mountains." The charismatic preacher's voice was growing louder, the words coming faster. "Faith uplifts the human spirit. Faith can heal all our ills!"

This was the kind of language Marcus needed to hear. It was nearly three years since botched surgery had triggered his facial neuralgia. Three years of daily pain, pain that seemed to worsen with every passing hour, pain that defied the doctors' best efforts to banish or even alleviate it.

One specialist had told him neuralgia was the most painful disease known to the medical community, as if Marcus should wear the fact as some kind of badge of honor. He knew exactly how painful it was. All he wanted was a cure.

Surely, after all he'd been through, one tiny miracle wasn't too much to ask for?

Marcus caught sight of something out of the corner of his eye, and turned his gaze from the pulpit to the nearby altar. Covered in a pristine white cloth with golden stitching, the altar was backed by an oversized heavy plaster sculpture depicting Christ in his agony on the cross.

Tiny sparks of bluish-white light seemed to be playing around the altar. Some of them rolled off the top, more like globules of mercury than flashes of light. Everyone else was fixated on Consody in the pulpit, and Raymond Marcus felt a sudden elation welling up inside him.

Lurching to his feet, he pushed past a couple of people and into the aisle. The bluish light grew stronger as Marcus walked purposefully toward the altar, his gaze never leaving it.

A miracle! The words soared in his mind like a hymn of praise. *There's going to be a miracle!*

A couple of feet from the altar, the pain in his face

forgotten, he stopped and reached out a hand toward the sparkling light that danced in front of him.

The altar erupted with a roar like thunder.

A dense column of blue energy shot straight up from it, engulfing Marcus's outstretched hand. He screamed in sudden, surprised pain as the skin on his hand and wrist began to blister. Dazedly, he smelled the reek of his own burning flesh and desperately wrenched his hand away.

He stared at his wrist in shock, unable for a moment to comprehend what had happened. His hand had disappeared almost entirely, leaving only a few strips of charred skin flapping off burned bone.

Dimly, he was aware of voices shouting and people leaping to their feet. Then the column of energy struck the cathedral ceiling, twenty-five feet above. Beams and rafters cracked and broke, then tumbled down into the church interior.

Raymond Marcus looked up, just in time to see the falling wooden crossbeam that crushed him to death.

As the energy beam burst through the sewer roof, Batman realized that the cathedral was directly above him. He knew that whatever the source of this lethal pillar of light, wherever it came from, the people inside were going to need help.

Ignoring Ratcatcher's curses and protests, Batman tied him to a set of iron rungs a safe distance away that led up to a sewer hatch.

"I'll be back for you," he growled.

Part of the arched ceiling had collapsed under the

power of the beam. Taking care that no part of him touched the energy column, Batman scaled the worn brick tunnel side and hauled himself up through the hole in the roof.

He emerged into a nightmare.

The column of blue light seemed to dance on the altar, still bringing sections of the cathedral roof crashing down on the people below. Dozens lay where they'd fallen, their bodies crushed and broken, while hundreds of others milled around in panic and confusion. The pulpit had shattered like matchwood under the weight of falling timber, and John Consody's lifeless body lay sprawled next to it.

Tonight, faith had not been enough.

Batman barked into the radio microphone that was stitched into the lining of his cowl. He knew that wherever Jim Gordon was, the message would be relayed to him. Emergency services would be there as fast as Gordon could rouse them.

A loud shriek cut across the babble of noise as the metal bands that once supported a plaster sculpture of Christ gave way. It toppled sideways slowly, directly toward a half-dozen caretakers who were trying to maneuver their patients' wheelchairs among the debris.

Batman ran toward the sculpture, throwing himself feetfirst in a double-footed dropkick that squarely connected with its heavy supporting strut. The falling statue twisted in the air as Batman's momentum altered its trajectory. It missed the small group by less than a yard as it crashed to the floor.

A fire extinguisher hung from a bracket on the cathedral wall. Batman wrenched it free and broke its seal, directing a jet of thick foam at the base of the column still playing over the altar.

The foam vaporized instantly. If anything, the energy column swelled rather than shrank.

Realizing it was futile, Batman hurled the metal extinguisher casing into the beam; it too was vaporized.

Now the pillar of energy was swirling above his head like a living thing. Shielding his eyes with his hand, Batman glanced directly into the beam—and felt as if he'd been punched in the gut. A figure was forming in the light, a human shape with a blood-stained torso and golden horns growing from its head.

What *was* this? And how was he going to stop it?

He slid two small metallic spheres from his Utility Belt and weighed them in his hand. He gazed back up at the shifting bull-headed figure in the pillar and felt his blood run cold as its red-glazed eyes swiveled to skewer him.

Batman's heart began to pound. Needles of fear lanced through his mind. Every nerve ending in his body jangled as a black hole of terror opened up at the very core of his being, threatening to suck him in.

Somehow, the bull-headed figure was laying bare the fears that Batman knew and accepted—and it was amplifying them, till they threatened to overwhelm him.

Batman shook his head violently, trying to deflect the malevolence that engulfed him. There was a moment of respite, and Batman seized it. He lobbed the two small spheres with unerring accuracy into the center of the light column.

The phosphor grenades exploded with a flash that lit up the entire cathedral. Just as suddenly, the bull-headed figure seemed to dissolve as the energy column twisted, then buckled.

As suddenly as it had appeared, it withdrew into the altar and vanished completely.

An eerie silence filled the church, broken only by sobbing and the cries of the injured. In the distance, Batman could hear the sound of approaching sirens. Jim Gordon had received his message.

The Dark Knight bent to help a woman trapped by broken pews. As he pulled her to her feet, mercifully uninjured, the vision of the bull-headed figure seemed to linger. What was it? Why had it done this?

When he returned for the Ratcatcher, half an hour later, he still had no answers to his questions.

"This is Rayne Taylor, reporting from Gotham Cathedral, where at least a dozen people have died in a freak tragedy . . ."

Cassandra stared hard at her radio, mentally challenging the reporter's statement. She had never owned a television, because she suspected its subtle electrical fields might disrupt her empathic abilities. But she always listened to the late news on the radio before retiring for the night.

She didn't need to hear the names of the dead to know that Raymond Marcus was among them. Her vision had come true.

Her heart heavy, she switched off the radio and sat down on a window seat, staring out at the lights of the city. Sometimes she wished she'd never inherited her grandmother's talents. Empathy could be more of a curse than a comfort.

She sat there for a long time, dazed and numb, before the tears came and she found herself crying for a man who would never find his miracle.

CHAPTER 4

Brief Encounters

Boston, October 27

An evening shower of rain had cleansed the city, washing off the day's dirt and freshening the air. The manicured lawns of the mansions on Thurber Avenue had turned a deeper shade of green, mottled by dead leaves the rain had stripped from the trees.

Princess Diana of Themyscira, daughter of Hippolyta, the Queen of the Amazons, stood in the bay window of Ambassador Wester's house, watching a large black-and-white cat as it patrolled the moonlit, tree-studded garden. Behind Diana, a small diplomatic party was in full swing, a murmuring babble of voices backed by quiet jazz music from a state-of-the-art sound system.

The men wore tuxedos and the women were expensively and fashionably dressed, but Diana didn't feel out of place in her red, blue, and gold costume. Silver bracelets given to her by the gods themselves glinted on her wrists, and a golden lasso was slung from her belt.

Her peripheral vision caught a flash of color moving through the trees near the foot of the sweeping gravel drive that led up to the million-dollar house. Diana frowned. A moving spark of blue light? What could that be?

"You are bored with our company, Princess? Or do I call you Wonder Woman?"

Diana half turned, her long, thick, black hair swinging against her bare shoulders. Sergei Vasily, the billionaire Russian businessman in whose honor the party was being held, stood close behind her. His steely eyes and slim mustache gave his face a distinguished look, but Diana wasn't fooled; she'd heard the stories about this man and his ultraviolent clashes with the gangs of the Moscow Mafia. Somehow, Vasily had always come out on top.

"Your choice, Mr. Vasily." Diana's voice was deep and rich. "And how could I possibly be bored by some of the most interesting people on the East Coast?"

Diana nodded slightly toward the main body of the party. The ambassador himself was on the small dance floor, his movements jerky and uncoordinated compared with the lithe grace of the pretty model he danced with. Vasily's girlfriend, Diana noted.

A group of wealthy Silicon Valley investors was animatedly swapping information with Vasily's senior staff, and a gaggle of the younger guests were laughing loudly as they grouped around the punch bowl.

"Ah, if you were only a beautiful princess, that would be enough," Vasily told her with easy charm. His gaze flicked down to acknowledge her costume. "But you are also a super hero, ambassador from the ancient gods and goddesses to the atheists of our modern world. If I were you, I would most certainly be bored."

Diana glanced outside. The blue light was gone. A car pulled up, and a couple of latecomers crunched across the gravel to the front door. There was obviously no threat.

Diana turned away from the window as Vasily reached out to take her hand.

"Come, we will dance," he said with imperial authority, a man clearly not used to being refused. "I am sure our host will have some Russian music for us."

Diana smiled and followed him through the throng.

Outside, the prowling cat's attention had been caught by something near the end of the driveway. A small globule of blue light hovered in the air, darting between the trees, heading toward the lot next door. Motionless, the cat waited behind a neatly trimmed Japanese cherry tree, its eyes glinting with anticipation.

The blue light moved closer, and the cat leaped from its hiding place, one paw reaching up to slash it with unsheathed claws. As the cat connected with its prey, the globule pulsated suddenly and pain shot up the animal's leg. The cat gave an indignant screech, then turned tail and bounded back up the drive.

As if satisfied, the light bobbed and continued on its way.

St. James's Church had stood on this spot for a century and a half, long before the street had a name and the mansions were built. It was a small, compact building with barely enough space to hold the Sunday congregation, but its graveyard was immense.

The blue light zigzagged between some maple saplings, then arced over the wooden panel fence that separated the garden from the cemetery. As it hovered six feet above the neatly clipped grass between the sea of tombstones, lines of force began to emanate from its interior. Like tiny streaks of lightning, the energy lines darted through the burial ground, homing in on the graves.

As the light touched each grave marker it expanded and brightened, causing a tracery of fine blue veins to sparkle and spread across the tombstones. An eerie silence fell, broken only by the hooting of a nearby owl and the occasional muffled peal of laughter from the party next door.

Suddenly, the lawn in front of one tombstone began to ripple slightly, as if something was trying to force its way up from below. A skeletal hand burst through the surface with sudden force, knocking a long-dried bunch of flowers off the grave. The ground heaved and buckled as, a hundred years after it had been laid to rest, a corpse began to hoist itself out of the ground.

Throughout the graveyard, the scene was repeated a score of times and more. Long-dead bodies, festooned with scraps of moldering grave-clothes, hauled themselves out of what should have been their final resting place. Their bony limbs jerked and shuddered spastically as they rose to their feet, eye sockets empty and sightless.

Responding to some unseen signal from the still-hovering globule of light, the zombie corpses turned as one and began to shuffle toward the mansion next door.

Joe Krane, the Westers' security guard, had heard the cat's scream. Karnak, it was called, a reference to Horace Wester's time as U.S. ambassador to Egypt. Joe always carried a couple of cat treats in his pocket when he was on night patrol, and over the months he and Karnak had become good friends. He called the cat's name now, unwrapping a fish-flavored treat—Karnak's favorite. But tonight the cat didn't come running to greet him.

There was a loud crash from a thick patch of rhododendrons that skirted the fence between Wester's property and the church. Puzzled, Joe moved toward the noise, playing his flashlight at ground level. Maybe Karnak had caught that squirrel he'd been stalking for weeks.

A dreadful stench assailed his nostrils, and Joe fought down the impulse to gag. Surely the cat hadn't dug up something in the graveyard? Pinching his nose against the pungent smell of decay, Joe cautiously pushed his way into the bushes.

"Karnak?" he whispered.

A vision of unspeakable horror appeared in his flashlight—a skeleton with a grinning skull, scraps of rotting flesh still clinging to its frame. Joe opened his mouth to scream, but no sound came.

Before he could move, skeletal hands reached out from the darkness, grabbing at his arms and torso. Bony fingers closed around his throat, tightening with incredible strength until the world started to spin. Within seconds, blackness claimed him.

Inside, Vasily and Wonder Woman had just finished their dance. Diana couldn't honestly say that she was enjoying the party, but she comforted herself with the knowledge that she was doing her duty. Her mother, Queen Hippolyta of Themyscira, had appointed Diana ambassador to Man's World. It was her task to mingle with people, to share the millennia-long philosophy of the Amazon race, and to foster peace wherever she could.

Horace Wester came over to join them, red-faced from his efforts on the dance floor. He accepted a glass of punch, eager to discuss with Vasily the new joint-enterprise businesses they intended setting up in Moscow and New York. While the two men launched into a mutual tirade against over-enthusiastic government regulation, Diana smiled and made her excuses to leave.

The smash of breaking glass momentarily drowned out the Duke Ellington track playing on the stereo. Conversation died as party guests looked around quizzically, wondering if this was some new entertainment with which Horace and his wife were going to dazzle them.

Slowly the terrible stench of rotting flesh drifted into the high-ceilinged room.

Something's wrong! The words screamed in Diana's mind as she strode quickly past the Westers' expressionless butler and headed down the hall toward the front entrance, wrinkling her nose against the growing smell.

She turned a corner and approached the mansion's opulent reception area. The opaque glass entrance door had been smashed beyond repair. Several zombie corpses had hauled the Westers' master of ceremonies to the polished parquet floor. Blood spouted from a dozen places on the dying man's body.

Diana ran forward, grabbing one of the skeletons from behind. She yanked it off the dignitary's still-twitching body, surprised at the strength of the creature's resistance, and hurled it against the wall. There was a hollow snapping of bone. A leg broke off entirely, and the corpse pitched to the floor. Diana stamped hard on its scrabbling fingers, then turned her attention to the others.

Normally, Wonder Woman preferred discussion to violence. Part of her mother's instructions had been that she should attempt to spread the message of peace on Earth. That was hard enough, among a species that seemed to delight in waging war against its fellow members. But how did you preach peace to murdering zombies?

Fortunately, the ancient gods had smiled upon Princess Diana. They endowed her with the power of superhuman strength, gave her the Golden Lasso of

Truth, and provided the silver bracelets that had the ability to ward off any missile.

She thanked the gods silently, as three of the skeletons turned toward her. She saw jagged slivers of glass from the destroyed door, held like daggers in their fleshless hands. She dodged aside as the first zombie swung its weapon, deflecting the blow on the silver bracelet around her wrist. Then her fist shot out in a savage punch that took the zombie full in what was once its face. The monster's skull shattered in an explosion of bone.

But the headless body didn't fall. It merely redoubled its efforts to skewer her as its companions joined in the attack.

Wonder Woman rained a series of heavy blows on her attackers, smashing the rib cage of one and completely snapping the arm off another. Their glass knives went flying. But even with limbs and skulls shattered, the corpses fought on. Hands that were almost as strong as hers clawed at her body, and bony fists knuckled into her with blows that hurt.

From the other end of the hallway, she heard the sound of more breaking glass, followed closely by the screams of the Westers' guests. Gritting her teeth, Wonder Woman stepped up her assault.

Her fists sought out target after skeletal target. Her foot kicked out and up, the sole of her red-and-white knee boots landing squarely on a corpse's thigh. The bone snapped and, unable to retain its balance, the corpse toppled sideways to the floor. Even as it landed, Wonder Woman's foot stamped down hard on its skull, smashing it to smithereens.

Thirty seconds later, the hallway was littered with broken, disconnected bones, and Wonder Woman was streaking back to the party and the ongoing screams.

Her heart sickened as she entered the room. A large group of zombies had barged in through the window, and at least half a dozen people lay dead or wounded the thick Chinese carpet. Horace Wester was trying to wrestle a skeleton away from his wife, and Sergei Vasily was swinging a heavy, cut-glass lamp standard around his head, trying to hold several of the zombies at bay.

Wonder Woman plunged among them like a whirlwind, fists flashing and feet flying. Time and again her blows landed home, cracking bones and pulverizing skulls. The zombies tried to retaliate, but their strength—wherever they derived it from—wasn't up to the task.

On the sound system, the music of Duke Ellington still played, a surreal backdrop to the slaughterhouse that the Westers' home had become.

Soon, there was only one zombie left intact. It lurched toward Wonder Woman, the fractured bones of its companions crunching under its feet. Easily avoiding the creature's clutching hands, Wonder Woman unclipped the golden lasso that dangled from her waist. It spun in her hand, then dropped lightly over the zombie's skull and down to the bulge of its chest. She pulled the noose tight, and the creature halted in its tracks.

Forged from the girdle of the Earth goddess, Gaia, the magic Lasso of Truth forced anything caught by it to be rigorously honest.

"What power has resurrected you?" Wonder Woman demanded of the trapped zombie. "Why are you here?"

The monster's toothless mouth moved, as if it was trying to comply with her demand, but no sound issued from it.

Realizing that she would not get a response, Wonder Woman tugged hard on the lasso, yanking the zombie toward her, and her fist powered into its skull. Seconds later, it too was no more than a pile of disconnected bones littering the expensive carpet.

All around her were the sounds of moaning people. She heard Horace Wester speaking on the telephone, urgently calling for ambulances and police. Sergei Vasily was crouched on the floor, sobbing as he cradled the head of his lifeless girlfriend. The room was redolent with the reek of death.

Wonder Woman was filled with heavy sadness. Queen Hippolyta had also charged her daughter with safeguarding humans against any kind of outside attack.

Tonight, she had failed.

Keystone City

Kurt Glaser glanced at the bank of dials that comprised the dashboard in the cab of the subway train he was driving. Everything A-OK.

This was the last trip on his schedule, the long, winding journey from South Chever Station up under the city center and on to the suburbs. According to the

monitors, he was precisely on time, not a second early
or late. It was something Kurt prided himself on; in
thirty years of conducting trains, he had come to know
the Keystone City underground like the back of his
hand. He knew the times, stops, and destinations of
every train in the timetable.

The doors hissed shut with a low whoosh of pres-
surized air, and Kurt pushed the button that would
electronically secure them until the next station. He
heard the whistle from his rear-positioned guard, and
engaged the engine. Slowly, the train pulled away
from the platform and its garish lights.

Kurt sipped a soda and smiled softly to himself. The
train reentered the tunnel, the cab's headlamps illuminating the gleaming rails ahead as they rolled into the
darkness. This is where he was happiest, in the air-
conditioned car as it sped underground, tunnel walls
only a foot away on either side of the rushing engine.
Kurt wasn't a big people person.

He didn't need the monitor map, with its pulsing
lights, to tell him to slow for the signal ahead. After so
much time, Kurt liked to think he could have driven
any route blindfolded.

Behind the engine, the cars carried only a fraction of
their rush-hour load: late workers heading back to the
welcome of their families, a few homeless people coming in to the big shelter on Main Street.

The train slowed. Through the toughened glass
window, Kurt saw the signal ahead blink from red to
green. He eased up on the brakes, and the train effortlessly regained its speed.

As the train neared the signal, Kurt frowned and lowered the soda bottle from his lips. There was a bluish glow around it, casting a few sparks out into the surrounding darkness.

Looks like the signal's about to short out. Kurt reached out to the radio mike that kept all drivers in constant touch with the centralized control system. *Better call it in—*

The thought died in midstream as Kurt's eyes opened wide in amazement. The mysterious blue light had detached itself from the signal and was hovering and pulsating six feet above the tracks.

"Kurt?" Section Controller Jack Icke's voice crackled from the cab speaker. "You have something to say, buddy?"

"Yeah, you bet," Kurt began. But scarcely had he got the words out when he broke off again.

The blue globe of light flew toward him at incredible speed and hurled itself at the cab window. Instinctively Kurt threw up one hand to protect himself. But the Plexiglas remained intact as the light passed right through it.

There was a tingle like static electricity as the ball touched his skin. Then Kurt's mind went blank, and his entire body spasmed with bone-deep pain as the globe of light sank into his flesh.

"Kurt? Kurt, you still there?" Jack Icke asked.

But Kurt Glaser *wasn't* there. His consciousness was stilled, his identity usurped. Whoever—or whatever—was controlling him reached out to crush the crackling intercom, splintering it into pieces. Warning lights flashed red on the monitor panel as the train's speed began to increase dramatically.

Wally West stood on the platform of the Blane Street subway station, the taste of Paloma's Pizza still tangy in his mouth. "Best in Town," Paloma's advertising claimed, and Wally couldn't disagree with that. He'd been to the football game, a dreary defensive ordeal that could have been a classic if only both sides had opened up. At least the pizza was good.

As his alter ego, the Flash—the Fastest Man Alive— Wally could have run home in less than a second. But that would be defeating the purpose of his evening— to relax, for once, and forget all about superspeed. He'd seen the game, he'd eaten the pizza. It was only a fifteen-minute subway ride.

Pleasantly full, Wally leaned against a pillar, only half paying attention to the evening newspaper he held. The warning bell rang out to announce the imminent arrival of a train, and Wally tossed his newspaper in a trash can as the lights approached from the darkness of the tunnel.

"Train approaching," a disembodied voice blared from the station speakers. "Stand clear of the platform edge."

As if on cue, several commuters moved disobediently toward the platform's edge. Long use of the subway system had made them jaded about its safety rules and regulations. This was the one time they should have heeded the announcer's warning.

Instead of slowing to a halt, the train accelerated.

Wally West caught a fleeting glimpse of the driver's face as the train flashed toward him.

It's not going to stop! he thought, seeing the blank, almost zombielike cast to the conductor's features.

The deafening roar of the train echoed through the station, and Wally saw sudden panic on the faces of those commuters standing close to the edge. Traveling at this speed, the train's slipstream would suck them down onto the tracks as it sped by.

Wally moved at the speed of thought itself. His costume, a manifestation of the speed force, appeared around him, his mind willing it into being.

A microsecond later, Wally West was transformed into his super hero identity—the Flash, the Scarlet Speedster, the Fastest Man Alive.

Once, Wally was a boy, a kid like any other. Until the accident. While visiting his uncle, police scientist Barry Allen, an unlikely combination of chemicals had exploded in the lab. Wally was drenched and knocked unconscious. When he came to, he found that he had mysteriously acquired the ability to control every single molecule in his body—to make them speed up so much that he became effectively invisible.

Since that day Wally had dedicated himself to mastering his newfound powers and putting them to work on behalf of humankind. He was honored to be asked to join the Justice League of America. When not battling against threats to the planet, shoulder to shoulder with his fellow super heroes, the Flash worked for the benefit of the citizens of Keystone City.

The train was shooting through the station in a nightmare of noise, moving so fast it swayed dangerously from side to side on the rails beneath its wheels. Wally saw distressed faces at the carriage windows, people screaming as they clung to the straps, rocking against the train's motion.

Suddenly, the last carriage was streaming past. Even as the vacuum created by the train's speed pulled at the people on the platform's edge, the Flash was a red blur running toward them at incredible speed. He grabbed the belt of an overcoat as its wearer overbalanced and began to fall forward, yanking the man back to safety before he even realized he was in danger.

Then the Flash's body was between the other passengers and the track, the shockwave created in the air by his speed gently shifting them back from the edge.

It happened so fast, the passengers had no idea what was going on. As the train's rear lights disappeared out of the station, the Flash didn't hesitate. He leaped down onto the track without breaking stride and streaked after the out-of-control train.

His legs pumping like pistons, the Flash raced along the track in the wake of the speeding train, his superspeed allowing him to quickly overhaul it. He saw the terrified faces of the passengers in the end car as he caught up with it, and his mind sifted swiftly through the alternatives.

He could try to unhitch the cars from the engine, leaving them to slow down and stop naturally. But that was a delicate maneuver to try and perform when the train was moving at a good eighty miles an hour through the confines of the tunnel. He could swing himself up into one of the cars and apply the emergency brake, but a sudden halt at this speed might unbalance the whole train and send it rattling off the tracks.

No, there was only one way to stop it. He had to incapacitate the driver and use the main brakes to bring the runaway engine under control.

It wouldn't be easy: there was less than eighteen inches of clearance on either side of the swaying train. It would take only one unexpected jolt, and all of the Flash's vaunted speed would do him no good as he was crushed between the train and the unyielding tunnel wall.

The Flash judged his moment perfectly, leaping two steps sideways, accelerating at unbelievable speed as he moved into the narrow gap between the train and the wall. His eyes scanned what he could see of the track ahead, looking for railside obstructions. If he hit a signal, or even a discarded workman's tool, he knew that he faced death, or at the very least severe injury.

A few hundred yards ahead, the Flash saw the glow of a red stop signal. Beyond it, he knew that the tracks crossed; one of the Suburban Line trains had right-of-way. Unless he could halt this train now, there was going to be an accident of cataclysmic proportions.

The Flash accelerated, his feet almost flying as he leaped lithely from the end of one concrete sleeper beam to another, leaving carriage after carriage behind him. He drew level with the engine, casting a final glance at the fast-approaching red signal as he made his move. If he got it wrong, there was no hope of a second chance.

Grabbing the handle on the outside of the door, the Flash swung both legs smoothly off the track, bringing his feet up to smash through the toughened glass of the window. An instant later he was inside.

Kurt Glaser's eyes stared straight ahead, blazing with an unnatural light. There was a slight smile on the man's lips, as if he was looking forward to the crash that was now only seconds away.

"Brake!" the Flash yelled.

Kurt Glaser didn't even turn to look as he threw out one fist in a savage backhand blow. Taken by surprise, the Flash barely managed to jerk his head aside in time. Glaser's fist whistled past his chin, embedding itself in the cab wall with a fearsome crash.

Superstrength!

Before the possessed Kurt Glaser could react, the Flash's fist shot out, delivering a rapid-fire series of triphammer blows to the driver's head. Glaser went down like a tenpin, sprawling unconscious on the floor of the cab.

Through the cab window, the Flash saw that they were almost on top of the signal. Desperately, he grabbed the brake handle and pushed it forward to its furthest extent. The train wheels screamed as the potent air brakes bit, sending up an explosion of sparks.

The brake shuddered and shook in the Flash's hand as he fought to hold it in position. For a moment, he thought the engine was going to jump the tracks. He knew that the sudden deceleration would be throwing the passengers around in the cars behind—but better that than a headlong smash into another train.

The Flash breathed a deep sigh of relief as the train ground to a halt a dozen yards beyond the signal, but still a good way short of the cross track. There was a roar of moving air, and he saw the lights of the Suburban Line Special speed by in front of him. Only then did he realize just how close they'd come to disaster. Another half second and . . .

The Flash dismissed the thought. In the hero business, you'd go crazy if you dwelled on all the near misses. For the first time, he glanced down at Kurt Glaser. There was a momentary flicker of blue light, then Glaser groaned and opened his eyes with an obvious effort.

He stared uncomprehendingly at the Flash, then lapsed back into unconsciousness.

The Flash fingered the emergency button that would sound a distress call in the control center. Then he set off toward the rear of the train to ensure the passengers were all right.

As he went, his mind seethed with unanswered questions.

Cape Canaveral, Florida

"Almost midnight, the end of October, and it's still eighty degrees out here. I'm telling you, Clark—it's not natural!"

Jimmy Olsen dabbed at the perspiration beaded on

his forehead with a handkerchief. His flaming red hair was damp from humidity, collecting into the tight little curls he hated so much, the way it always did when he was wet. Florida had been enjoying a late-season heat wave as a ridge of strong high pressure lay unmoving offshore.

Beside Jimmy, Clark Kent used a spotted kerchief to wipe the fog off the lenses of his heavy-rimmed glasses. "Perhaps if we put in a complaint to NASA," he said lightly to his younger companion, "they'll relocate the space shuttle launches to Metropolis. We'll be able to cover them for the *Daily Planet* and still be in bed by midnight."

"In bed?" There was a note of mock scorn in the young photographer's voice. "You really are a homebody, aren't you, Clark?"

A small smile played around the corners of Clark's mouth. *If Jimmy only knew,* the reporter thought to himself.

They were seated in the press stands erected specially for the launch, a full quarter-mile away from the mighty Saturn-class rocket that would follow the shuttle *Lincoln* into the upper atmosphere. Over the past few years the public had grown used to shuttle launches; they were no longer the newsworthy events they once had been.

Tonight's blastoff was something special, though. For the first time ever, an American astronaut would be going into orbit accompanied by his Russian and Chinese counterparts. Their mission had a dozen different objectives, from observing the behavior of fungi cultures in a zero-gravity environment to monitoring the network of communication satellites that was slowly but inexorably drawing Russia and the People's Republic of China closer to the American way of life.

"It's about time." Jimmy aimed his binoculars at the complex of prefabricated buildings that surrounded the launch site. "That's the vehicle carrying the crew appearing now."

Clark pretended to follow the young man's gaze with his own binoculars and saw a white, futuristic but chunky-looking vehicle powering up the removable ramp toward the crew entry hatch. Clark had already done his interviews with the flight leaders, Martin Spears, Grigor Mendel, and Li Xing. The laptop computer that was connected to his cell phone had automatically sent his feature article back to editor Perry White in downtown Metropolis. Jimmy had shot his close-ups of the astronauts, and now he wanted one final photo of the shuttle lifting off into the velvet, starry sky.

Clark saw the figures step out of the vehicle at the end of the ramp. They turned, and each raised a hand in recognition of the distant watchers in the press stands before stooping to squeeze through the entrance hatch.

There followed a long, boring wait in the oppressive nighttime heat as the shuttle crew ran through their prelaunch checks.

Jimmy passed the time swigging from one of the liter bottles of water he'd been buying ever since they'd arrived in Florida the day before. He checked and rechecked his camera, making sure the proper distance and light conditions were programmed in. There would be a very narrow window of opportunity for him to snap the breathtaking shot he wanted, and he was determined nothing would go wrong.

Clark Kent's thoughts were more philosophical. More than anything else, he wanted peace in this world of humans he had adopted for his own. As his alter ego, Superman, he did everything in his power to safeguard humankind against attack, be it from insane earthly supervillains or threats from outer space. The vast powers bestowed upon him by Krypton, the planet where he'd been born, and the yellow sun under which he now lived, ensured that few if any threats could withstand the Man of Steel.

But in his heart of hearts, Clark knew realistically that the world would only find a rest from hatred and war when humanity learned for itself the virtues of co-operation and universal tolerance. These were values that could never be forced on people, but had to be gladly and willingly embraced if any lasting change was to be made. An international space shuttle crew might not sound like much, but it was a step in the right direction.

Clark suddenly remembered the Justice League engagement the month before, at the site of the Gotham Dam disaster. Funny how none of the other Leaguers, like Aquaman, Plastic Man, or Zauriel, rubbed him the wrong way. Only Batman.

Superman had always felt uncomfortable with the fact that Batman operated outside the law. A vigilante, rather than a hero. Yet he had to admit that Batman always got the job done. Still, if it was so hard for them to get along in perfect harmony, small wonder that whole nations found it much more difficult.

Though deep in thought, Clark was far from inactive. His eyes scanned the area ceaselessly, his X-ray vision probing deep into the space base's most hidden corners. No accident, no unforeseen sequence of events, could be allowed to hamper this historic moment.

Just then, on the far side of the base, his amazing Kryptonian vision detected something strange. There was a sudden flare of blue light, so brief that it disappeared again almost immediately.

"Did you see that?" he asked Jimmy, but the photographer's binoculars were still trained on the rocket.

"The ramps have withdrawn, the hatches are sealed," Jimmy intoned. "The stablizers are pulling in. The countdown will begin any minute now."

Clark got to his feet. "Excuse me a moment," he said hurriedly. "Must be the heat—I feel a little faint."

"Take off your tie and unbutton your collar," Jimmy suggested, not looking up.

But Clark was already gone, sidling past the other news and camera teams assembled on the press stands. He reached the bottom of the wooden steps and, surreptitiously checking to make sure he wasn't observed, slipped into the dark shadows beneath.

Less than a second later he emerged again, his formal suit gone, replaced by the bright red-and-blue costume of Superman. His red cape streamed behind him as he flew at speed across the base, heading toward the spot where he'd seen the mysterious blue light.

There was nothing there.

Superman's brow furrowed. He'd caught only a glimpse of the light, but that had been sufficient for him to realize it was neither natural nor man-made. He hovered a few feet higher above the tarmac surface, his eyes flickering back to the rocket and its precious cargo. What he saw there made his blood run cold.

The shuttle's massive engines were just igniting in a sea of white-hot flame that blasted down into the thick concrete silo and came spilling back up over the edges. But a shimmering blue globe had materialized on the giant gantry that kept the craft upright. The same light he'd seen only moments ago.

Superman took off again, cleaving through the air with great speed. As he flew, his superhearing picked up distant shouts and comments from the press area "What the hell is *that*?" "It's some kind of UFO!" "I can't get a focus on it!"

As Superman flew closer, the light turned in the air and bobbed, as if acknowledging his presence. He could see a fine tracery of electrical force rippling within its confines, the lines brightening as they converged at the globe's center. Without warning, a jagged streak leaped from the globe, zigzagging through the air at the speed of thought.

Before Superman could avoid it, the lightning streak struck him full in the chest. A hundred thousand volts seared through his body, throwing him backward as if he were a rag doll and not the mightiest man on Earth.

At least it's declared its intentions, he thought grimly, fighting to regain his balance against the shocks that continued to rebound off his invulnerable body. Then the lightning ceased, and the bluish orb seemed to sink into the metal of the gantry, as if it were being absorbed.

The gigantic rocket was starting to lift now, hovering a few dozen feet above the silo's strengthened base, preparing for its leap into the atmosphere. In disbelief, Superman saw one of the gantry's huge steel beams bending and twisting like a living thing. Suddenly, it recoiled and with incredible speed bounced back to slam into the side of the rocket. Swiftly it drew back again for another blow.

Laserlike beams of heat sprang from Superman's eyes. As they struck the section of gantry, it began to glow red, then white with fiery heat. Then there was a silent explosion as it disintegrated in huge drops of molten metal.

But the blue light's destructive work wasn't finished yet. Even as the rocket started to rise, so gradually it looked like it was moving in slow motion, the blue light reappeared. It dropped like a stone toward the casings of the rocket's huge engines. As it fell, the roiling electrical energies inside the ball of light grew fiercer, spinning faster and faster.

Superman flew headfirst toward it. He could see that the temperature in the silo beneath the rocket was climbing, as if the globe was magnifying the engines' discharge. It was only seconds away from a catastrophic explosion.

No! I won't allow it . . . I can't allow it!

Superman filled his lungs with the hot night air, then expelled it swiftly as a long, cool stream of frozen superbreath. For almost a minute he hovered there, locked in a life-or-death struggle with the orb, trying to cool down the massive amounts of heat that emanated from it.

I'm not going to beat it this way, he realized with a sinking heart. For every few degrees that his icy breath managed to cool the silo, the globe merely heated it up again.

Kicking into forward flight, Superman swooped as fast as he could. At almost the speed of sound he careened into the sphere of light, his hands grabbing for some kind of hold on it. Its surface was smooth, almost plasticlike in its consistency. But beneath the exterior he could feel the power of concentrated energy.

He carried it a hundred yards away from the silo in a fraction of a second. Then, as if becoming conscious that its schemes were being thwarted, the light orb began to pulsate in his hands.

"Sorry, but I'm not going to see what else you have in store," Superman snarled.

With an abrupt movement he tossed the spinning, throbbing light ball high into the air. As it reached the apex of its flight, Superman blasted his heat vision into it with as much power as he could muster.

The ball spun faster, striving to absorb the energy of his Kryptonian vision. But in vain. Its motion ceased

totally, and the roiling energies in its core glowed in-
candescently. For an instant it flared intensely—

And then it was gone as suddenly as it had arrived.

Superman watched as a hundred tons of rocket regained its equilibrium and went shooting high into
the air, trailing flame. He just hoped that Jimmy Olsen
had managed to get the photograph he wanted.

New York

The domed glass roof of the Manhattan Museum of
Ancient Art gleamed dully in the feeble moonlight
that managed to penetrate the city's neon electric
glow. The doors had closed to the public many hours
ago, and now the building was in darkness except for
the moonlight and the occasional gleam of the pa-
trolling flashlights of the security guards.

"Geez, this place gives me the spooks!" Don Bradley
breathed quietly.

His flash beam played over the display cases full of
artifacts in the Neolithic Hall: stone axes, hammers,
flint scrapers, animal bones. He gave an involuntary
shiver as the light picked out a replica of a shaman's
mask hanging on the wall, its mouth distended in an
ugly snarl, the deep eye sockets black and mysterious.

"That thing's uglier than me!"

"You only been here a week," Don's fellow guard,
Louie Beltrani, pointed out. "You'll get used to it. Me, I
been here eighteen years. It's all water off a duck's
back."

"Yeah . . . but can you imagine what it would be like

to *wear* that thing? You'd have to be some sort of psycho to begin with."

Louie Beltrani pursed his lips in disapproval, blowing out through his mustache. Ever since he was a kid growing up in Rome, Louie had loved the lure of the ancient world. Surrounded by the remains of emperors' palaces, the Colosseum, and the Via Appia, he felt a bond with the past that Don, New York born and bred, would never really be able to share.

"Different folks"—Louie shrugged—"different strokes."

He ambled off down the marble floor, heading for the life-size diorama of a tribal group and their dwelling during the last Ice Age. Louie always liked to stand there for a few moments alone, just thinking about what life must have been like for these people. Short, brutal, dangerous, and perishingly cold. And yet, against all odds, they'd survived. Without them, there would be no civilization now, no New York, no museums.

Thirty yards behind him, Don Bradley was still staring at the mask as if mesmerized, unable to tear his eyes away. For even as he'd started to walk on, he'd seen the mask's eyes light up with a brilliant cobalt-blue flare. Don opened his mouth to call to Louie, but he felt suddenly dazed and disoriented, unable to remember what he was going to say.

Slowly and deliberately, he reached out and unhooked the grotesque wooden mask from its hanging. The blue light shone hypnotically. Trembling slightly, knowing he was about to do something he shouldn't,

Don turned the mask over and held it in front of his face. Vaguely wondering why he was doing this, he tied the plaited reed fastening behind his head.

Instantly, a ripple of energy surged down to flood through his body. His thoughts seemed to float a vast distance away, so far that he couldn't tell what they were. He felt his heart throb thunderously in his chest. A terrible rage grew out of nowhere, filling his mind, so strong it turned the edges of his vision red. A low, guttural snarl escaped his lips as he snatched up a large flint-headed ax from the neighboring display table.

"What'd you say?" Louie Beltrani called over his shoulder, his attention still wandering back in the misty depths of human history.

Hearing a clatter behind him, Louie turned to see a figure from a nightmare leaping toward him, eyes blazing, stone ax raised high above its head. Then the razor-sharp flint edge sliced down through his skull, cleaving it in two.

Louie was dead before his body hit the floor.

Snarling and growling, Don Bradley held up the bloodied ax. His tongue reached out through the mask's mouth, licking off blood and flecks of gray matter. Then, with surprising delicacy, he used the ax to shave off several splinters of wood from the desk-top. Piling them together, he struck the ax against a stout flint grinding stone. Sparks leaped from the impact.

A dozen blocks away, Kyle Rayner was kicking back, taking it easy.

Stretched full-length on his living room sofa, a can of soda on the table and the football game on cable, Kyle felt life didn't get much better. Unless he had a commission. As a freelance artist, Kyle never felt secure unless he had at least three jobs lined up.

Or, of course, unless he was wearing his Green Lantern duds, using his power ring to blast some threatening supervillain.

Even super heroes deserve a night off, he told himself, quickly amending it to: *Especially super heroes deserve a night off.*

Kyle held the chilled soda can against his cheek for a moment, glad that he wasn't in Florida but here, where it was more than twenty degrees cooler.

On-screen, the cheerleaders had left the field and the players were running on. Kyle pointed the remote control and turned up the volume.

"—just joining us, this is Mike Dare live from the—" the commentator was saying, but the rest of his words were completely drowned out by the scream of sirens out on the street below his window.

Kyle groaned. Just one of Manhattan's constant irritants. He counted three fire engines and at least a half-dozen cop cars as they sped past a dozen floors below.

Something big, he thought, already mentally bidding farewell to two hours of sports. *Maybe they could use my help.*

Kyle strode across the room and hauled back the thin curtain across the window. Leaning out, he saw the flashing lights fade into the distance. A burning red glow lit up what little he could see of the night sky.

As fast as he took to think it, Kyle was soaring up the concrete canyon after them. Only now he was dressed in the dark, verdant costume of Green Lantern, his eyes masked, the power ring glowing emerald on the middle finger of his right hand.

He felt the air rush past him as the ring's limitless power carried him down the street fifty feet above ground level. Now that he was outside, he could hear the sounds of angry flames and cracking glass. Blazing sparks were drifting high into the night.

The ring reacted immediately to Kyle's mental impulse, carrying him over a block of higher buildings where he could actually see the burning museum for the first time.

The place was an inferno, the flames roaring like a maddened mob as they sucked in air from the surrounding streets to feed their growing intensity.

Instantly, Kyle sent a thin green beam shooting down from the ring to probe the conflagration for signs of life. Nothing.

Not surprising, he thought. *No human could survive in that heat.*

Fire crews were already spilling over the pavement as police grouped to hold back the gathering crowd of evacuees from neighboring buildings, along with the usual assemblage of nosy spectators. Swiftly the firefighters advanced as close as they dared to the blistering heat before their hoses started to gush.

Kyle knew it would take them hours to bring this fire under control—and that was assuming they managed to prevent it from spreading to the rest of the block.

Another thought flashed through his mind, and his alien power ring produced another miracle. The entire museum was suddenly sheathed in a bright green bubble. As the flames licked in vain against it, a hole a yard in diameter opened near the bubble's base. The blades of a fan took shape in the hole, flashing emerald as they spun faster and faster, sucking out all the air inside the containment area.

With no oxygen to fuel its growing hunger, the fire died back as if the heavens themselves had opened and the Deluge descended. Green Lantern held the dome in place by force of will, opening windows here and there to allow access to the firefighters' hoses. It was all too easy for the embers of a fire to flare up again as soon as its oxygen supply was restored.

Kyle Rayner had never wanted to be a super hero. In fact, he'd never wanted to be much of anything. He thought he was happy just living his life, doing his own thing, getting by with whatever commissions his artwork brought him.

Until one night he met an alien in an alley behind a dance club.

The weird little blue being in red had spoken to him, though Kyle was so bemused he could scarcely take in its words. Something about being the very last of the Green Lanterns, the galactic peacekeepers, and that Kyle was chosen to be his successor. The Guardian then handed Kyle his green, glowing power ring, making him promise he would use it wisely.

Then he was gone, leaving Kyle wondering if he was the victim of some practical joke. Or maybe even the unsuspecting stooge on one of those hidden-camera TV shows.

But when he tested the ring—which is limited only by his imagination and willpower—Kyle discovered precisely what it was capable of, and the tremendous energy it contained. Soon his whole attitude changed. He found that doing good made him feel good. For the first time, his life seemed to have a purpose. He could help people who needed it. He could be a hero.

Suddenly, something crashed into Green Lantern's back. The ring automatically protected him from attack, but even through its force field he felt the impetus of the blow. He turned to look over his shoulder and caught a glimpse of a large stone ax as it plummeted toward the street.

A misshapen figure balanced on the flat roof of the building beyond. It was obviously humanoid, but something about the way it held its body reminded Kyle of a great ape. Its face was covered by some kind of horror mask with protruding fangs and bright blue light blazing from its circular eyes.

Even as Kyle watched, the figure launched itself at him from thirty yards away. As it soared effortlessly through the air, Kyle stole a glance at the museum. All of the flames had disappeared, but smoke drifted up from still-smoldering rubble. If he took away the shield now, the firefighters might perish in a reawakened inferno.

Kyle wasn't really afraid, because he knew the ring would protect him from whatever this assailant could do. So he braced himself, ready for the impact. But it never came. Instead, the weird figure spiraled in the air and came to rest, hovering six feet in front of him.

"What's your beef?" Kyle snapped, mentally preparing himself in case he had to go on the offensive.

In answer, the creature's eyes blazed ever more fiercely. They seemed to be spinning, spiraling round and round, dissolving Kyle's will as he felt himself fall under their malevolent influence.

Incredible, he thought with sudden shock. *This thing is trying to hypnotize me—one thing the ring won't defend me against!*

He felt as if his mind were turning to jelly, his thoughts drifting away into nothing. His deteriorating willpower was no longer enough to power the ring's efforts to contain the fire.

Almost in a dream, Green Lantern saw the protective shield fade and vanish. At once, flames reignited in a dozen places.

A firefighter screamed as the smoldering ground beneath him flared up in a blast of flame. It was the man's sheer terror that jerked Kyle back to reality.

Instantly, a beam of solid green light flashed from Kyle's ring. But before the hovering figure could take evasive action, the beam slammed into it with the force of a steam hammer.

There was a sudden haze of blue sparks, and the creature plummeted downward. Another beam shot from the ring, grabbing the tumbling figure in a pair of emerald pincers. Green Lantern lowered the body gently to the ground, then turned his attention back to the fire.

Only when he was satisfied that the museum was in no further danger did he return to the prone body propped against the wall.

It was a man in a security guard's uniform, a shaman's mask strapped to his face. The blue light in the eyes had disappeared, and his body was now lifeless.

Carefully, Green Lantern slipped off the mask and looked down at what had been the face of Don Bradley.

CHAPTER 5

Captured!

The Moon, October 28

The glaring sun cast deep black shadows across the lunar landscape. With no atmosphere to protect the rocky, crater-strewn landscape, the daytime temperature soared. In just twelve hours' time, as lunar night fell, it would plummet to a marrow-freezing hundred degrees below zero.

It was a world that had been dead for more than four billion years. A world hostile to all life-forms. The ideal place for the Justice League to build their base.

The Watchtower rose from the pitted surface like a monstrous artifact left behind by an ancient alien civilization. A wedge of concrete and steel towering to a height of almost a mile, the Tower was the team's official headquarters.

In the spacious penthouse boardroom, the windows were darkened Plexiglas to shut out the sun's torturous heat. Oxygen was provided by a gaseous exchange membrane J'onn J'onzz had built. Artificial gravity was generated deep in the machine rooms under the lunar surface. And the boardroom interior was softly illuminated by light produced from solar panels on the building's sun-facing sides.

Batman had called this extraordinary meeting from his lair in Gotham, then teleported here to preside over it. He sat at the head of the vast conference table, in the convenor's chair, his face grim as he recited the official roll call.

"Wonder Woman. Green Lantern. Flash. Superman." As he read out their names, each hero nodded. "J'onn J'onzz was also requested to attend, but sends his regrets. He's engaged on other business."

"Just us five?" Superman queried. "What about Aquaman? Plastic Man? Zauriel?"

The JLA had around two dozen members and affiliates, but at any one time more than half of them were likely to be involved in their own personal crimefighting endeavors. However, that wasn't why Batman hadn't called them in.

"Each of us seated here was involved in something last night," Gotham's Dark Knight answered. "I had Oracle program everything I knew into her computers. There's a ninety-eight percent chance—virtual certainty—that all of last night's activities were connected."

Once, Oracle had been plain Barbara Gordon, niece of the Gotham City police commissioner. Inspired by Batman, she adopted the guise of Batgirl to fight crime. But the Joker, on one of his psychotic sprees, had put an end to that, leaving Barbara crippled. Now wheelchair-bound, she could no longer physically battle against criminals. Instead, she had turned herself into a high-tech wizard, and her high-powered bank of sophisticated supercomputers lay at the heart of the League's abilities.

Fed by a network of orbiting satellites, Oracle's system specialized in trawling through trillions of bits of seemingly random information, searching for underlying patterns and connections. Patterns that would have remained unseen by any individual showed up with startling clarity when exposed to her lightning-fast number crunching.

A monitor screen stood at each occupied place around the table. At Batman's signal, they flared into life, streams of data running down their green-glowing screens.

"Appearance of a mysterious blue light. Three of us faced a human foe who was apparently possessed, while Wonder Woman dealt with a pack of reanimated corpses." Batman enumerated the points of similarity as they lit up on-screen. "Murder and destruction for no obvious reason. All encounters took place within a very limited time frame. Temporary engagement with a super hero, leading to the defeat and disappearance of the foe. Further inexplicable blue lights . . ."

"Your point is made, Batman," the Flash put in. "Can we cut to the bottom line? Has Oracle fingered any particular villain for this?"

"It sounds like one of our more powerful enemies,"

Wonder Woman mused. "Dr. Destiny, maybe? The strange manifestations fit with his power to induce dreams and nightmares."

"Or Brainiac?" Superman suggested. "He certainly has the mental powers to produce last night's effects."

Almost imperceptibly, Batman shook his head. "Not according to the computers. While individual events might point to particular supervillains, the overall pattern does not support that hypothesis."

"I'm sorry, but then, what hypothesis *does* it support?" Superman asked, slightly exasperated.

In reply, Batman nodded toward his own monitor, where the computer bank's conclusions were scrolling down the screen: *Unknown enemy. Unknown power source. Unknown motivation, though testing is indicated.*

"Testing?" Green Lantern frowned. "Testing *what*, exactly?"

"Us." Batman's tone seemed to drop even lower than normal. "Whatever our foe was, it targeted the five of us. Not precisely, of course, but every one of its manifestations occurred within a one-mile radius of our presence, as if they were designed to draw us out, engage us in conflict."

"Only to be defeated and disappear?" Superman was skeptical. "Not much of a test."

"That depends on what it wanted to learn," Batman continued, no trace of emotion in his voice. Although Batman had tremendous respect for Superman, it was tempered with caution. Unlike every other member of the League, Batman had no superpowers of any kind. Everything he knew, every skill he possessed, had been won through hard work and determination. It made him extremely wary when dealing with beings whose phenomenal powers were a gift, like Green Lantern, or a confluence of nature, like Superman.

But Batman had no hesitation in calling on their powers whenever it was necessary.

He turned to Green Lantern. "If all of last night's attacks *were* made by one central source, Oracle has been unable to locate it. Perhaps your ring might achieve more success?"

Under his mask, Green Lantern's eyes twinkled. Less than a year ago he had been an unknown, struggling artist. Now, he routinely rubbed shoulders with the greatest heroes on the planet. And his abilities were just as integral to the team's functioning as anyone else's.

Lantern rose to his feet, for a moment swaying under the Watchtower's artificial gravity, which was slightly less than that on Earth. He walked across to the huge electronic map of the planet that dominated one entire wall of the penthouse, and pointed his ring at it. The rest of the world disappeared in a twinkling of electronic lights, to be replaced by an expanded map of the United States.

A needle-thin beam of emerald light lanced from the ring, pointing in turn to each of the heroes' base cities: Gotham City, Metropolis, Keystone City, Boston, New York. A fine tracery of green appeared around each location, expanding and contracting as tendrils shot out seeking to establish connections.

Green Lantern shook his head in wonder, still awed by the power ring's abilities.

The others watched in silence as green lines quickly formed, joined up, split apart, and vanished again. Less than a minute later, a single image was frozen on the map. Lines joined each city to the others, with one finer line—barely noticeable compared with the others—leading back to a single location.

"According to the ring, we have our source." Lantern had turned his back on the map to face the others around the table. "Just outside Gotham City."

"Yes," Batman said emphatically. "It's the last place the five of us gathered together. Remember Gotham Dam?" He paused for a moment, ensuring that he had their attention. "If Lantern's ring is right—"

"And I've never known it to be wrong!" Green Lantern interrupted, grinning.

"The source of all last night's misfortunes is here," Batman finished, "in the stepped pyramid uncovered by the dam burst."

Dark clouds scudded across the night sky, blocking out the moon's light.

It was well after midnight, but the lights of the surveying teams working on the remains of the Gotham Dam still burned. The dam had provided water for most of western Gotham, and the electricity generated by its giant turbines brought heat and light to almost a million people. It needed to be up and running again as fast as possible.

A half mile away, the truncated pyramid was a

black, undifferentiated mass protruding from the
scoured valley side. Following Robert Mills's tragic
death, and Peter Glaston's disappearance, the Gotham
Police Department had closed off the entire site for
forensic analysis. Though Commissioner Gordon himself had spearheaded the investigation, his inquiries
led precisely nowhere.

All they could suppose was that Glaston had suffered some sort of mental breakdown, murdered his
tutor, and then fled—taking Professor Mills's head
with him. A photograph and a description of Glaston
had been sent to every police force in the state, but so
far there hadn't been a single sighting.

In deference to Professor Mills, the university authorities had abruptly canceled all further excavation.
The murder attracted the worst type of publicity they
could get, and the university's president was worried
that it might affect future funding levels. Better to
withdraw from the public eye—for a while, at least.
The pyramid was potentially the single most important find ever uncovered in North America, and it
merited long and in-depth study. The digging teams
would return, but only when the furor had died away.

Now, the pyramid was deserted and lifeless, hardly
even visible beneath the foreboding sky. Had anyone
been watching, they'd have seen a flash of light from
the flattened summit, ten times brighter than the
cloud-obscured moon.

As the light from their teleportation device died
away, the five Justice League heroes found themselves
standing atop the pyramid. The Flash breathed a quiet

sigh of relief; every time he used the teleporter he remembered the movie about the fly and the man whose disassembled molecules had become jumbled up beyond repair. Still, even he couldn't run from the moon to Earth.

"It feels barren—empty," Wonder Woman pointed out. "Not at all what you'd expect if it's the nexus of the energies we encountered last night."

"Use your telescopic vision," Batman told Superman. "Check out the whole site."

The others waited as the Man of Steel stood, swiveling a few degrees every second or two, his gaze directed down at the structure beneath their feet.

Superman had been conceived on the distant planet Krypton, a world circling a giant red sun that was slowly dying. When the energies at Krypton's core threatened to destroy the planet, the scientist Jor-El built a rocket to carry his unborn son to safety.

So Kal-El, who would come to be known as Superman, had come to Earth, where the radiation of its much younger and more active yellow sun resulted in many of his godlike superpowers.

"There's one small interior chamber," Superman announced at last, "and that's it. The rest of the pyramid is of solid construction, alternating layers of granite and chalk." He studiously avoided meeting Batman's gaze as he went on. "Looks like we may be here on a wild-goose chase."

The words were barely out of his mouth when the small plateau beneath their feet started to shudder and shake.

"Fall back to the edge!" Batman called out.

The center of the summit had begun to heave violently. Either a very localized earthquake . . . or something was trying to burst its way through from the interior.

"Lantern, see if your ring can tell us what's going on here," Batman shouted.

"But there's nothing in there," Superman said, puzzled.

"Nothing tangible, maybe," Green Lantern agreed, "but it would seem there's some kind of unusual energy configuration. Might take me a few minutes to find out more—"

But he didn't have those few minutes. With a roar like crashing storm waves, the center of the plateau erupted in a fountain of rock and debris that shot fifty feet in the air before falling back on the League.

"I'll try to contain it!" As he spoke, Lantern's ring sent out a stream of energy that coalesced into a dome-shape, a smaller version of the trick he'd used last night to subdue the blaze at the museum.

The violent eruption stopped, but only briefly. As if it had been conserving itself, the energy again surged upward, blasting into Green Lantern's capping dome with such force that the dome was blown aside. The Emerald Guardian himself was knocked off his feet.

"Whew," he breathed, taking Wonder Woman's proffered hand and hauling himself upright. "Have to admit, I wasn't expecting *that*!"

A thick column of cobalt-blue light extended a hundred feet or more into the air. The energies within the column swirled and roiled, crackling with flashes of a strange electricity that seemed to throw off little globes of fading light.

The five heroes stared soundlessly at it for a long moment, at a loss over what to do next.

"I see . . . something in there," the Flash said at last. "Look at those patterns."

The light inside the column writhed like a living thing, tortuously weaving this way and that as it gradually began to acquire a faintly humanoid form. But there was something animal about it, too. As horns began to sprout from the giant figure's head, Batman suddenly realized why it seemed so familiar.

"The same figure I saw at Gotham Cathedral!" he exclaimed. "The monster that killed all those people!"

"It's not a whole lot different from the thing that attacked me, too." Green Lantern nodded in agreement. "About ten times bigger, is all." He remembered the feeling of looking into the eyes of the shamanic mask, the mesmerizing power that had seemed to sap his will and replace his thoughts with . . . something alien.

"You told us it tried to hypnotize you?" Batman asked.

"What of it?" Lantern said curtly.

Batman shot his companion a puzzled look. It wasn't like Green Lantern to be so snide. "Everybody go careful," he cautioned. "We don't want it happening again."

Without warning, the light column expanded in

width until it covered the entire summit, enveloping the startled heroes before they could react.

Suddenly, they found themselves fighting for their lives.

Green Lantern was astonished to find himself surrounded by a thick, blue-green mist that seemed to cling to his body.

He ordered his ring to clear it, but as fast as the green beams dissipated the mist, more appeared, so thick he could barely see his hand in front of his face.

I could be at this for days and not make any difference, Lantern concluded, futilely trying to brush away the dull turquoise tendrils that wafted round his face. *Time to try a different tack!*

Another thought, and the ring responded at once, creating a green spotlight that shone brighter than the noonday sun. It penetrated the mist, but only partially. Not enough for Lantern to see what was happening to his companions.

How come I can't even hear them? he wondered anxiously. *Surely this thing hasn't managed to kill them?*

The thought tailed away, to be replaced by a feeling of what he could only call dread in the pit of his stomach. Something was moving through the mist toward him, something ancient and powerful and unspeakably hideous.

It walked on all fours, its feet scaly and clawed. Its body was massive, covered in armored plates like a dinosaur. A knob of sharp spikes bristled on the end of its long, heavy tail. Huge jaws opened wide, showing foot-long teeth festooned with scraps of meat and rotting flesh. And its cobalt-blue eyes blazed with a hatred that he could actually feel.

Obedient to Lantern's every whim, the power ring armed him with a double-bladed battle sword. As the monster lunged at him, its drooling jaws snapping, Lantern swung the sword with all his might.

His blow embedded the blade deep in the huge beast's skull. Blue sparks flew, and a wild shriek of pain assailed Green Lantern's ears.

He raised the sword to strike again, but already it was too late. The beast's nightmare jaws snapped shut around his torso. In agonized disbelief, Lantern felt the creature's teeth puncturing his flesh as if the ring's protective field was no longer in place.

Burning pain, the likes of which he'd never felt in his life, scorched through him. And the whole world seemed filled with his own terrified screams. . . .

The bull-headed figure's massive hand had closed around Superman's body, lifting him high off the ground and squeezing with a power the Man of Steel found hard to believe possible. Bracing himself, he flexed every muscle in his body in an effort to break free, with scant success.

At any moment, he expected to hear Martian Manhunter's telepathic voice inside his head, detailing what he and the others must do to overcome this predicament. But J'onn wasn't here, and the only thoughts in his head were his own.

Exerting all of his fantastic strength, Superman

managed to pry the figure's treelike fingers apart for a fleeting moment. Everything was swirling blue-green light. He could see no sign of his comrades.

Superman blinked, bringing his heat vision into play. He trained the focus of the narrow beam on the fingers that held him in their unbreakable grip, the heat quickly mounting until it felt like the surface of the sun. Black smoke poured from the creature's charred flesh, and Superman seized his opportunity as its hand relaxed its grip slightly.

With one superhuman effort, the Man of Steel broke free. Powering into flight, he tried to put distance between himself and the sixty-foot-tall bull-headed figure. But no matter how hard he tried, he could only move a few inches. The air was thick and viscous, and the more Superman struggled against it, the harder the air seemed to cling to him and slow him even more.

"Batman? Superman?" Wonder Woman's voice sounded thin and hollow as she narrowed her eyes and tried to pierce the weird turquoise fog.

Can't see anything . . . but they were right beside me only moments ago!

There was a spine-tingling roar behind her and she whirled, instinctively dropping into defensive pose as she braced for attack. Nothing there. Another roar, closer now, but coming from somewhere off to her right. Wonder Woman turned quickly. There was nothing but thick mist.

Like the sea mist in the mornings off the coast of The-

myscira, she thought, with a sudden, uncharacteristic stab of homesickness.

Suddenly, from out of the fog, a stone club smashed into her skull, thrown or swung with such force that it disintegrated into dust on impact. Normally impervious to physical violence, Wonder Woman staggered and almost fell. Recovering her balance, she heard a low swish as something cleaved through the air toward her.

This time she raised both hands, and a second heavy club ricocheted off the silver bracelets she sported on each wrist. Wielded by hands she couldn't see, the weapon swung at her again and again, and Wonder Woman's own hands became a blur as she fought to anticipate and ward off the blows.

Thoughts chased chaotically through her head, tumbling over each other: *How long have I been here? Where are the others? What in the name of Themyscira is going on?*

Her mind seemed to be seizing up, crammed full of a million thoughts all clamoring to express themselves at once. Grimly, she shook her head, trying to clear it. And that was all the opening her unseen foe needed.

A dozen clubs thudded into her simultaneously. Still trying to fight back, Wonder Woman fell to her knees, snarling defiance. But a second wave of blows rained down on her, coming in from all angles, bombarding her with blinding pain.

Her vision seemed to fill with stars, before darkness mercifully claimed her.

* * *

Only the Flash's reaction had been swift enough when the light-column swelled.

He'd moved back instinctively, but at superspeed, so the expanding light barely touched him before he lost his footing and fell off the pyramid's top course. He hit the sloping side once, rolled, and crashed heavily to the second course ten feet below.

Cursing beneath his breath, ignoring the pain that flared in his left ankle, the Flash scrambled back to his feet and looked up. No column of light. No Justice League members.

Nothing at all.

The moon was blanketed by a black mass of clouds, and not a beam of light broke through. The Flash stretched a tentative hand toward where he figured the up-sloping pyramid wall should be. There was nothing there.

This is absurd! The Fastest Man Alive, hamstrung like a blind animal!

He started to walk to the end of the course, but before he'd even completed the first step, a sudden thought struck him. He paused, stooping to feel for the ground before him with his hand. Nothing. Anxiety growing within him, he turned around and repeated the maneuver. Nothing behind him either.

It was as if he were perched on the tip of a narrow stone plinth. The only solid ground was beneath his feet, and around him absolutely nothing but thin air. Unlike Superman and Wonder Woman, Flash couldn't fly. It was a talent he'd never missed, because when you were as fast as he was it was no problem to go anywhere in the world on foot.

Granted, he could manipulate the molecules of his body to keep him hovering in the air. But as far as he could tell, he was standing on the only solid ground. Where the hell could he hover *to*?

He'd have given almost anything to have heard Martian Manhunter's voice inside his head, telling him exactly what was going on. As a member of the Justice League, you got used to doing things as a team. It was only when team dynamics stalled that you realized how dependent you'd become.

The Flash squatted on his haunches, feeling despair creep over him. Whoever had laid this trap couldn't have made a better one for the Scarlet Speedster.

Even as the light had flared out to swallow them, Batman had cursed himself for making a mistake. He *knew* that the previous night's encounter had been some sort of testing ground for the heroes. He should have known they'd be targets!

Now he found himself alone in the strange blue-green fog, with neither sight nor sound of his companions. His mind raced, sifting through the possibilities: he might have been transported to another location, even another dimension. This might all be an illusion, the work of some warped master conjuror. Or maybe it was the others who had been transported elsewhere. . . .

Batman had faced hundreds of villains over the

years, each with his own weird and twisted power. He'd learned long since to accept nothing at face value, and to question everything. He riffled through the files of his memory, but found no name connected with this type of modus operandi.

What was that?

A shiver of fear ran through him like a jolt of electricity, jamming his senses. Had he heard a rustling around his feet? Was he just imagining the cool, slimy touch of something like a tentacle, wrapping itself around his boots? He wore infrared lenses in his mask, but even with enhanced vision he could see nothing except the all-pervading mist.

He kicked out with a foot, and encountered nothing. Just his imagination—though that fact itself caused him to worry. Batman wasn't in the habit of imagining things.

Something he couldn't see brushed against his cowl. He heard a dry, chattering voice whispering like an insect in his ear, a long stream of savage blasphemies and murderous threats. Despite himself, a small knot of terror was growing in the pit of his gut.

How could he fight what he couldn't see? How could he resist an enemy who didn't seem to even exist? How could anyone deal with disembodied voices?

The whispers in his ear became more insistent, leering obscenely, describing in sickening detail what was going to happen to him.

We'llcutoutyourheartandfeedittoyourfriends! We'llripoff yourlimbs! We'llsuckthemarrowfromyourbones!

Suddenly panic-stricken, Batman pulled a handful of tiny concussion grenades from his Utility Belt. Tossing them underhand, he sent them scattering in front of him like a handful of corn seed. There was a five-second delayed fuse on each, and he pulled his cape over his head as he turned his back to wait for the explosions.

The first grenade went off with a wet sound like a razor slicing through flesh. The second emitted horrible, high-pitched laughter. The others exploded in a series of small pops, followed by a redoubling of the odious voices hissing in his ears.

The knot of terror pulsed within him, quickly turning into a hideous dread that seemed to penetrate every pore of his body. Beads of perspiration broke out on his forehead. His heart raced, and his hands felt clammy. He was going to die here—horribly and painfully. He knew it with a certainty that was almost physical in its intensity.

A thin sliver of logic slipped between his terrors. *Fear is a gift*, he reminded himself. *Fear is a message from the subconscious mind. Fear is a warning.*

Yet there was nothing here to be wary of, just a strange blue-green mist. Voices in his ears might be uncomfortable and unsettling, but on their own they couldn't harm him.

Then why do I feel terrified?

Of course! The answer struck him with the force of a hurricane. This wasn't his own fear, his own terror, his own dread. This was being imposed on him, forced on him by some external source. Something, or someone, was tampering with his feelings, manipulating them, trying to drive him crazy!

Thinking the thought was enough to bootstrap him momentarily out of the fugue. Almost immediately, he felt the knot of terror reseed itself in his stomach. Whatever his enemy was, it wasn't giving up. He had to take action and extricate himself from this madness.

It was impossible to get any sort of bearings within the all-encompassing mist. Batman had no option but to entrust himself to his own earlier observations—to assume that his unconscious mind had noticed, and filed away, everything it could about the pyramid.

Trusting himself completely, Batman suddenly took three strides forward and dived headfirst off the summit.

The blue-green mist remained where it was as his body burst through it into the darkness of night. He tucked his head into his chest, bringing both hands up to break his fall an instant before he struck the pyramid's sloping side. He somersaulted once, then his feet hit the next course down.

Unable to check his momentum, he plunged over the side of the second course. This time he wasn't so lucky, landing awkwardly and rolling down the slope only half in control. His head struck against a knob of protruding granite, half dazing him.

In daylight he might have been able to make it to the foot of the pyramid. In darkness, even with his night lenses, it was an invitation to death or serious injury.

The trees!

A vivid picture of the stand of cottonwoods growing almost at right angles out of the bank below flashed into his mind. Batman didn't hesitate. As his feet hit the third course down, he launched himself out into thin air.

One second—two—and for a moment he thought he'd blown it.

Then branches whipped against his face and chest, snapping under his weight, carrying him with them as they plunged down toward the ground.

He landed with a bone-jarring thud on soft grass and soil. He lay there for a moment, breathing deeply, regaining his composure. Leaning against the tree trunk for support, he hauled himself shakily upright and looked around.

The turquoise fog had disappeared.

His fellow Justice Leaguers had disappeared.

And the Gotham Pyramid was no longer there.

CHAPTER 6

Dialogue with a Madman

Gotham County, October 28

The dechromed black Rolls Royce's six-liter engine purred as the sleek car cleaved the darkness, heading for the lights of Gotham City.

"Where to, sir?" In the soft leather driving seat, Bruce Wayne's English butler, Alfred Pennyworth, kept a watchful eye on the speedometer set in the walnut dash. It wouldn't do to be stopped by an overzealous highway patrol officer. Not tonight. Not with the cargo he was carrying. "The Batcave?"

Reclining in the car's spacious rear, Batman thought for a moment. He'd already used the Rolls's built-in computer to send a message to all of the Justice League's reserve members, informing them of what had happened. Many were absent on personal business, but the others were now placed on high alert. "No," he said at last. "Take me to Arkham Asylum."

Alfred raised one eyebrow askance, but voiced no question. "Very well, sir," he agreed, in his rich English tones. Obviously his master was deep in thought. When the time came for Alfred's opinion, Batman would ask.

Their employer-employee relationship was a public display, a mask to conceal their mutual respect and genuine friendship. Trained at one of England's finest colleges, Alfred Pennyworth was an ex-actor and combat medic who turned to domestic service when his father died. He made the perfect butler for the Waynes, a model of efficiency and a walking encyclopedia on all things social and domestic.

Alfred also made the perfect aide for Bruce Wayne's alter ego, the Batman. He was discreet, honest, hardworking, and reliable. He was a talented actor who taught an eager Bruce everything he knew about disguise. And he could keep a secret.

When Alfred had first discovered that his young master aimed to lead a double existence, he'd been appalled. Little more than a teenager, Bruce would be inviting all manner of violence and danger into his life. When rational discussion failed to dissuade Bruce from his self-appointed task, Alfred took the only decision a man of honor could.

He became the Batman's entrusted aide.

When the vigilante was on patrol, Alfred manned the control console in the cavern buried deep under Wayne Manor. He did the research that different cases called for. And he was a sounding board, as well as a fountain of good advice.

As with Batman himself, what started as a part-time interest soon became a full-time vocation. Alfred knew that, with every villain Batman put behind bars, with every innocent victim he saved, Bruce Wayne was atoning for his own parents' death. It became Alfred's mission in life to help his young master in any way he could.

Bruce never knew where the older man found the time—or energy—to keep Wayne Manor, the family's sprawling mansion, in order too.

Now, Batman's mind was racing. He had used his satellite phone's secure line to call Alfred immediately after he'd recovered from his ordeal at the pyramid. Wonder Woman and the others were gone, spirited away, perhaps captured or dead. The pyramid itself had disappeared as if it had never existed, like a hologram without its light source.

The Justice League had faced a being of immense power, and Batman didn't have a single solid clue as to its purpose or motivation.

Over and over, he reviewed the events of the past few nights. Was there anything that jarred? Anything that sat uneasily with the normal flow of events?

Just about everything!

No matter how hard he thought, or what angle he approached it from, Batman always came up with a big fat zero.

There were only two possible clues that might lead him somewhere, and both of them were pretty tenuous. First, the history of the pyramid might shed some light. No doubt Alfred would be happy to do some research on it, or on similar ones found elsewhere.

And second, there was *fear*. Batman had rarely experienced that kind of terrified dread before. Perhaps only once, when as a child it had really sunk home that his parents were never coming back. That he was alone in the world. Forever.

He knew of only one man—apart from himself—who specialized in fear.

Professor Jonathan Crane, a.k.a. the Scarecrow.

Arkham Asylum, the home for the criminally insane, stood on a wooded hillside several miles outside Gotham City center. High brick walls topped with razor wire kept unwelcome intruders out, and would-be fugitives in.

Its crowstepped gables and Gothic turrets rose above the beeches and elms, scraping at the sky like fingers silhouetted against the moon. Here and there windows were lit, backlighting the thick metal bars that guarded them. Dozens of gargoyles brooded at the corners of the roof, their fierce glares and bared fangs designed to keep all evil at bay.

In that, the gargoyles had failed. Arkham Asylum housed more evil than all other penitentiaries and institutions in North America combined. Its rambling corridors and Victorian rooms were home-away-from-home to archvillains such as the Joker, Two-Face, and the brutal Killer Croc. At any one time, it might be expected to have Clayface, the toxic Poison Ivy, and the

Ventriloquist and his dummy Scarface within its somber walls.

As Alfred guided the Rolls Royce around a bend in the road that ran past the asylum grounds, the sunroof whispered open and Batman exited. There was a brief sense of a shadow swooping upward, of black scalloped wings taking to the air.

The car continued on its way without slowing, making for the little-known back roads that would take it to Wayne Manor. Alfred had some research to do.

In the branches of a tree that overhung the road, Batman briefly paused to consider his route. His nightscope brought the hundred-year-old building into focus.

He saw the stooped shape of Jeremiah Arkham passing a window, making his long night rounds. Batman had a lot of reasons to criticize Jeremiah—especially over security lapses—but he knew that the asylum owner cared deeply for his charges. He genuinely wanted to make some of the most evil people in the world well again.

Until he succeeded, Batman would be there to pick up the pieces.

As Jeremiah passed, Batman made a snap decision, then moved into action. He swarmed up into the higher branches until they became too thin to bear his weight. A bat-line carried a grapnel to a main branch of the ancient elm that stood opposite the one he was situated in, and he swung across the road twenty feet from the ground.

Batman knew the location of every closed-circuit TV camera in the grounds, and timed his passage to coincide with their swiveling lenses. Two permanent security guards patrolled the gardens and woods with German shepherd dogs. Batman waited patiently till they'd stopped to share a cigarette and a joke before he moved again.

Twenty seconds later he was seeking handholds on ivy stems thicker than his wrists, as he clambered up the asylum wall.

Built as a private house around the same time as Wayne Manor, the asylum was a product of a bygone age, when media magnates and railroad tycoons vied with one another to build the most luxurious palace for their families. No expense had been spared, vast fortunes had been spent. But whereas the Waynes had gone from strength to strength, the family that built Arkham had lost its wealth and been forced to sell its palace.

Now, both buildings hid their innermost secrets from the world of man.

Batman stepped off the spreading ivy that encased half the frontage, onto a foot-wide ledge that ran along the third-floor level. Back to the wall, he moved swiftly along it until he came to a darkened, bar-covered window. He rapped loudly with his knuckles. No reaction.

He rapped again, and this time was rewarded by a strange, strangled sound, "Hrraaao," like a cross between a laugh and a death rattle. The sound of a very disturbed man.

Inside the bars, the leaded glass windowpane swung open.

"Clancy?" The voice was sibilant and menacing. "Is that you, my trusted lieutenant?"

"Afraid not, Scarecrow. I busted Clancy three nights ago. He's sweating in a holding cell on Blackgate Island."

Batman moved so Scarecrow could see his cowl. The sight brought an immediate howl of dismay as Scarecrow physically recoiled. "Hraiii!"

Moonlight streamed between the bars, enabling Batman to see the figure inside. The body seemed stooped and twisted, yet still tall and with a wiry strength. It was enclosed in a costume made from burlap, with sticks of straw jutting from the cuffs at wrist and ankle. A sackcloth hood covered the head, topped by a ridiculous floppy hat. The eyes that blazed out from slits in the hood were the eyes of a madman, not the eyes of respected university professor Jonathan Crane.

Jeremiah Arkham believed in allowing his charges to live out their fantasies. That way, he was more likely to gain their trust. He'd discovered long ago that forcing them to wear asylum drabs provoked more trauma than it was worth.

"Come to gloat, have you?" Scarecrow hissed accusingly. "After all, you put me here." The crooked body straightened, and Scarecrow went on contemptuously. "Despite the fact I'm not insane. *You're* the one who's crazy!"

Batman was silent, letting the villain unburden his unhinged venom. He needed Scarecrow in a good mood.

"Look at you," Scarecrow went on scathingly. "You dress like a bat. You fly around at night. You hide your face behind a mask. Isn't *that* insane?"

"Far from it." Batman shrugged. "I'm not the one who left two security guards crippled by fear gas. It wasn't me who condemned their families to a lifetime of misery."

"Collateral damage," Scarecrow replied loftily. "There's always fallout when a repressed society tries to smother the creativity of its true individuals. Those guards stood between me and my destiny."

"You mean the Assyrian clay tablets you stole? You think books are worth more than life?"

"Books are worth more than anything," Scarecrow returned, his long skinny arms wrapping themselves around his body in a strange hug that seemed to reassure him. "Books are the repository of all knowledge. Books are more precious than gold!"

Batman adjusted his stance on the ledge, leaning in closer to the villain. "I haven't come here to argue with you, Crane."

Scarecrow bristled. "Professor Crane is out," he announced coldly. "Scarecrow is in."

As a child, Jonathan Crane had been severely traumatized by a flock of birds. Perhaps his vivid imagination had been fired by some illicit viewing of the Hitchcock movie, or perhaps he really had been attacked. No one but him would ever know. For years he'd hidden his growing psychosis from the world, until it had erupted one day in the psychology class he taught at Gotham University.

The good professor turned a gun on his students—
purely to illustrate a point, of course. The university
authorities didn't see things the same way. His foolish-
ness cost Crane his job, and so began his abrupt slide
into poverty and obscurity. Crane didn't bother too
much about lack of recognition, but he badly needed
money for buying his life's obsession: books.

He turned to crime, adopting the sinister imagery of
the Scarecrow. Birds had frightened him; scarecrows
frightened birds. Now Jonathan Crane—alias the
Scarecrow—would frighten everybody. Fear became
his stock-in-trade.

His scientific genius allowed him to concoct a range
of gases that could inflict fear, or terror, or dread, on
anyone who absorbed them. As his ambitions grew, he
experimented with gases that caused fear of specific
things. Scarecrow loved to watch an arachnaphobe,
for instance, imagining he was covered in revolting
spiders. Or a claustrophobe believing he was entombed alive in his coffin.

"Scarecrow," Batman said pointedly, "I'm here for
two reasons. First, to verify that *you* are here, and not
some ringer while the real Scarecrow goes on a ram-
page."

"I'll have you know, sir," Scarecrow said haughtily,
"that I would personally deal with any such imposter.
There is but one of me."

"Relax. I've heard more than enough to know it's
you." He paused, knowing how strange his next
words would sound. "Secondly, I want to ask you a
favor."

In the pale light Batman watched as the hood's rough-stitched mouth widened in a grin.

"And what, precisely, would you want from me?"

"A recipe," Batman said curtly. "For one of your fear gases."

Scarecrow stamped his straw-filled boot petulantly on the floor of his cell. "Oh, yes," he drawled sarcastically, "I do have a certain reputation as an altruist to maintain. I mean, I always bestow favors on lunatics who have me locked away!"

"I'll give you something in return," Batman offered.

Scarecrow didn't react.

Batman tried again. "I'll give you a book. A first edition."

The Dark Knight knew his enemy well. If there was one thing Scarecrow cared for with a passion that defied explanation, it was books. In secret stores and warehouses throughout the city, the Master of Fear had a collection of millions that he had bought or stolen over the years. It was his ambition to own every book in the world, from those written in ancient Egyptian hieroglyphs to the latest bestseller.

Beneath his grotesque hood, Scarecrow's eyes lit up. "A first edition?" he repeated, savoring each word. He drummed his fingertips lightly against his sack-covered mouth. "By whom? Shakespeare, perhaps? Marlowe? Spenser?" His voice turned disdainful. "Or are we talking Agatha Christie and Jackie Collins?"

"We're talking *Universe*," Batman said softly. "Scudder Klyce's *Universe*."

Scarecrow sneered. "A work of genius, yes. But

valuable? I'm certain I can purchase a copy for only a modest fee."

"The author's personal copy?" Batman asked. "In mint condition, with handwritten margin notes, and a previously unpublished addendum?"

Suddenly, Scarecrow's hands shot up to grasp the cold metal bars. "Do you jest with me, sir?" he cried theatrically, genuine anguish in his voice. "Is this another of your fiendish schemes to torture a poor man incarcerated against his will?"

Klyce's *Universe* was one of the most peculiar of all American books. Published privately in the early twentieth century, it was an idiosyncratic and highly original interpretation of existence, a "verifiable solution of the Riddle of the Universe," as Klyce himself put it. Only a thousand copies had ever been printed, and most of them had disappeared from view.

But the author's own copy was a rarity of great distinction.

"I would give much to possess this book," Scarecrow said piously. "My services for, say, the coming year? Or a blank check drawn on an offshore account in the Windward Islands?"

"Nothing so expensive," Batman assured him. "A recipe will be enough. For a very special fear gas."

Scarecrow visibly swelled with pride. "Name your terror, my man!"

"Just one thing—" Batman's voice dropped an octave. His eyes were dangerous slits, and the self-styled Master of Fear had to suppress a distinct shudder at the menace the vigilante projected. "Double-cross me, and I will ensure you stay in Arkham for the rest of your life."

He paused to let the words sink in, then added, "The hospital wing."

Scarecrow raised both hands, palms facing out, in a gesture of compliance. "My word, sir," he protested, "is my bond!"

Somewhere a dog was howling at the moon, as Batman swung again into the trees and out of the asylum grounds. He vaulted down onto the grass verge and, keeping to shadows, ran toward the nearest buildings, half a mile away.

Once there, he would disappear among the rooftops. When dawn came, and it was time to retire to the Batcave, one of the many Batmobiles hidden around the city would be his transport.

Bruce Wayne had found the old book in the cavernous attic of the Manor, still wrapped in heavy, ornate paper, a Christmas gift to his great-great-grandfather, possibly from Klyce himself. But the old man had died on Christmas Eve, and there would be no celebration in the Wayne household that year. Since then the book had waited in its dusty home.

It was a high price to pay to a criminal, Batman knew. But the formula Scarecrow had given him might prove invaluable. An insurance policy against . . . he didn't know what.

He would be busy in the Batcave labs tonight.

CHAPTER 7

Witches' Night

Gotham City, October 28

Cassandra had scarcely slept for forty-eight hours.

Every time she closed her eyes, she saw the broken, lifeless body of Raymond Marcus. On its own that would have been bad enough, but looming over the dead man, a symbol of murder and destruction, was the bull-headed beast she'd seen in her tarot vision.

Real fear gnawed away at her. She knew in her bones that her vision *meant* something. It hadn't just been a warning for the tragic Marcus. Cassandra couldn't explain it, not rationally and logically, because card reading, palmistry, and the other fortune-telling arts she practiced weren't rational themselves. They depended on the brain's right hemisphere, the pattern seeker, the home of the unconscious.

Cassandra just *knew*, in a way she didn't understand

and was afraid to analyze, in case picking her empathic gift to pieces destroyed it for all time.

She'd canceled all her appointments and put a CLOSED notice on her apartment door. That had brought the only smile she'd enjoyed since Marcus's visit, as she toyed with scrawling DUE TO UNFORESEEN CIRCUMSTANCES on the sign. A great advertisement for a fortune-teller!

She spent a day in the battered old armchair that had once belonged to her grandmother, flicking through the pages of reference books taken from her small library shelves. There were a lot of entries regarding bull worship—it had been commonplace for a long time in the ancient world, particularly during the zodiacal Age of Taurus, more than three thousand years ago.

Widely regarded as the most advanced race in antiquity, the Egyptians had worshiped the sacred Bull of Apu for centuries. Bulls' bodies had been mummified in a way that suggested they were as important as the pharaohs themselves. Over the years, more than a dozen of the massive bull tombs had been unearthed during official excavations.

On the Mediterranean island of Crete, the people worshiped bulls on a daily basis. Thousands of vases and pottery items had survived from the Minoan culture, many of them illustrated with the "bull dance." Graceful youths of both sexes took their lives in their hands and vaulted over the angry bulls' backs.

And, of course, lurking in the heart of the famous King Minos's maze was the most feared bull of all, the

Minotaur. Half man, half animal, it prowled the miles
of subterranean labyrinth beneath the royal palace
bringing death to any intruder in its domain.

Bull worship died out sometime before the birth of
Christ, but even in the modern world remnants of the
old ways survived. Every summer in the Spanish
town of Pamplona, a herd of wild bulls was released
into the narrow winding streets. No teenage boy could
call himself a man until he'd "run the bulls," sprinting
through the medieval town with several dozen maddened animals in hot pursuit. Nowadays, even the
tourists joined in.

There were literally hundreds of mentions of bulls
in her books, but only one Cassandra kept returning
to.

It was a crude drawing of a beast found on a shard
of pottery from ancient Lebanon. Scholars took the
half human, half bull to be a representation of the
Middle Eastern storm and war god, Baal. In the pan-
theon of gods, Baal had been a rising star who was finally elevated to the status of Jehovah's number-one
enemy.

The lines of the drawing were too thick, the perspec-
tive all wrong, but the artist had captured one thing
perfectly: pure evil seemed to shine from Baal's
brutish eyes.

But by the end of the day Cassandra was no closer
to an answer.

Then she heard the news from cities across America. The security guard in New York who'd run amok,
burning down his own museum; when they found his

body, he was wearing a horned shamanic mask. Underneath, his flesh had been stripped to the skull. The Keystone City subway driver who claimed he'd been possessed by "a weird blue light." The near-aborted shuttle launch in Florida, where Superman was said to have battled with a "mysterious globe of blue light."

Cassandra didn't know how, but it was obvious to her that these events were connected. Something terrible was starting to happen, and she felt as if she were the only person aware of it.

Now, in the afternoon of the day after these incidents occurred, she found her feet carrying her toward Gotham Cathedral. It hadn't been a conscious decision. In fact, at first she didn't even know where she was going. But some part of her obviously did, and it was with a feeling of shock that she found herself standing across the street from the badly damaged church.

POLICE LINE—DO NOT CROSS was stenciled on the yards of tape stretched along the bottom of the wide steps that led up to the cathedral entrance. There were a couple of police cars parked down on the street, and a solitary policeman chewed gum as he stood vigil. Close to him were a dozen large bunches of cut flowers, placed there by grieving relatives of the victims and the public, who had heard the news on TV and radio. It was one of the few ways people had of showing solidarity with others in a time of grief. A way of saying, "We feel for you, even if there's nothing else we can do."

Cassandra gave a mental shrug. The cathedral was obviously off limits. Perhaps she should just go home again.

But whatever impulse had brought her here was stronger and more daunting than an official police line. Despite her best intentions, Cassandra marched straight up to the young cop. He saw her coming, her striking platinum hair framing her pretty face, and straightened his cap.

"Can I help you, ma'am?"

"Someone I know died here the other night." Cassandra spoke without thinking. "I'd like to go in and pay my respects."

"I'm sorry, ma'am. I can't allow that."

At that moment, a group of men and women in plain clothes, accompanied by a couple of uniformed officers, exited and began to make their way down the steps.

"Okay, Andy," one of the officers called, "Forensics are finished now. You stay until the EPA arrives to check the site."

"How long?"

The policeman shrugged. "If they're not here in a couple of hours, call in."

The young cop gave his colleague a thumbs-up sign and watched as the group drove off before he turned back to Cassandra. She wasn't there.

As soon as the young guard had turned away, Cassandra seized her chance. She stepped behind one of the tall pillars at the cathedral entrance, out of sight of the small group on the steps.

The cathedral's studded oak doors stood half open.

and as she slipped through them Cassandra felt that she was entering another world. The traffic noise from the street could no longer be heard, and the air inside was calm and still and peaceful. Stained-glass windows filtered the light, casting a warm golden glow.

Twisted roof beams lay here and there where they'd fallen, two of them on top of a row of smashed wooden pews. A Bible had fallen open among the debris, a poignant reminder that faith didn't always save, at least not in this world.

She stood for a moment at the top of the aisle leading up to the altar, bowing her head and making the sign of the cross above her heart.

Cassandra was no Christian. In fact, it was only a few centuries since the church would have burned her at the stake as a witch. But she had great respect for all religion. Humanity had always believed in something far greater than itself, something that was sensed rather than known: an order higher than mere mortals, where all the banalities of evil made sudden, perfect sense. Who was she to judge how they worshiped it?

Her head still slightly bowed, Cassandra walked down the aisle, footsteps echoing on the checkered tile floor. She was puzzled to see chalk scrawls on the floor, until she realized they were the outlines of bodies. She wondered which one marked where Raymond Marcus died, searching for his miracle.

Cassandra said a short, silent prayer that in death he would find relief from the pain that had plagued him in life.

Unsure what to do next, Cassandra looked around her. The ornately carved pulpit was little more than matchwood, and several of the cathedral's impressive stained-glass windows had been damaged beyond repair. A jagged hole gaped in the center of the altar recess—she remembered the radio announcer saying that a bolt of energy had come bursting up through the floor.

The altar table itself had been fragmented by the impact, barely recognizable slivers of wood lying everywhere.

She bent to pick up a short length of fractured wood, feeling a little guilty as she gingerly touched it.

Upon lifting it, she was immediately plunged into a vision of another world, as daylight turned into darkness.

Cassandra saw a street she didn't recognize, but knew from the buildings that it was someplace in Gotham. Indistinct crowds of people thronged the street, laughing and moving along in dancelike steps. A firecracker cartwheeled into the air, its bangs and crackles punctuated by the laughter of the crowd.

Now she could see the people more clearly. Every one of them wore a mask. Some were cheap plastic replicas of celebrities and presidents, while others bore the image of skulls, animals, and even characters from children's cartoons.

"Trick or treat?" she heard a young boy in a mask call out, and realized that this was Halloween. Witches' night. In olden times, it was a celebration of another year safe from evil. It was also when ordinary

mortals had to take extraordinary steps to banish evil
for the coming year.

The whole city seemed to be engaged in the street
party. The sides of buildings were lit up with neon
signs. Holograms depicting jack-o'-lanterns were projected in the air. Mobs of people streamed from all directions. Music boomed from the open doorways of a
dozen bars and diners. A group of teenage girls wearing pop-star masks and carrying lit candles led an impromptu dance on the pavement, bringing traffic to a
halt.

Suddenly a bearded student, his face made up to re-
semble a werewolf, pointed upward. Cassandra
looked, and her blood turned to ice water in her veins.

Towering over the street, a thousand feet high, was
the horned monster she'd seen in Raymond Marcus's
tarot card.

Terrified, Cassandra tried to drop the fragment of
wood she held. But her fingers were locked rigid
around it, and try as she might she couldn't move
them. The church interior was like a distant dream.
Reality was now witness to the Halloween street
party.

The music had magically halted. The dancing girls
stood rooted to the spot, gazing up. The shrieks and
laughter of the joyous crowd were silenced, and a
grim oppression seemed to settle like a blanket on the
whole street.

The massive figure moved for the first time, tilting
its head downward to look at the silent figures on the
street far below. A huge drop of blood slid from the

creature's stained pelt, splashing over a group of people as it landed on the tarmac.

Its eyes blazed red, then cobalt blue . . . and all hell broke loose.

Jagged streaks of lightning leaped from the behemoth's eyes, striking a half-dozen different buildings. Huge chunks of masonry broke free, tumbling end over end, smashing to the ground amid the recent revelers. Cassandra saw the bearded student in the werewolf makeup fall, flattened by a billboard that had dropped from ten stories above.

The air was full of frightened screams, and the terrified crowd scattered in panic as the whole city began to crumble around them. Gaping holes yawned in the streets, swallowing a thousand people at a time. Flames leaped from several buildings as gas and electricity lines were severed.

Human blood ran through the gutters in surging rivulets.

"Ma'am?"

Suddenly, Cassandra was back in the cathedral. She was still on her knees, but the sliver of wood had fallen from her hand. Her heart was beating at an incredible rate, trapped in her frozen body. She couldn't see for the tears that filled her eyes.

"Are you all right, ma'am?" The young policeman stood behind her, his face concerned. Although they'd taught him how to handle situations like this at the police academy, somehow, it hadn't prepared him for the real thing. "You really shouldn't have come in. I . . .

I'm sorry about your loss," he added, feeling totally inadequate.

In silence, Cassandra allowed him to take her arm and lead her back outside.

She had foretold Raymond Marcus's death. As if on cue, the man had died. Now she needed to find out what *this* vision meant . . . and how to prevent it from coming true.

There was only one man she knew who could help her. But first, she would have to find him.

The sun was a distant yellow disk, planet Earth invisible against its glare.

J'onn J'onzz stood on his native world of Mars once more, his feet planted on the very rim of Olympus Mons, the highest mountain on the Red Planet. Once, it had been a popular attraction for his people, offering the best views of any location on Mars.

Six miles below lay the great plains. Beyond Mangala Valles, Daedalia Planum stretched away to the south. To the west, the rugged Tharsis Montes blocked off all further view, but he knew that behind them lay Noctis Labyrinthus, the Maze of the Night, and the massive impact basins of Argyre and Hellas.

Strange, he thought, *these new names, when once I knew them only by their Martian designations.*

Perhaps he should have told NASA, when they first started sending the Voyagers and Explorers to document his world. But Martian vowels and syllables are unpronounceable for any human being. So he said nothing, and on Earth Latin and ancient Greek became the new language of Mars.

At least the old names will live on . . . while I live on.

Every year he came here, for an hour, a day, or a week—for however long it took him to purge the lure of the Red Planet from his system. A lifetime of memories was locked up in the ubiquitous red dust and black basaltic boulders that littered the plateau.

He turned to look northeast, toward the massive Boreale Chasma. Far beyond it, frozen in two hundred degrees of cold, was the northern icecap; under it lay the vast subterranean reservoirs where the precious water had seeped away. One day NASA was in for a major surprise.

Somewhere down on the plain, wan sunlight twinkled off gleaming metal. Something left behind by one of the NASA expeditions, a surface rover. Billion-dollar junk, glittering like a jewel amid the debris of his world.

The land had been living once, and it had teemed with green. The inhabitants—J'onn's people, the very roots of his existence—had been like sentient beings everywhere: good, bad, indifferent, and every moral shade in between. He had a wife then, and the most beautiful daughter. He also had friends. He had a life.

And then a devastating plague had claimed everything, not just from him, but from Mars itself. Apart from J'onn, not a single soul had survived the contagion that spread faster than they could burn the bodies of the dead.

As powerful emotion swept through him, he sank to

his knees. One hand touched the ground, and he scooped up a handful of dust, letting its dreams and memories trickle slowly away through his fingers. It swirled gently in the thin, almost nonexistent atmosphere, and settled slowly to the ground.

Dust to dust . . . like the bones of my people.

He raised his eyes beneath his craglike brows, squinting against the setting sun to make out Earth. His adopted world.

J'onn thought of the friends who'd taken him in, treated him as one of their own, given purpose back to his life when he saw only misery ahead of him. He would always owe a debt to Superman and the members of the Justice League.

But in his heart he would always be a Martian, a Red Planet warrior, the last of his race.

He leaped outward, almost overcompensating for the weaker gravity, and soared down for several long, glorious minutes. The past was long gone, but while he held it sealed in his memory, in some way it would live on.

Then he landed on the plain and strode off into the red, dusty distance over the bones of his people.

CHAPTER 8

The Darknight Detective

Marlbuck Point, October 29

"And how can I help ye, laddie?"

Hamish Stewart's lilting Scottish accent cut through the quiet of the late-October noon. He stood beside the scuffed Dodge Charger that had pulled up beside him, its top down. Hamish's expression was polite as he ran his eyes over the car's driver—a broad-shouldered man with silver flecks in his hair, wearing heavy-rimmed glasses.

"Mr. Stewart?" the man asked. "I'm Dag Rawlings. I'm a—"

"Journalist, aye?" Hamish finished for him, gesturing toward the notepad and tape recorder that lay on the passenger seat.

"You're very astute, sir." Dag smiled as he unlatched the door and swung his legs out of the car and onto the gravel road. He reached back in for a sturdy walking cane and leaned on it as he stood. "But actually, I was about to say writer. There's a difference."

"Oh, I know that fine," the sturdy, middle-aged Scot replied. "I'm a writer of sorts myself. Historical research. Two books published, working on the third."

"Well, sir, I won't take up much of your valuable time." Dag squinted his eyes against the golden autumn sun as it reflected off the car's side mirror. "I'm here to see Jenny Ayles."

"Maybe," the older man mused, "but the question is, does she want to see you?"

"It's all right, Hamish," Jenny Ayles called, her footsteps crunching on the gravel as she hurried up to join them. "Mr. Rawlings called me last night. I said I'd see him. I should have told you—it just went completely out of my head."

Hamish Stewart grunted and looked at his watch. "Aye, well, just be sure ye don't take too long. I'm on a tight budget, as I'm sure ye know."

"I should know," Jenny muttered under her breath as Stewart strode off. "You remind me often enough!"

Dag smiled, his perfect white teeth marred by a broken crown at one side. "Bit of a slavedriver, is he?"

"Let's walk over to where I'm working," Jenny said, before answering his question. "No, Hamish is a joy to work for. But he has to fund his own research, because his book advances are so small."

She led him off the track and through a thick clump of bushes to an open grassy area beyond, Dag's limp slight but noticeable as he walked. They were on a small plateau about fifty feet above the ocean, and

Dag could smell the salt in the cool breeze. He'd driven up to Marlbuck Point from Gotham City in the noon sunshine, leaving behind the docks and industrial zones as the Dodge climbed the narrow, twisting road that hugged the rocky coast. Only forty miles from town, yet it was like another world.

The grass in front of them was scarred with several neat trenches, about eighteen inches wide and several feet deep. A thin young man in a "Save the Planet" T-shirt was on his hands and knees, sifting through a spoil heap with painstaking slowness. He glanced up briefly to acknowledge their presence, then bent back to his task.

Jenny stopped at the end of a trench and looked around to survey the whole site. "You'd never believe there was a village here once," she said almost wistfully.

"You're kidding."

"No. See—evidence of a hearth." She pointed to a patch of upturned soil a few shades darker than the rest. "Charcoal. Stake holes in the ground there—" Her finger swiveled, indicating a few small indentations. "Rotted wood in them. They supported houses, maybe six hundred years ago. At least, if Hamish's theories are correct."

"Yes. I've read his books."

Jenny looked at him in surprise. "You have? That's a first—I've never met anyone who's read them. Apart from myself, and Jamie." She nodded toward the young man. "And he's Hamish's son."

"Mr. Stewart believes that members of a Scottish

clan settled parts of the east coast of America centuries before Columbus 'discovered' it, right?"

"With good reason," Jenny said defensively, though there had been nothing in Dag's tone to say that he was skeptical. "We've unearthed quite a lot of circumstantial evidence. We just need something concrete now, like an inscription, or maybe a tool."

She broke off, playing nervously with a strand of the blond hair that framed her face. "But you're not here to ask me about Hamish, Mr. Rawlings," she said at last.

"That's true." Dag nodded toward a tussock of sea grass. "Mind if we sit down, Miss Ayles? My leg . . ." he added, by way of explanation.

Dag carefully lowered himself onto the grass, and Jenny seated herself cross-legged on a rock a few feet away. "As I mentioned on the phone," he went on, unstrapping the tape recorder from his shoulder, "I'm investigating the Gotham Pyramid."

Jenny pulled her cardigan closer around her, though the sun was warm in spite of the sea breeze. "And that's all I'm willing to talk about," she said, almost sternly. "The pyramid."

Dag nodded. "I'm a writer, not a tabloid reporter. It would be helpful if you could tell me everything you remember about the pyramid, no matter how irrelevant it seems."

Dag glanced meaningfully at the tape recorder, and Jenny nodded. He switched it to "record" mode, and held the microphone loosely in front of her.

Jenny hesitated for a moment, collecting her

thoughts. "Well, come to think of it," she began, "when our team first stood on top, a shiver ran up my spine. I didn't know if it was excitement, or fear." She shook her head. "But it certainly affected Peter. My boyfriend," she added. "From the moment we arrived, he was bad-tempered and impatient, picking fights for no reason. I thought it was because he was so excited. He had this theory, you see—that the pyramid was constructed for a shaman, a witch doctor, if you like. A sorcerer. Someone who wanted to control the pyramid's energy system."

"Energy system?" Dag's eyebrows furled. "How do you mean?"

Jenny gazed at the sunlight reflecting off the restless ocean, and sighed. She hadn't bothered explaining Peter's theories to the reporters who'd quizzed her, the ones who were interested only in scandal. But now she found herself telling Dag everything Peter had confided in her over the years. His belief in telluric energy, the natural flow from high- to low-resistance points of the earth's magnetic field. His theories about human exploitation of piezoelectric forces, and how the mind could interact with their electromagnetic fields. His wild ideas about undiscovered energy forms produced by currents in the deep magma layers under the earth's crust.

Dag listened attentively, interjecting the odd question, careful to keep his voice level so as not to betray the mounting excitement he felt at Jenny's answers. Perhaps this wasn't going to be a wild-goose chase after all. He was beginning to see hidden connections between events, and was particularly interested in Jenny's description of a worldwide energy grid that connected hundreds, if not thousands, of ancient sites.

Hamish Stewart ambled past them a couple of times, pointedly looking at his watch and muttering to himself, but he made no effort to interrupt the interview.

When Jenny finally began to run out of words, the sun was starting to sink toward the horizon, lengthening the shadows on the grass. The breeze had become markedly cooler.

"I seem to have taken up most of your afternoon," Dag apologized. "Thank you. I only hope I haven't reawakened painful memories."

"I've never forgotten, Mr. Rawlings," Jenny said with sudden passion. "I think about what happened every day. I have nightmares more nights than not." She hesitated briefly, as if coming to some inner decision, then rushed on. "That's why I left the university. Everything reminded me of Peter."

She paused, then added, "And Professor Mills."

Dag could tell that Jenny wanted to talk—that she needed someone to listen to her. Deliberately, making sure she saw what he was doing, he reached down and switched his tape recorder off.

Jenny's eyes flicked up to look into his, and she blinked to hold back a tear. "The tabloids just printed what they wanted," she said sadly. "They twisted everything I said, made Gotham U sound like a hotbed of sex and sin. They even made things up. But it wasn't like that at all!"

She was quiet for a long moment, her eyes distant, wrapped in memories. "Peter was a genius," she said almost dreamily, then quickly corrected herself, "*Is* a genius. Robert Mills himself said Peter has the potential to revolutionize archaeology. But he's also very temperamental. He can be very . . . difficult with those close to him."

Another silence before her words came pouring out. "It was like that in Peru. Last year. Peter and I quarreled—it was over something trivial, I can't even remember what. But he said some hurtful things to me. I was upset."

Conflicting emotions crossed her pretty face, guilt and misery and grief all jumbled up together. "Robert . . . comforted me. One thing led to another, and . . . well, sorry to be so blunt, but Peter walked in on us."

"And you think that gave Peter motivation for what happened at the pyramid?"

"Yes. No. I don't know." Jenny was close to tears. "The Peter I know would never do a thing like that, not under any circumstances. But I told you—he started acting strangely as soon as we climbed the pyramid."

Hamish Stewart passed again, and Dag got to his feet. Jenny saw him wince with pain as he straightened his bad leg. She stood up herself and reached out a hand to shake his.

"Thank you, Mr. Rawlings," she said sincerely. "I feel a lot better now. I guess I needed someone to listen to me."

"That's something we all need," Dag agreed sagely. "Thank you again for your time, Ms. Ayles."

He took a couple of steps, then turned back to her as if he'd forgotten something.

"Oh, one last question, if you don't mind." He slipped his hand in his pocket and brought out a sheet of folded drawing paper. He opened it, and Jenny squinted at it in the fading light. "Does this mean anything to you?"

There was a pencil sketch on the sheet, showing a human figure dressed in animal pelts and wearing a bull-like horned headpiece. Jenny stared at it and shook her head. "Sorry," she told him. "It looks like some kind of tribal shaman—similar to the ones depicted in cave art in some areas of Europe. But I'm afraid I don't know enough about the subject to be any more precise. I can recommend some books, if you like."

"Excellent." Dag refolded the sheet and stuffed it back in his pocket.

Jenny reeled off a short list of titles he might find interesting, then watched as Dag retraced his steps along the footpath and through the bushes. She heard the sound of his car engine start and caught a fleeting glimpse of the glow from his taillights as the Charger bounced back along the gravel track toward the highway.

She felt drained, but strangely more at peace than she had since Peter's disappearance. Even Hamish Stewart's pointed comments about "the wasted afternoon" didn't faze her.

As far as Dag Rawlings was concerned, the afternoon had been far from wasted. He had learned more than if he'd spent a week in a library.

The Dodge barreled back down the highway toward Gotham in light traffic. The rush hour had started, but most vehicles were headed in the opposite direction, out of the city.

Dag thumbed a button on the dashboard, and the glove compartment popped open. He reached over to take out a moist towelette and rubbed it across his head. When he tossed it aside, it was smeared with the silver highlights from his hair. Instantly he looked twenty years younger.

As he continued on, his tongue pushed at the broken tooth in the corner of his mouth, dislodging the small plastic camouflage cap. He spat it out.

Jenny Ayles and Hamish Stewart—and anyone else who'd seen him that afternoon—would remember a middle-aged man with a broken tooth and a bad limp. Not the most elaborate disguise he'd ever used, but it had served his purpose.

No one would ever connect Dag Rawlings with the man who really drove the car—Gotham City's billionaire playboy, Bruce Wayne.

Celebrity TV shows and newspaper gossip columns often reported on Bruce Wayne's comings and goings, after all, he was reputed to be the city's wealthiest man—and its most eligible bachelor.

According to the reports Wayne was a fop, a handsome but weak-willed man whose major mission in life was to spend the vast fortune his father had bequeathed him. His exploits on the ski slopes of the Italian Alps or in the sun-drenched resorts of South Africa gave the tabloid reporters reams of column space as they speculated on who he was dating, who he had dumped, and who had dumped him.

He'd been romantically linked with supermodels, Hollywood actresses, and the daughters of European aristocracy.

Not one of them would recognize the man who sat at the wheel of the Dodge, his face grim, eyes intent on the road ahead even as his mind raced to integrate everything he'd learned from Jenny Ayles.

Too many coincidences, he thought. *All of this is connected somehow—Robert Mills's murder, Peter Glaston's disappearance, the weird blue lights, the unbelievably powerful figure who faced the Justice League . . . and beat them. But how? What are the connections?*

Wayne took the service road for the Gotham Narrows Bridge and was halfway across it before he saw the golden beam of light that lanced upward from a city roof. It was focused on a single low, dark cloud, and as he drew closer he could make out the shimmering shape of the Bat-Signal projected on the cloud's base.

Commissioner Gordon needs to see the Batman.

A half mile past the end of the bridge, Wayne turned the car off the main road into the old Industrial Zone. Back in the nineteen thirties and forties, a nationwide network of rail lines had terminated here, bringing raw materials from the hinterland to feed Gotham's insatiable factories. When the new, postwar light industries started to expand, they relocated to the area of the docks, abandoning the I.Z. to the rats and vandals. Now even the vandals had moved on, leaving a ghost town stripped of everything that had even a glimmer of value.

Wayne dimmed his headlights and drove swiftly through the rutted, disintegrating streets. There were no streetlights here, but the so-called playboy knew exactly where he was going.

As the Dodge approached a crumbling red sandstone warehouse, Wayne depressed a button on a small infrared control panel concealed behind the car's radio display. Immediately, a section of brick work slid back, revealing a space just large enough for the Dodge to squeeze through.

The secret doorway closed automatically behind him as the car shot inside, drawing to a halt in the deep shadows. Over the years, parts of the building roof had collapsed, falling into the interior, leaving mounds of rubble and glass heaped up on the store room floor.

Wayne slid out of the car, with not a trace of the limp he'd feigned that afternoon. It was almost pitch black in here, but his movements were smooth and confident; obviously, he knew the place well.

A cursory check assured him no one had been here since he'd last taken the Dodge out in the early hours of the morning. The thick dust on the floor hadn' been disturbed, and the all-but-invisible lengths of cord that he'd threaded across the open areas were unbroken. He stepped quickly over them, carefully keep ing to the brick stepping stones scattered here and there, seemingly at random, as he made for an indistinct, six-foot-high pile of rubble.

He bent suddenly, reaching underneath a twisted pile of corrugated steel panels. His fingers encountered hard, cool plastic and sought out the control buttons set into it.

The air shimmered for a moment as the hologram projector shut off. The high pile of rubble was suddenly revealed for what it really was—the sleek, menacing lines of the Batmobile, the Batman's high-tech car.

Wayne held the palm of one hand against the infrared reader pad recessed in the car door. Soundlessly, the door slid open. If he'd been an intruder, several hundred volts would have sent him on his way.

Seconds later the Batmobile shot out of the building its massive engine barely ticking over, all of its lights running on infrared mode. It wheeled in a tight semicircle and sped toward the junction with the highway into downtown.

The man seated behind the wheel, hidden by smoked glass and steel plate, was no longer Bruce Wayne. A lightweight cowl covered his head; short, stubby, batlike ears jutted up from it. His eyes were hidden behind a mask, the bat-symbol emblazoned on his chest.

He was already doing well over a hundred miles an hour as the car hit the near-deserted highway.

* * *

Three miles, and fewer minutes, later, Batman parked in the stygian shadows of a narrow city center alley.

The Batmobile's roof slid noiselessly open. A grapnel snaked upward, and Batman swung himself up into the nighttime rooftops. Swinging, running, and diving, never setting a foot wrong, he made his way swiftly toward Police Headquarters.

A huge electronic billboard blazed on a building roof. ONLY 2 DAYS 2 GO! its flickering neon letters declared. Beneath them was an array of grotesque masks, their features lighting up and darkening again in an eye-catching display that had been the talk of the city when it was first erected a week earlier.

MEGA-MASKS was emblazoned along the bottom of the board. WE PUT THE 'HELL' IN HELLOWEEN!

Batman grimaced as the inertia reel of his line swung him past the face of the massive billboard, his trailing cape briefly covering the winking neon lights. Halloween was far from his favorite time of year. It always seemed to draw out the worst of Gotham, as if the old legends about it being witches' night were firmly grounded in reality—as if, under their masks, people's inhibitions disappeared. And, of course, it provided the perfect cover for criminal activity.

Villains like Scarecrow always seemed to be revitalized as the autumn nights heralded the coming winter. Last year it had been the turn of Cornelius Stirk, the cannibal, who'd escaped from Arkham Asylum and brought terror to the city for days before Batman managed to return him to his padded cell.

But this year promises to be the worst of all. The unwelcome thought ran through Batman's mind. *The Justice League's mightiest members gone—captured or abducted by who knows what? And me armed with only a handful of suspicions and even fewer leads.*

He shrugged the nagging thought aside. Jenny Ayles had given him much to consider, and once he dealt with whatever emergency Jim Gordon was calling him to, he'd devote himself full-time to trying to piece Jenny's data into what little he already knew.

There was a sense of some grand scheme behind all the seemingly disparate events of the past month or so. It would take time and hard thought before he could begin to pin it down.

Batman flexed his ankles and knees as he dropped fifteen feet through the air, landing atop the roof of the insurance company building that stood next to Police HQ. Slightly below him, at the far end of the roof, he could see two figures waiting by the huge lamp that projected the Bat-Signal. Jim Gordon was unmistakable, his overcoat collar turned up as he hunched himself against the cutting wind that blew at this height above the city's concrete canyons. There was a dull red glow as he puffed furiously at the pipe clamped in his teeth.

Obviously fallen off the wagon, Batman thought, knowing that Gordon was having difficulty implementing his decision to quit smoking. The stress of the job made it doubly hard for the lifelong nicotine addict to break his habit.

Batman's eyes narrowed as he saw that Jim Gordon's companion was a woman. She was bundled up in a dark cape, a scarf knotted over her hair. And it was her hair, struggling out of its covering in platinum locks, that gave her identity away.

Batman had met Madame Cassandra once before. At his wits' end while striving to bring to a close one of the Joker's insane murder sprees, he'd turned to Cassandra for help. She'd been of little assistance, but he remembered her as a sincere and serious young woman.

Not a sound betrayed him as Batman dropped down onto the lower roof. He moved through shadows thrown by the forest of air-conditioning boxes toward the waiting couple. Only when he was half-a-dozen feet away did he cough slightly to alert them to his presence.

He saw Cassandra start visibly, but Jim Gordon was long used to Batman's surreptitious comings and goings and had learned to take them in stride.

"Sorry about this." Gordon turned toward the shadows, and Batman saw that the older man looked uncomfortable, even embarrassed as he briefly nodded in Cassandra's direction. "She refuses to talk to anyone else. If I've brought you here on a wild-goose chase, call me an old fool and—"

"Never that, Commissioner," Batman said quietly, keeping it formal for the benefit of the girl.

Batman's friendship with Jim Gordon went back a long way, to the very first nights when Batman took to the rooftops as the city's guardian. A dozen years earlier, eight-year-old Bruce Wayne had stood by, young and terrified and helpless, as his parents were gunned down before his eyes in a street robbery gone wrong. The boy's life seemed to end then.

Later, when terror had turned to grief and then to guilt, the child had knelt on his parents' grave and made a solemn vow in their memory.

"Mother, Father, I promise you this," Bruce Wayne said, the tears that rolled down his cheeks lost in the driving midnight rain. "Someday, somehow, I will prevent other innocent people from dying. What happened to you will never happen to anyone else, if I have the power to stop it!"

For more than a decade, young Bruce Wayne worked obsessively to attain the goals he'd set for himself. Regular punishing exercise turned him into a perfect physical specimen. He developed reading and memory skills until he could recall almost anything he'd ever seen at will. He expanded his general knowledge until his head swam with facts and figures, and took in-depth courses on subjects as varied as forensic science and the psychology of criminality.

He traveled extensively, training under a variety of masters: detectives, martial artists, and gymnasts. The Wayne fortune meant that he could afford to employ only the very best teachers.

Finally, when he was twenty-one, he decided that his training had come to an end. After all these years, he was ready. It was time to fulfill the promise he'd made to his parents. Time for justice.

He chose the image of the bat as his disguise because it inspired fear, particularly in criminals. It never ceased to amaze Batman how the much-maligned bat was reviled as a demon, a symbol of evil and a harbinger of death, throughout the world.

But Bruce Wayne would be the bat-demon from heaven. He would help ordinary people. He would bring justice to those who mocked it. He would bring law to the lives of those who hated it.

And it would all have ended within weeks, had it not been for James Gordon.

Gordon had broken a long-running corruption racket in his own force in Chicago. Memories were long, and a lot of cops didn't like one of their own who blabbed. So Gordon was transferred to Gotham City as harsh a way as any for a policeman to be punished.

Jim Gordon was appalled both by the lawlessness of Gotham, and the ineptitude and corruption of its police. He immediately saw an ally in this new vigilante—the "Batman," as the media called him. Both men thought the same way, both would confront any danger in the cause of what they knew was right, and both loved justice with a passion.

Sometimes, lying awake late into the night, Gordon had wished that he too could become a costumed crimefighter. No paperwork to bury him, no boss to order him around, no more petty squabbling and jealousies from his subordinates. But Gordon had a wife and child, and he owed it to them to build a reliable and stable career.

Not long after Batman's presence in Gotham had first become obvious, a police team had laid an ambush for the vigilante. Committed to never using firearms, Batman found himself trapped in an empty house surrounded by more than a dozen sharpshooters. He'd already taken one bullet, a high-velocity rifle shot that seared through the flesh of his thigh and made it difficult to stand, let alone run.

Without Jim Gordon's help, Batman would have died that night.

The righteous cop followed the dictates of his conscience. He turned a blind eye when it was needed most, and allowed Batman to escape to fight again another night. To become one of the few men in the world that Gordon would trust with his life in the war against crime.

A lot had changed in the past dozen years. Jim's good work saw him promoted again and again, until he'd eventually become Commissioner. But in the interim, his wife left him, taking their son with her. His niece Barbara was shot and crippled by the Joker; now, unknown to her uncle, she had become the mysterious Oracle, whose computer expertise was invaluable to the Justice League.

Finally, Jim's hopes of finding new love were smashed when his second wife, Sara Essen, was murdered.

Only one thing hadn't changed: through everything, his friendship with Batman had endured, unwavering.

"I'll wait out of earshot," the commissioner said now, snapping off the heavy switch on the Bat-Signal projector. The stylized black bat disappeared from the clouds.

"No," Cassandra said emphatically. "What I have to

say might sound crazy, but the police should hear it, too."

Gordon nodded his agreement, and Cassandra's brow creased as she tried to penetrate the roof shadows. She knew Batman was there, she'd heard his voice, but there was nothing in the darkness she could pin down as a human shape. She could feel his presence, though, steady and calming.

"Please, go on," Batman said, as if he sensed her dilemma.

"As you know, I'm an empath," Cassandra began, her voice quiet and steady. "In scientific terms, my unconscious mind picks up tiny signals from other people and amplifies them. Sometimes, I can extrapolate these feelings into the future, so I can tell what's going to happen before it does."

She broke off abruptly, afraid that Jim Gordon would laugh at her. Batman already knew of her abilities, but the pragmatic commissioner didn't. However, Jim had studied psychology, and knew that 90 percent or more of all communication took place at a level below the threshold of conscious perception. In fact, Gordon's own department increasingly used slow-motion videos of criminal interrogations to reveal far more than their words ever could. The telling of a lie could be pinpointed exactly by the film.

"The night of the attack at Gotham Cathedral," Cassandra continued, "I had a consultation with a client. I had a full-blown vision. My first ever." Her voice became husky with emotion, and she stopped for a second to compose herself. "I saw that my client was going to die at the hands of a bull-headed monster."

A shiver ran down Batman's spine, a feeling most people might have put down to fear. But Batman knew it for what it was—a signal that another piece of this unfathomable jigsaw was starting to fall into place.

"I advised my client to go home. He ignored me, and paid the price. He . . . he was crushed to death later that night at the service."

Jim Gordon frowned. It was his job to catch whoever had killed those people in the cathedral, but despite throwing every police officer he could at the case, so far he didn't have a single lead.

"That's it?" the commissioner asked Cassandra, unable to keep the disappointment from his voice.

"It was enough for me, Commissioner!" Cassandra shot back at him.

Jim accepted the rebuke with a muttered apology. Easy for him to forget how deeply and personally death always touched those affected by it. He saw a dozen or more corpses every week of his life; it was sometimes hard to remember that each one had its own tragic tale.

He turned away to fire up his pipe again, and Cassandra went on in a low voice. "Next day I went to the cathedral to pay my respects. I had another vision, much more powerful than the first." She halted to moisten her suddenly dry lips—a gesture, both men knew, that what she had experienced truly frightened her. "I saw the bull-headed man again, but this time he was gigantic. He towered over Gotham City like a god."

"Or a devil," Batman added, so softly she didn't even hear.

"Lightning came from his eyes and his hands. Buildings burst into flame. The whole city was on fire. People were dying—men and women. I could hear children screaming—"

Cassandra broke off, her shoulders heaving as sobs racked her body. Tears welled up in her eyes and poured down her cheeks. Unnoticed, Batman had taken a couple of steps closer to her. His arm extended around her shoulder, drawing her against him, letting her feel the calm strength of his body. A man who had mastered his fear.

Her sobs subsided, and she tilted her head back so she was looking up directly into the vigilante's masked eyes.

"It's going to happen," she said, as evenly as she could. "I *know* it's going to happen. The whole city was on fire!" She reached up to knuckle away fresh tears. When she spoke again, there was a vehement edge to her words. "You have to stop it, Batman. *Somebody* has to stop it!"

Jim Gordon heaved a sigh. He could have been in his snug office for the past half hour, wading through some of the paperwork that deluged him every day. "Guess I am that old fool after all," he began, but stopped as Batman spoke.

"Cassandra, what you've just told us fits very closely with another case I'm investigating. Think carefully now—" His voice was still soft, but contained the authoritative tone of a man used to getting his own way. "Was there any indication of a time scale in your vision? I mean, anything that would allow you to judge exactly when this was going to happen?"

"Why, yes." Cassandra hadn't paid much attention to the detail of what she'd seen, she'd been too traumatized by the death and destruction. But the date had been obvious. "Everyone was wearing masquerade costumes. And face masks. Halloween . . . it'll happen on Halloween."

"All Hallow's Eve." Batman's voice was grim. "We have only two days from now. . . ."

CHAPTER 9

The Stone King

Peter Glaston was alive, but dead. He still existed, his body still moved and acted, his mind still thought.

Only, it was someone else's existence that filled him, crowding Peter out until he was no more than a spectator in the theater of his own life. His body moved at the volition of an intruder. The thoughts of his conqueror blasted his own into wisps of gibbering trivia.

Glaston was still inside the hidden chamber of the Gotham pyramid. He didn't know whether or not he'd been here since he found it, because his memory seemed to be playing tricks on him. He remembered bright light, like a fountain of shining blood, erupting in Gotham Cathedral. Yet he'd never been to the cathedral. He remembered a subway train screaming down its tracks at breakneck speed, a rocketship blasting off into orbit, a man with a green ring.

He remembered dead men walking.

Something had possessed him. A spirit . . . a ghost . . . a consciousness. It had gained access the moment he fell through the ceiling of that sealed chamber, bursting into his brain like an exploding star. As if it had been lurking across the countless centuries, waiting for him.

It had made him dig like a dog in the hard-packed soil. Clutching the ancient ax in Peter's hand, it had used his lips to emit a guttural shriek of triumph. And when the blade rose and fell, burying itself deep in Robert Mills's skull, it wasn't Peter Glaston's thoughts that guided it.

He remembered Mills's blood and brains splashing over him, horrifying him to the point of violent nausea. He'd tried to vomit, but with no control over his physical self, even that was denied him.

He watched helplessly as his own hand was guided to Mills's chest. The stone blade began to slice through the professor's rib cage, and Peter's nausea reached fever pitch. He had a brief, sickening memory of holding aloft Mills's heart, still pumping weakly, slippery blood dribbling down his wrist and arm. Then Peter had lost consciousness.

When he came to, it was with that mixture of fear and relief that invariably accompanies waking from a nightmare.

Thank God it's over! his mind cried with blessed relief.

But when he tried to move his hand, nothing happened. It was as if the nerve endings that interfaced between his body and his brain had been severed. He realized for the first time that he no longer owned himself, that he'd been taken over, turned into a puppet—a tool to be used at the whim of its new owner.

The terror he'd felt then abated somewhat. The blind panic that had filled him at no longer being in control of his own actions, his own mind, had gradually eased. Though he felt its malice, its malign pleasure in hurting others, whatever had taken him over seemed to bear him no evil intent. In fact, it ignored him completely, as if he was completely irrelevant to whatever it planned. Sometimes he found himself wondering if it even knew that he was still there.

Cowering in a corner of his own mind, Peter Glaston tried to fathom what had happened to him. Some kind of possession, obviously. But by what? And for what purpose?

His senses still carried information: he could feel a hairy animal pelt against his skin, hanging in loose folds over his shoulders and back. Did he really remember a field suffused with moonlight, the stone blade in his hand slicing through the jugular vein of an Aberdeen Angus bull? Was it possible he had danced in a meadow at night, a slow, shuffling counterclockwise movement, chanting obscenely as he smeared himself with the dead beast's innards?

His body reeked of stale blood, so maybe his memories were authentic. There was a weight pressing down on his head, and every now and then something warm and slick slipped from it to slither down his neck. Had he really hacked off the bull's head, crouched for an hour as he carefully skinned its flesh before setting it on over his own head? Was it blood and animal brains that dripped and slid down his body?

Peter reawakened from his reverie with a start. After a long period of inactivity, as if his possessor had been asleep, his body was moving again.

The interior of the chamber seemed to have grown, somehow. Incongruously, Peter was reminded of an old British television series he'd seen, about a space traveler whose craft was a phone booth on the outside, yet as big as a football stadium within. A tesseract, Peter recalled from his freshman science class. At least his memory was still his own.

Unless the intruder had access to his memories, too.

Twigs dipped in animal fat and set ablaze threw out a smoky light that flickered across the room interior, but failed to penetrate the deepest shadows. Peter saw shapes on the wall—spirals and sticklike human figures, lozenges and palm prints—all outlined in blood that had darkened as it dried. The remains of the bull's head lay heaped on the altar stone, giving off an indescribable stench.

Peter watched in fascinated horror as his hand, with no input from him, closed around the base of a burning, fat-soaked torch. Words that he didn't recognize, whose meaning was a mystery to him, spilled from his mouth in a guttural dirge.

His feet were bare, and the rough soil rasped against his soles. Seemingly of their own volition, they carried him deeper into the stone-lined chamber.

With a sense of shock, he saw the figures there. Totally motionless, jutting from a massive block of stone that must have weighed fifty tons, he mistook them at first for carefully carved, life-size sculptures.

He heard his own voice rise and fall, a new tone in it now, as if he were praying. His hand moved the flaming torch in slow, spiraling circles. Its guttering light fell on the figures, and Peter felt his stomach churn as he realized what they were.

The Justice League of America.

He'd seen their pictures in a dozen newspapers, watched footage of their exploits on the television news. They were even present the day the pyramid was uncovered by the dam burst.

Superman was unmistakeable in his blue costume and red cape. The dark-haired female with the tiara, a red star emblazoned in its center, was Wonder Woman. The black-and-green symbol identified Green Lantern. Peter had never seen the Flash before—any photograph of the Scarlet Speedster tended to show only a red blur—but deduced it was him from the golden lightning streak that crossed his chest.

Four of the mightiest heroes in the world . . . and Peter Glaston held them captive!

No, not me, Peter corrected himself. *Whoever has invaded my mind and stolen my body. Why did I think it was me?*

Somehow, the heroes' bodies had been imprisoned in the living rock, as if the stone had grown organically around them, the way that, over years, a tree will grow to envelop a nail hammered into its trunk. Their hands were free but, here and there where they touched the rock, they too seemed to be absorbed.

Only their heads and upper torsos were showing; the rest of them was buried in the solid granite. Their eyes were closed, and Peter would have thought them dead had it not been for the tiny fluttering movements of their eyelids.

Like they're in REM sleep, he thought. Rapid eye movement was one of the physical manifestations of the dreaming mind. *But what does this all mean?*

The pain seemed to have been burning in him for all eternity.

Huge jagged teeth pierced his midriff. He could feel them, chafing against his innards every time a muscle so much as flexed. Staying still was agony, yet even the slightest movement sent him into a paroxysm of suffering.

Time and again Green Lantern tried to focus his will, to send a single coherent thought to the ring that was supposed to have protected him, but had failed.

What in the world could be strong enough to overcome—

The thought died stillborn as fierce pain radiated from his abdomen, jangling nerves all over his body. He couldn't even tell if he was screaming or not.

Next to Green Lantern—although she might have been a thousand miles away, for all he was aware of her existence—was Wonder Woman.

She'd wakened from unconsciousness to find her world in darkness. Her first thought was that she'd gone blind, that somehow in her battle atop the pyramid with her unseen foes, her sight had been affected.

She'd tried to stand up, but her legs refused to bear her weight, sending her sprawling on the rough rock.

The others need me, her mind called over and over, with mounting urgency. *They might be in any kind of danger. I can't give up. I have to help them!*

Again she'd tried to rise, swaying slightly as she struggled to find her balance without her eyesight to assist her. A massive blow landed on the back of her neck, its impetus sending her sprawling again. Groggily, she rolled onto her back, striving to bring her bracelets up so they could intercept any further assault.

But the attack came from all angles, slamming painfully into every part of her body, giving her no chance to protect herself.

Stone on skin, stone on bone! Had she said that? If not her, then who? Did she just think it? Was her mind playing tricks now, her senses deceiving her?

Wonder Woman was almost relieved when the deeper darkness appeared again, expanding slowly to engulf her in its cool, unfeeling shadows.

Superman seemed to have been flying for hours. How could this be? At superspeed, he'd have long since been carried into outer space.

But I can still breathe, he thought. *Not space, then. So where?*

None of his extraordinary senses were of use to him. He strained with his X-ray vision, but couldn't pierce the eerie blue-green fog that surrounded him. He stilled his breath and listened intently, but his superhearing picked up no sounds at all. He tried shouting, vaguely hoping that he'd get some sort of echo that he could home in on. But he couldn't even hear his own voice.

He tried to recall what he'd been fighting against, but his memory wouldn't function. Instead of his enemy, he pictured events from his past, but they rolled by so fast he could scarcely keep pace with them.

A flash from his childhood: a baby in a rocketship.

Krypton—the giant planet that was his home—exploding.

A middle-aged couple—he knew them well. What were their names? Ah yes, Ma and Pa. Martha . . . and Jonathan . . .

Superman tried to shake his head, to banish these unwanted thoughts. Though he could have sworn his head didn't move, the memory traces disappeared, winking out of existence like the embers of a dying fire.

But Superman's relief was short-lived. His mind immediately filled with images of Batman. Batman fighting, swinging, thinking, scoffing.

This is ridiculous! I can't even control my own thoughts!

Unable to think clearly enough to formulate a better plan, Superman flew on. And on. On a journey that was taking him nowhere.

Speed is the answer. The Flash kept saying the words over and over to himself. *It has to be!*

He'd never found himself in any trap where his speed couldn't break him free.

Captive in a solid steel cell? His molecules could vibrate at exactly the same frequency as his prison walls, allowing him to slip through them like a ghost. Or his fist could act like a powerhammer, striking a thousand times in the breadth of a single second, finding a weak spot and pummeling it until it shattered. Or, from a standing start, he could accelerate so quickly that by the time he crossed the cell he'd be traveling at thousands of miles an hour—enough to demolish any wall.

But this was different. He was surrounded by nothing but turquoise mist. No ground of any kind, solid or otherwise. For a long time the Flash thought he stood on the point of some eldritch needle of stone. Perhaps he could run down its side, using his speed to keep his balance. Might be a problem when he reached bottom—if he hit solid rock while vibrating at the wrong frequency, he'd have as much chance as a fly against a windshield at a hundred miles an hour.

The risk's worth it, he assured himself. *The League might need me . . . they must, otherwise they'd have come to my rescue!*

He squatted down, using first one hand and then the other to feel whatever was underneath the ground he stood on. No needle of rock. Nothing at all.

Frustrated and angry, the Flash settled back onto his haunches.

Speed is the answer, he thought. *It has to be!*

Peter Glaston wondered why he had lit a fire amid the remains on the altar stone.

Animal fat hissed loudly as it burst into flame.

Greasy black smoke rose in rolling tendrils, quickly filling the chamber. Peter felt it rasping at his lungs, and coughed harshly. Whoever was controlling him might be used to breathing smoke, but Peter wasn't.

His arms were suddenly thrown wide, his head tilted back, his open mouth already beginning a singsong chant. Peter didn't understand a word his lips were saying—a curious mixture of grunts and semi-words that bore more resemblance to the rants of acute schizophrenics than to any language he knew.

But the meaning of the words resounded through his consciousness, their ageless wisdom in sharp contrast to the doom-laden way they resonated. *The Universe is an endless cycle of endless cycles. The world spins around the sun spins around the galactic center spins around in a supercluster that spins around . . .*

What is now will not be always. What is gone will return.

Blasphemers rise, blasphemers die. The world spins around. Flame cleanses, and the seed grows. The sun spins around. After the flame, the foul will be sweet. The galaxy spins.

The fire grows.

The sun will cross the sky once more in its eternal dance of life and death. Then the world will be cleansed. What is gone will return.

Trapped deep within his own mind, Peter Glaston was suffused with fear. There was going to be a cleansing. Planet Earth was to be purged.

On Halloween.

CHAPTER 10

Enter the Martian

Gotham City, October 29

"Are you sure you want to go through with this, Cassandra?" Batman asked. "It might be dangerous. There's still time to back out."

Cassandra sat in the passenger seat of the Batmobile, cocooned in the mesh of a safety harness, as Batman drove them at speed through the deserted back streets of downtown Gotham. Climate control kept the vehicle's interior at a pleasant temperature, and Cassandra found that staring at the soft glow of the myriad lights on the dashboard was strangely soothing.

They'd left Gordon at Police HQ, his skepticism tempered by the knowledge that Batman took Cassandra's vision seriously. Now, worried himself at what the future had in store for his city, Gordon was redoubling his officers' search for the missing Peter Glaston. Batman had assured him that when they found Peter

Glaston they would also find the bull-headed monster who was the key to this mystery.

An idea had occurred to Cassandra while she'd been telling Batman and the commissioner her story. She hadn't said anything at the time, but the thought continued to gnaw at her as Batman guided his futuristic vehicle through a maze of roads and alleyways.

Central Gotham had never been built on a city grid, and its tangled traffic system was a stiff test for even the best of drivers.

Finally, as a green light saw them streaking through an intersection, Cassandra turned to Batman.

"I've been thinking," she began slowly, as if still unsure that the decision she'd reached was the right one. "According to the newspapers, the archaeology expedition retrieved some artifacts from the pyramid. Perhaps if I could touch one of them . . ."

"You think you might have another vision?" Batman finished for her.

Cassandra nodded. "I can't guarantee it, of course. And I have to admit, I'm a little afraid. But if all this is really as serious as it seems, I'm willing to do anything to help you get to the bottom of it." She paused, then added, "After all, Gotham's my city, too."

Batman immediately switched direction, the Batmobile's four-wheel steering spinning its oversized body through 180 degrees in less space than a sub-compact automobile would take.

The university campus was a couple of miles straight out on Fox Boulevard. Scant minutes later they were pulling up in the shadows of a tree-lined residential street, a few moments' walk from the archaeology building.

"You're absolutely sure now?" Batman asked again. He would never willingly endanger any innocent bystander. But how could a vision imperil anyone? I might spook Cassandra, maybe even terrify her, but i would have no power to physically harm her. Anc who could say what they might learn?

Cassandra's only reply was a slight smile anc furtive nod, and Batman hit the button that openec the car's gull-wing doors with a slight hiss of com pressed air. They slid out. A touch on a tiny remote control, and the sleek vehicle's chameleon-like light sensitive paint began to change, blending it in with the tree-dappled shadows.

Hugging the darkness, Batman led her toward the unfenced campus. Security lights shone here and there on the pathways, pools of bright light accentuating the darkness beyond their glow. Batman pulled up shor under an old, overhanging linden tree, its dry leaves rustling in the night breeze. Every now and then, one of them fell fluttering to the ground.

A finger to his lips told Cassandra to remain silent They waited motionless for several minutes until they heard footsteps growing louder. A uniformed security guard came around the corner of the building, his gun snug in its hip holster, a powerful flashlight in his hand. Periodically he shone its beam into the darkness, checking for intruders.

At last, satisfied there was nothing amiss, the guarc headed away from them to continue his patrol.

"He'll be back in twenty-three minutes exactly," Batman whispered gruffly. "Plenty of time for us to get inside."

Cassandra wondered how he knew, but didn't ask. It wouldn't have surprised her to find that Batman had memorized the patrol movements around every major building in town—as well as their internal layouts and escape routes. Which, of course, he had. Long experience had taught the Dark Knight never to leave anything to chance.

Cassandra started forward, but Batman grasped her wrist, shaking his head. He pointed up to a corner of the building, where a matt-black closed-circuit TV camera swiveled slowly on its bracket.

"Wait till the lens swings away from us," Batman ordered, "then stay close to me."

Seconds later, they were standing in a recessed staff entrance at the side of the building. Batman had taken a small metal tool from his belt, and Cassandra watched him insert it and twist it carefully in the lock.

With a slight click, the lockpick settled into the tumblers, and Batman pushed open the door.

Cassandra wondered if there was no end to this enigmatic man's talents. She raised her eyebrows and shot him a quizzical look.

"Any good lockpick can pick any good lock," he told her as they made their way inside and he quietly pulled the door closed behind them.

"It'll be ironic," Cassandra pointed out, "if, next time Commissioner Gordon sees us, we're under arrest for breaking and entering."

Cassandra fancied she saw the slightest of smiles cross Batman's lips. But when he spoke, there was no humor in his voice.

"There's no point alerting the commissioner about this until we have a result. Or not." Fleetingly, Batman wondered if he should say any more. But Cassandra was willing to risk herself—she deserved to know. "Besides," he continued, "I haven't told Gordon quite how serious the situation is."

"What do you mean? Surely things couldn't be much worse."

"Yes. They are." Batman nodded curtly. "The bull-headed beast that you saw has already captured four members of the Justice League."

He chose the word "captured" with care. For all he knew, Superman and the others were already dead. But he couldn't allow himself to think that way. He had to believe they were alive until events proved otherwise.

"It's only fair that you should know," he added pointedly. "We're dealing with real evil here, and it has a lot of power to back it up."

Cassandra shivered at his words, but didn't respond.

A narrow corridor led them to the main hallway, their progress illuminated by the powerful beam from Batman's penlight. They made their way across the checkered floor of black-and-white marble and passed the hall's only exhibit, the glass-encased skull of a flesh-eating dinosaur. It had been discovered in the mud of Gotham Docks by one of Robert Mills's predecessors during a routine dredging operation.

Six-inch-long teeth glinted in the flash beam as they passed it.

Gotham City has a long, long history, Batman thought. *It's at least sixty-five million years since beasts like that roamed our hills.*

Set against that, the seven or eight generations of the Wayne dynasty were mere pimples on the skin of time.

Batman stopped suddenly, spinning around in a blur of movement, dropping into a defensive martial-arts pose. He froze for several seconds, every sense at full alert, striving to penetrate the darkness. Then he relaxed.

"Thought I heard something," he said by way of explanation.

They passed a glass door with the word LIBRARY etched in it, and Batman stopped again. He turned the door handle and pushed. It was open.

"Now might not be the best time," he told Cassandra, thinking of the books Jenny Ayles had recommended to him earlier that day, "but I want to check something out."

Cassandra followed him into the lighter, airy library. There were a dozen skylights set into the ceiling, and moonlight poured in to illuminate the interior. Batman scanned the floor-to-ceiling bookshelves with his flash, quickly pulling out a half-dozen titles from different sections. He carried them to a reading desk, sat down, and handed the flashlight to Cassandra.

"Keep it trained on the open pages," he told her.

Puzzled, Cassandra did as she was instructed. She

could read some of the titles—*Lost Civilization of the Stone Age, Ancient Voices, The Origin of Consciousness*—but they meant nothing to her.

Using some of the books as a prop, Batman leaned one volume against them and opened the cover. He closed his eyes briefly, using one of the many meditative techniques he'd learned during his research in Tibet to calm his mind. His eyes blinked open again, defocusing until he could see no detail on the pages before him. The black type seemed to become three-dimensional, standing out several inches above the white background of the page.

Cassandra watched in astonishment as he began to flick through the pages, turning them over at a rate of more than one per second.

He can't possibly be reading them, she thought, but kept her silence as Batman sped through the books.

Less than ten minutes later, he closed the last one, pushed the pile aside, and got to his feet. Swiftly, he replaced the volumes in their positions on the shelves. He led Cassandra back out into the hallway, explaining as he went.

"The technique imprints the pages directly into the subconscious mind, making it available for later conscious recall."

"Oh. Right."

"Trust me. It works."

The items Mills's team had recovered from the pyramid were still under active analysis. They found them neatly filed in an unlocked examination room, cocooned in bubble wrap and plastic storage bags.

"Any preference?" Batman asked, reading off the handwritten label on each bag in turn. "Shard of pottery. Charred animal bone. More pottery. A jet bead."

His eyes flicked to scrutinize Cassandra's face. Her lower lip quivered slightly, and he reminded her gently that this wasn't compulsory, she could still back out any time she wanted.

"I'm afraid," Cassandra admitted, relieved to put the feeling into words. "Afraid I'll see something . . . evil again."

"Fear is the messenger, not the message," Batman told her. "If you feel you shouldn't do it, there's no shame in that."

Cassandra forced an uneasy smile back onto her lips. "No, my mind is made up." She reached out to take a plastic bag from Batman's hand, and read the label aloud. " 'Burned rib. Aurochs.' "

"A type of primitive cattle," Batman responded to her uncomprehending glance.

The plastic seal parted easily as Cassandra tugged it.

"This is called psychometry," she said, more to try to calm herself than explain to Batman. "Picking up—for want of a better word—vibrations from inanimate objects. Psychometrists believe that everything experienced by an object is somehow recorded into the structure of the object itself."

Batman nodded. He'd been taking an interest of late in the cutting-edge advances in quartz technology. Scientists had discovered that the near-infinite crystal lattices in a piece of quartz were capable of recording phenomenal amounts of data. Anything that might be of use in the fight against crime was a magnet to Batman.

"Normally it's not something I do," Cassandra was saying, "but after my experience in the cathedral . . ."

She let her words die away. Closing her eyes, her fingers closed gently around the three-inch fragment of blackened bone, teasing it from its clear plastic envelope. At once an electric tingle caressed her fingertips, then sent what felt like a thousand volts of electricity coursing up her arm.

A window opened to another world.

"I see . . . people dancing," Cassandra began. "A long time ago. It's night. They carry flaming torches, weaving in circles around the base of . . . something." She screwed up her eyes, trying to force the vision to become clearer. "It's the pyramid—the Gotham pyramid! Many of the people are afraid, others are dancing like dervishes."

She tilted her head back, her closed eyes squinting upward, as if the real physical movement would allow her to see more in her mental picture. "There's someone at the top. He's surrounded by timber and brushwood. He's setting a torch to the pile and it's blazing up.

"Wait!" The word was expelled in a sharp hiss. "There's another light. A blue light. It's merging with the flames, like the whole pyramid is on fire."

A fire festival! The thought flashed through Batman's mind. *At certain times of the year they were supposed to cleanse the energies of sacred sites.*

Aloud, he said nothing, unwilling to disturb Cassandra's deep concentration.

"The whole sky is lit up with brilliant color," the empath went on. "People are cheering. I think some may be screaming. There's a giant figure growing out of the pyramid top. Wait . . . it's the bull-headed creature! People are afraid of him. He's a . . ." She paused, momentarily at a loss for the word. "King," she finished softly.

"The Stone King." A deep, husky voice spoke from behind them, and Cassandra's eyes snapped open in sudden fear. Batman had already turned, eyes narrowed under his mask, to face the repulsive being that stood there.

Its head and face were almost completely hidden by the bull's skull it wore, and the thick animal skin that covered its body stank of stale blood and corrupted flesh. Raw, red eyes bored into them.

"I am the king who was," it grated haltingly, as if finding the words it wanted was a distinct effort. "The king who will be. I am the Stone King, who completes the cycle."

"Far from it!" Batman said accusingly, his voice harsh. "You're Peter Glaston, a postgrad student at Gotham U. I don't know what's gotten inside your mind, Glaston, but—"

The sunken red eyes began to glow, and Batman moved with instinctive speed.

"Cassandra, look out!" he called, stepping sideways so that the girl's body was shielded by his own.

A searing beam of energy crackled toward them.

The bolt took Batman full on his chest-symbol, the triple Kevlar layer below cushioning the worst of its effects. That was one of the reasons Batman had adopted it—it made such a tempting target for any assailant to aim at.

The sheer impact blasted him off his feet and sent both him and Cassandra careening into a wall. He felt the thin plasterwork crack and give beneath him as his body smashed right through it.

Batman turned his uncontrolled fall into a roll, deftly springing to his feet. As the Stone King's gaze swiveled, its eyes once more beginning to glow, Batman grabbed Cassandra's hand and pulled her through the jagged hole into an adjacent display room.

She was barely through when a second, stronger energy bolt exploded around them.

Cassandra's body went limp and sagged against Batman. Her eyes were closed, and her breathing was slow and shallow.

Batman cursed quietly to himself. She must have been knocked unconscious by the second bolt. Swiftly, he dragged her unresisting body behind a heavy oak desk. She would be relatively safe there while he dealt with this monster.

The dividing wall shattered suddenly, and the Stone King strode leisurely through the enlarged hole.

Batman didn't wait for another onslaught. Phosphor grenades had stopped this thing in Gotham Cathedral, presumably because they interfered with its energy patterns. Maybe they'd do the same now. Batman moved away from the desk, decoying their at-

acker to follow him to a safe distance from the unconscious medium.

"Where's Superman?" Batman demanded. "And
he others. What have you done with them?"

The Stone King snarled, an animal sound, spittle
spraying from its mouth. Batman figured he wasn't
going to get the answer he sought, and sent three
small spheres spinning through the air toward the inhuman figure, primed to detonate on impact.

But the Stone King saw the danger, and a web of
fine blue beams emanated from his fingertips. The energy net caught the grenades, lowering them gently to
he bare wooden floor.

Batman had already pulled a half-dozen Batarangs
from his belt. He sent the lightweight plastic disks
whirling at his foe, faster than the eye could follow.
Each Batarang had a solid lead core, and landed with
enough force to knock out a champion boxer.

The Stone King ignored them as they thudded into
him, ricocheting off with next to no effect. Tiny streaks
of lightning sizzled around his fingertips before unit-
ing into one massive bolt that split the air with a
shriek as it hurtled at Batman.

The Dark Knight dived full-length to one side, feeling the heat of the lightning as it passed a foot above
his head. There was a bright flash as it destroyed a display case full of silver and turquoise jewelry from the
Peruvian tombs at Sipán, and Batman used the extra
light to get his bearings in the unfamiliar room.

On his feet again, Batman bounded across the floor,
coming to a halt beside a red fire extinguisher clipped

to a wall. He snatched it from its strapping, the heel of
his other hand slamming into its release button. He
whirled and aimed the unwieldy cylinder, and the
Stone King roared with anger as he disappeared in a
curtain of thick foam.

It won't hurt him, but perhaps it'll blind him long
enough for me to—

Holding the heavy cylinder by its end, the Dark
Knight swung it into the mass of foam. There was a
satisfying metallic thud as the extinguisher hit its target, and even though he couldn't see him, Batman felt
the Stone King stagger under the blow.

He swung the cylinder again—once, twice, three
times—striking home with unnerring accuracy. On the
fourth swing, the Stone King stepped forward unexpectedly. A powerful backhand swipe sent the extinguisher flying from Batman's grasp. Then, before the
vigilante could take evasive action, the creature followed through with a punch that almost took Batman's head clean off his shoulders.

Batman staggered, the small of his back catching
against the top of a low display case behind him. Then
the Stone King was on him, hands clawing at his ad-
versary's throat, fingers tightening with unbelievable
pressure as they began to squeeze.

Batman gasped for breath, sickened by the stench of
decay, already beginning to feel light-headed, unable
to breathe from lack of oxygen. In vain his hands
struck at his opponent, seeking a pressure point or a
weak spot. Whatever he did, the Stone King seemed
invulnerable to it.

With a sudden crack the glass display case shattered, and Batman seized what might be his last chance. He brought his legs up, positioning his feet against the Stone King's chest. Exerting all of his remaining strength, he straightened his knees, at the same time yanking hard at the creature's pelt.

The Stone King howled with anger as he went sailing over Batman's head, impacting against the door frame with such force that the wood splintered.

Batman leaned against the wreckage of the display case, massaging his rasping throat, striving to get his breathing back to normal. Scarecrow's fear gas was still in his Utility Belt, if he could only reach it in time.

But the Stone King recovered first, a new hatred glinting in his red eyes as he prepared to renew their battle.

Desperately, Batman flung himself aside as the Stone King lunged, sweeping his fist in a downward arc that disintegrated what remained of the cabinet.

All right, Manhunter, the thought flashed from Batman's mind. *I could use a little backup now.*

"Excuse me." The Stone King turned at the sound of a new voice.

J'onn J'onzz, the Martian Manhunter, stood a dozen feet away.

Before the Stone King could react, J'onn dived at him, grasping the hairy, reeking body in a near-unbreakable bear hug.

Even as the Stone King flexed his muscles, exerting all his strength to try and break free, J'onn's grip tight-

ened around the creature's chest. Suddenly, he
brought into play his Martian ability to change the
density of his molecules. In an instant, each brawny
arm weighed half a ton.

The pressure he exerted was phenomenal.

A high-pitched scream of intermingled rage and
pain burst from the helpless Stone King's lips as his
body began to disappear. Hands and feet dissipated
into thin air, the effect quickly raveling through his entire body until it swirled like mist in a wind.

Then he was gone, and J'onn unfolded his arms. The
sudden silence was broken by glass shards breaking
underfoot as Batman moved to where he'd left Cassandra. She was still unconscious, but was she okay?

With one hand Batman checked that her pulse was
still steady; with the other he hit the emergency button
on his tiny cell phone. He spoke a few words into the
receiver, then thumbed it off before turning to the
green-skinned Justice Leaguer.

"Thanks," Batman said. "Though you might have
saved me a few bruises if you'd joined in earlier."

J'onn was surprised. "You knew I was there? Even
though I was invisible?"

Batman shrugged. "From the moment you followed
us into the building."

J'onn should have guessed. Batman was the greatest
detective in the world. His senses were honed to an incredible degree. During their career with the League
J'onn had seen him do a hundred things that no other
man could.

"I wasn't sure what you were up to, so I decided to

tag along," Manhunter explained. "I tried to contact Superman and the others when I returned from Mars. When I failed, I came to Gotham. My Martian vision revealed the Batmobile's hiding place."

Batman nodded. He'd been wondering how Manhunter found him.

"I wasn't sure if your actions were a deliberate ploy to attract the Stone King," J'onn went on. "So when he appeared, I thought it best not to interfere unless I absolutely had to."

"And I didn't want you to interfere," Batman admitted, "unless it was necessary. I did still have one trick in my book, but I couldn't get to it in time."

Just then they heard the distant click of a key in a lock, and a security guard shouting, "Who's there? Come out with your hands up. I'm armed!"

Batman took one last look at Cassandra, lying as if asleep, then motioned J'onn to follow him through another exit.

They left the building and vanished into the night, the wail of an approaching ambulance telling Batman his call to the emergency services was being answered.

They were seated in the Batmobile before either of them spoke again.

"The girl was very brave," J'onn said. "I hope she will be all right."

"She has no physical wounds," Batman told him. "I think it's just the effect of shock on her sensitive mind. I also think the risk she took may have paid off."

Batman had taken off his gauntlets and pulled a small plastic tube from his Utility Belt. He squeezed it

into his palm and rubbed the cream into various parts
of his body that had been cut or bruised.

"Synthetic shark cartilage," he told J'onn. "Speeds
up healing."

Quickly, Batman ran over the whole story, from the
disappearance of the rest of the team to the events that
had led up to tonight's break-in.

J'onn was incredulous. "So the Stone King is the rein-
carnation of a five-thousand-year-old shaman who has
possessed the body of a young student? And he has
power enough to defeat Superman and the others?"

"He certainly did something with them." Batman's
voice was grim. "He appears to be one of the most
powerful enemies we've ever encountered. And he in-
tends to kill everyone in the world . . . in just over
twenty-four hours!"

CHAPTER 11

Earthlights

The Moon, October 31—All Saints' Eve

The view of Earth was spectacular.

The planet hung in the velvet darkness of space. Behind it, the sun glittered like a fiery yellow diamond, a beacon of hope in the vast inky cosmos.

High in the Watchtower, Batman and J'onn J'onzz had no time to appreciate the beauty outside. Both were seated at workstations, punching in data for Oracle's computers to sift, appraise, and analyze.

One entire wall was taken up by a telecommunications screen that showed a map of the world. Twenty feet high by almost forty feet long, it dominated the room, dwarfing the two heroes. As they entered their data, lights representing various places throughout the world flashed on the giant screen.

"Satellite scans show seismic disturbances in Peru,

Mexico City, Ireland, and eastern Europe," J'onn J'onzz reported.

"Infrared cameras show heat buildup in the following areas," Batman said in clipped tones. "Pacific Ocean—specifically at Easter Island. Japan—at Mount Fuji. Hawaii—several islands involved."

As he spoke, his fingers flew with speed across his keyboard. Every now and then he glanced up at the giant world map, as the sites he named lit up on it.

"And the computers' conclusion is . . . ?" Manhunter asked, not looking up from his own screen.

"Potential volcanic eruptions. Within hours, not days." Batman didn't dwell on the ominous thought. "I've already put all active and reserve League members on red alert."

"Perhaps we could use a few of them here to help monitor this data."

Batman shook his head. "If Cassandra's vision was correct, they're going to be needed all over the world."

J'onn J'onzz ran his eyes down the list of green figures and coordinates that filled his personal monitor. "Electromagnetic field imaging shows increasing anomalies at the following locations: Stonehenge in England, Delphi in Greece, three separate locations in India. Minor anomalies detected in the Tibetan Himalayas, at Angkor Wat, and the Forbidden City in Beijing." J'onn shook his head wearily, his bald, green pate reflecting the cool glow of the room's lighting. "And that's not all—there are predictions for further electromagnetic disruption at a whole series of secondary sites, including the Serpent Mound in Ohio."

Batman felt as if he was compiling a death list for planet Earth. "Increased seismic activity predicted," he read aloud. "Iran. Afghanistan. The Caucasus region of Russia. South America, from Ecuador to the Sacred Valley of the Incas in Peru."

He was silent for a moment as vivid memories impinged on his mind. Gotham City had suffered its own cataclysmic earthquake not so long ago. Whole streets had collapsed in piles of rubble. Subway tunnels were submerged. Entire districts had gone up in flames. Vermin and disease ran riot, and survivors were faced with no source of power and no functioning economy.

Tens of thousands had died, hundreds of thousands had been injured, and millions were turned into refugees overnight. And that was just one quake.

Several years ago now, and Gotham was still in a long, slow recovery.

Batman shuddered to think of the result if Oracle's extrapolations were accurate. Seismic disturbance could affect half the world, or more. The damage and loss of life would not only be colossal, but incalculable.

"And the missing pyramid?" J'onn asked.

Batman gave a small sigh of frustration. "Location still unknown."

He added, "Location of our four colleagues still unknown, location of the Stone King also still unknown."

J'onn had tried tracing the heroes with his telepathic powers before he and Batman used the teleporter to return to the moon. Eyes closed, mind focused to a single point, he'd tried sending out waves of mental messages. Theoretically, the range of his telepathy was unlimited, but in practice his mental emanations could be affected by a variety of things. Electromagnetic activity was capable of throwing him completely off, while even strong radio waves could set up interference patterns that turned any message into random noise.

Despite his best efforts, J'onn was unable to contact any of the missing members of the Justice League. No sign of the Stone King had shown up on his "mental radar."

It was as if they, and the pyramid, had disappeared into thin air.

"Perhaps they have been transported to another dimension," J'onn stated, as a sudden idea occurred to him. "That would explain the failure of my telepathy—and also why none of our instruments detect them."

"It's possible," Batman admitted, "but unlikely. The Stone King's quarrel seems to be with people. The energy increases are taking place on Earth, where we can observe and measure them. I find it hard to imagine the shaman doing this from any place except the planet's surface."

The cool, measured tones of one of Oracle's programmed computer voices broke in on their discussion. *"I am intercepting a transmission from the space shuttle* Lincoln. *It appears to have relevance to your current search. Shall I patch it through?"*

"Yes," Batman said curtly, and at once the grainy voice of Martin Spears could be heard over the Watchtower speakers.

"Houston?" the shuttle commander was asking, a note of disbelief in his voice. "Are you getting this? We can see what appears to be a column of bright blue light streaming up from some place in the Arctic Circle. Our orbit's not in synch with it, so we can't pinpoint the map coordinates."

Both Batman and J'onn were already on their feet, hurrying over to the plasticized glass viewing balcony. Steel panels slid automatically aside at their approach, triggered by the floor-set motion sensors. Naked sunlight streamed into the enclosed balcony as the duo slipped filter shades across their eyes.

"This is incredible! It must be twenty miles high now," the commander's voice went on. "Can you back us up on this, Houston? It's not some kind of space hallucination, is it?"

There was a long silence, as if the ground team in Houston were as stunned as the astronauts at this unprecedented phenomenon. Orbiting craft often reported unusual light displays, both in the upper atmosphere and on the planet's surface. Spectacular auroras had been filmed by previous shuttle crews. But in over thirty years of manned space flight, nothing like this had ever been seen before.

Batman squinted beneath his shades, narrowing his eyes against the sunlight, trying to make out anything abnormal near the earth's North Pole. The moon was nearly a quarter-million miles away from the earth, while the space shuttle orbited not much higher than 350 miles. He was going to need the telescope.

"There!" J'onn J'onzz breathed, his keen Martian vision zeroing in on the pulse of light. "By the souls of my ancestors . . . look at that!"

The light column must have been ten miles in diameter, a massive pillar shooting ever higher. As it reached the upper limits of Earth's atmosphere, almost a hundred miles from the planet's surface, its top spread out in a blue-sparking canopy that grew at amazing speed to cover half the planet.

Then, suddenly, it was gone.

"Did you see that, Houston?" Even dampened by the operations room speakers, there was no mistaking the urgency in the astronaut's voice. "I repeat, Houston—do you copy? The whole column just vanished, like somebody switched off a light!"

"We copy, *Lincoln*," a voice from NASA crackled. "Over."

Batman removed his eyeshade, more troubled than impressed by what he'd seen. He hit the button that controlled the shutters, and as they slid silently back into place, he and J'onn returned to their workstations.

"You don't think . . ." J'onn began. He hesitated, as if unwilling to put the thought into words, before finishing slowly. "You don't think the Stone King has started early?"

Batman ran his eyes over the columns of data that constantly flowed across his screen. "According to this, the light was a visual phenomenon only. None of the other instruments picked it up."

He closed his eyes, deep in thought. When he spoke again, it was with a slight shake of his head. "No, I don't think he's started early. I think he's testing what-

ver powers he has, awakening the ancient energy
enters. He's making sure that he'll be ready . . . when
ne time comes."

J'onn defocused his vision, allowing himself to drift
nto the calm center of his being.

"We're fast running out of time," he said softly, "and
still don't understand what this is all about." He gath-
red his ragged thoughts, then went on. "The spirit of a
tone Age shaman has possessed a university student.
Jow he's going to destroy the world. But *why?*"

"Presumably because he doesn't like what we've be-
ome," Batman countered. "Peter Glaston was a highly
ntelligent young man. There's no saying what the Stone
King might have extracted from his memories."

This was a scenario League members often adopted
rhen faced with a problem that baffled them. Talk
bout it, toss it back and forth, all the time looking for
ome tiny fact that had until then escaped their notice.

"Pollution, environmental destruction, global warm-
ng," Batman went on. "They didn't have these prob-
ems five millennia ago."

"He has access to seemingly unlimited power," J'onn
aid musingly. "The energies of the planet itself."

"And he can discharge those energies in highly de-
tructive ways."

Batman gestured to the huge electronic map, his un-
onscious mind releasing what he'd learned in his
eading at the university the day before.

"Almost all of the sites shown there were sacred to
ne or another human culture or religion. According to
enny Ayles, Peter Glaston believes they stand on points

of power, part of a grid or network that once covered every continent. It's probable from the increased activity that the Stone King is trying to kick-start the grid again, and use it to annihilate modern society."

Under his craggy brows, the Martian's blue eyes stared fixedly. He remembered the red dust wastes of his homeworld, the rock-strewn deserts that covered all that had once been green and fertile. He remembered a world once thronging with people, now dead and barren, a planetwide graveyard.

J'onn J'onzz had come to love Earth. It twisted him up inside to think his adopted home was slated to suffer a similar fate.

"But in the final analysis," J'onn said at last, "the Stone King is a foe like any other we've faced. Somehow, he can be beaten. What we have to do is discover his mind-set. If we can think like him, we can anticipate his actions . . . and beat him."

"We *can't* think like him," Batman said flatly. "Our brains are wired differently. I've learned the hard way, from battling the likes of the Joker these many years."

"Many scholars consider that prehistoric peoples were barbarians," J'onn persisted. "If that is the case, surely we can outthink him."

"That paradigm is changing quickly," Batman told him. "Rock art of thirty thousand years ago is highly sophisticated. There were flint factories in Czechoslovakia twenty thousand years ago. The city of Jericho was inhabited in 8000 B.C. Who knows how much people learned before Neolithic times?"

He paused for a moment, allowing his conscious

mind to retrieve more of what he'd read in the university library. "Their knowledge of stellar events predated ours by thousands of years. We still haven't duplicated the building techniques that let them move two-hundred-ton blocks of stone, the way they did at Ba'albek in Lebanon. Some accounts claim they had mastered sonic energy and knew how to use the earth forces for teleportation—"

"Which might explain the pyramid's disappearance," J'onn pointed out.

"According to one theory," Batman went on, warming to the subject, "the mind of ancient man was very different from our own. It was bicameral—two-chambered. Commands issued by the dominant right hemisphere of the brain were heard as audio hallucinations by the left brain."

"Voices in the head?" J'onn looked doubtful. "Isn't that one of the defining symptoms of schizophrenia?"

"It is. It's also what happens to me when you establish your telepathic link. There's something very powerful about hearing an internal voice. It instills obedience much more strongly than any external order ever could."

Which was precisely why Batman disliked the telepathic link procedure so much.

"So if the Stone King is controlled by an internal voice," J'onn asked, "he'd be impervious to anything we might say to him?"

"Yes," Batman agreed.

"Unless, of course," J'onn added hurriedly, "my telepathic powers can affect him."

"To do that, we have to find him." Batman continued to think aloud. "How can we save the others when we don't know where they are—or if they're even still alive? Where do you hide something the size of a pyramid?"

"Where indeed?" J'onn nearly leaped out of his chair as a sudden thought overwhelmed him. "Think back to the archaeology room. I was there, but you couldn't see me."

Batman understood instantly. "Of course, the *pyramid's* invisible!"

"Sometimes the obvious solution is the easiest to overlook," the Martian said ruefully. His voice took on an excitement that Batman couldn't mistake. "If the Stone King can harness natural energies to use against us, invisibility should also be within his power."

"Only one way to find out."

Batman was already striding toward the teleporter chamber, a technology any government or army on Earth would pay any price to possess. Which is why it was fitted with a number of fail-safe and self-destruct options. If it was ever found by anyone outside the Justice League, the whole Watchtower would be disabled and useless within minutes.

The duo stepped into the chamber, their recent frustration and sense of defeat nearly forgotten. There was a low hum as the machine sprang into life, and they were enveloped by a cool fluorescent glow.

Then they were gone.

CHAPTER 12

Ancient Voices

Gotham City, October 31

The pale morning sun streamed in through the hospital windows, casting a warm glow over the ward where Dr. Clay Valerian stood by Cassandra's bedside. She lay pale and still, her breathing shallow, her white-golden hair tumbled across her pillow.

A pretty young nurse the doctor hadn't seen before handed him the patient's notes. He hoped he'd be seeing *her* at the hospital's Halloween Hellraiser tonight. He smiled at the nurse and ran his eyes over the printed sheet attached to a clipboard.

"Found unconscious, Gotham U. lab," he read. "Cause of injuries unknown."

"Is she a student?" Valerian asked, but the nurse shook her head.

"We don't know who she is, doctor. She had no identification with her."

Valerian pursed his lips. Heartbeat, pulse rate
blood pressure—all body functions were performing
normally. Every test the hospital had taken came out
negative. Her only visible signs of injury were bruis-
ing and abrasions to her arm and back.

And yet she was unconscious.

Frequent blinking and rapid eye movement showed
her brain was still engaged, but the possibility of un-
detected damage remained high.

"Could be internal cranial bleeding," Valerian
mused aloud, the young nurse listening attentively
"though there are no other indicators. Nurse, arrange
a CAT scan, as soon as possible."

The nurse nodded and removed the receiver from a
wall-mounted telephone. She dialed a number, her gaze
running absent-mindedly over the woman in the bed.

Replacing the clipboard on the bedframe, ogling the
young nurse for a final time, Clay Valerian moved or
to his next patient.

Cassandra was a young girl again.

She was perched on her grandmother's knee, safe
and secure in the love that radiated from the old
woman. Grandma smelled of lavender, and her deep-
set wrinkled eyes made her look both ancient and
wise. They were seated on the old basket chair in the
apartment's window recess, looking out on the afternoon street life of Gotham City.

Grandma pointed to a man hurrying by on the other
side of the street, his head bowed, eyes riveted on the
ground despite the speed of his pace.

"A man in a hurry," Grandma said. "Not alert to what's around him. He's either deep in thought or worried sick. See his shoes, Cassandra—scuffed and worn. That overcoat may be shabby, but once it cost a lot of money. A rich man down on his luck?"

The old lady sipped from a glass of water. "Now, do you see that woman on the corner? Her makeup's smeared. She's been crying."

Grandma could look at anyone and, with her incredible eye for detail, produce their life story. She picked up on things that were in plain sight, but which most people either didn't notice or glossed over.

"Empathy is a gift," she used to say. "But like anything else on God's good earth, you can't afford to take it for granted. You have to work at it always."

Cassandra spent the happiest years of her life in that apartment with her grandmother. And now she had returned there again, to where she was safe and loved, where no bull-headed monsters roamed the streets, only men with scuffed shoes and women with tear-stained faces.

A visual flash: Ourobouros, hooped in a circle, the worm that eats its own tail. The symbol of life and death eternally consuming each other.

"The cycle will complete."

The words were like knives in Peter Glaston's head. Only, it wasn't his head any longer. He was just a passenger on someone else's journey. And yet, that was *his* voice.

He'd gotten used to the terrible smell of corrupt flesh, hardly noticed it anymore. He'd grown used to the ice-cold terror that sometimes gripped him. But he was becoming progressively more horrified as he learned the depth and scope of his possessor's plans. Until now, it had merely been flexing its muscles, making its preparations. Its actions had seemed to be isolated incidents, with no pattern to them that Peter had been able to discern. Now, he could see what the creature had been building up to.

There was going to be a cleansing, a disaster on a planetary scale. And there was nothing Peter could do to prevent this strange consciousness, this force that thought in words and symbols that Peter didn't fully understand, from carrying through with its insane quest.

Peter felt like he was coming apart, slowly disintegrating as the parasitic spirit that had invaded him leeched away his memories, his feelings, his very personality. Sometimes he could sense the intruder combing through his life, seeking anything that would aid it in its dreams of genocide. From Peter's mind, it had learned about super heroes, science, and God only knew what else.

Increasingly, the alien was doing things that Peter didn't know about. He had a confusing memory of a fight. Could he have been in confrontation with the Batman? Where had the pain come from, the pain that burned like acid?

Still he couldn't fit the images into a coherent whole. He knew that somehow, through ritual and sacrifice, the Stone Age sorcerer was harnessing the energies of Gaia—the Earth Mother herself. He intended to use them against the descendants of his own people.

Peter had come to only moments earlier, to find his body standing in front of a slaughtered rabbit, its entrails looped on the altar stone, warm and steaming.

Extispicy—reading the future from the patterns contained in the spilled entrails of a sacrifice. A philosophy student friend had used the word in a game of Scrabble once, and gained a record word score. Peter had never forgotten it.

The omens were obviously good, because Peter felt a warm, satisfied glow suffuse him. It—he—the Stone King was happy. The intruder was likely to be off guard, his mental defenses down. Maybe this was the time for Peter to reclaim himself, to fight for what belonged to him. His body. His life.

He was walking now, bare soles against hard-packed soil. Four figures trapped in living rock, like sculptures in a Paris park. Why were they captive? Peter didn't know if he'd forgotten, or if he'd never known. If they were his enemies, why were they still alive? What purpose did their continuing existence serve?

Yes, now was definitely the time to act, before his confusion became any worse.

He tried to prepare himself for struggle, for a battle of wills to be fought out in the arena of his own mind. But how does one fight a ghost? How do you drive out a malevolent five-thousand-year-old spirit?

Memory flash: breaking ribs and gushing blood. Something red and throbbing squirming in his hand.

A human heart? Peter wondered if a disembodied consciousness could vomit.

Truth is, Peter thought, *I don't have a clue. I'm afraid, and I don't mind admitting it. Better to wait. Yes, bide my time. My chance will come. Sooner or later, my chance will come.*

The Stone King held a chunk of quartz the size of a tennis ball in the palm of his hand. Slowly, his fingers closed around it, squeezing, exerting more and more pressure until—

Tiny pinpricks of light leaped from the quartz. First a dozen, then a hundred, snaking this way and that in the air, never colliding with each other as they whirled around at incalculable speed.

A practical demonstration of piezoelectricity!

Somewhere far away, Peter Glaston felt impressed. It looked like his theories weren't so far off the mark after all. That'd be one in the eye for the high and mighty Professor Robert Mills!

The quartz lights came together as if magnetized, coalescing into a larger, ovoid ball of plasma. Its internal shape shifted constantly, like the flames of a log fire. Peter gaped at it like a child seeing his first cartoon show. He fancied he saw pictures—of himself and Jenny, of heroes fighting to the bitter end, of distant cities burning.

The plasmoid ball dropped suddenly onto Green Lantern, playing around his head like the auras seen in medieval religious masterpieces. A tendril lanced out around Wonder Woman, then others to Superman and the Flash. None of the heroes reacted.

The light seemed to be performing its own crazed, intricate dance, shooting up in starbursts, rolling and twisting like a dervish in the Persian desert. Without warning it reared up, coiled itself like a living spring, then dove into the ground in a flash of cobalt blue.

The chamber lit up like the inside of a furnace, but the temperature didn't change.

Peter heard laughter issue from deep within himself, rumbling up through his diaphragm, bursting out to echo throughout the chamber. Laughter that might have come from the pits of hell.

Perhaps I'll wait just a little longer, then . . .

It was early afternoon in the Andes Mountains of Peru.

Three luxury tourist coaches and a host of battered minibuses baked in the dusty parking lot at the ruins of the fortress of Ollantaytambo, in the Sacred Valley of the Incas. Tourists of a dozen nationalities swarmed between the ancient walls, only half listening to the commentary of their guides.

Here and there, a few sat groaning on the ground or trying surreptitiously not to vomit. Altitude sickness. They should have heeded the guides when they recommended drinking coca tea. Far weaker than the refined powder, cocaine, the pale green brew had been used in the mountains for thousands of years for its beneficial properties. There was even a Museum of Coca in Cuzco, the old Incan capital.

Hiram Shipman was one of the afflicted, sitting with his back against a boulder, striving to hold down the

bile in his churning stomach and wishing his head
didn't feel like a blacksmith's anvil. It was the fourth
day of his tour, and he'd already missed the wonders
of the lost city of Machu Picchu, perhaps the most in
credible engineering feat ever undertaken by man.

At an altitude of around ten thousand feet, the Incas
had built an entire city on the vertiginous, near
vertical mountain peak. All Hiram remembered of i
was the bright green grass, because every time he
looked up he felt that his head was going to fall off his
shoulders.

Back at the hotel, someone else on the tour, a loud
mouth from Fort Worth, Texas, had suggested a cou
ple of *pisco* sours. Everybody and his dog knew tha
brandy would settle any stomach. Against his better
judgment, Hiram allowed himself to be persuaded
Three of the foul-tasting brandies later, he knew he
had made a serious mistake.

Now Hiram was going to miss Ollantaytambo, too.

Folklore had it that the stone fortress was built by a
senior Incan general. He'd fallen in love with the Em
peror's daughter, a sacred maiden forbidden to min
gle with the warrior caste. The couple eloped
accompanied by the general's faithful soldiers. Know
ing her father had a duty to the Sun God to reclaim
her, the couple built Ollantaytambo to hold the Em
peror at bay.

The massive walls withstood siege for many years
before there was a reconciliation. Everybody lived
happily ever after. That was then. . . .

Hiram was enjoying a rare moment's intestina

peace, his head back against the stone, eyes closed against the fierce sun, when he felt the earth beneath him move. He gagged, his throat on fire, because everything solid had long since been regurgitated.

There was a loud crack, and a chunk of the stone he'd been leaning against broke away. It hit Hiram in the small of the back, knocking him forward. His body twisted as he fell so that he landed on his back, looking up at the stronghold towering above him.

A bright blue light seemed to be emanating from the summit, two hundred feet above him. There was the noise of thunder, but louder than any Hiram had ever heard. A retaining wall near the top gave way, and car-sized boulders began to bounce and slide down the steep slopes.

Someone screamed, and Hiram realized it was he himself, as the entire fortress of Ollantaytambo began to slip down the hillside toward him.

"Race you to the top!"

Tony Torres grinned broadly at his eleven-year-old brother, Xuasus. He gestured upward, and Xuasus swiveled his eyes to follow.

The Pyramid of the Sun loomed above them, backed by an almost luminous blue sky. Mexico City's infamous polluted haze lay miles away. From this angle, the pyramid's steep sides looked as if they were sheer, a climb more suited to professional mountaineers than the tourists and families who straggled up them.

Xuasus snorted. A year younger than Tony, he always lost when they competed at anything. It was a school trip, and their teacher, Mr. Perez, had brought the whole class to visit the Avenue of the Dead and its two pyramids, an hour's drive from the city district where they lived. Xuasus would rather buy an ice cream and check out the souvenir stalls with the pesos his mother had given him.

"I'll do your chores if you win," Tony added slyly, and Xuasus's determination evaporated.

"It's a bet!" he cried, already leaping onto the first of the hundreds of stone steps that made up the pyramid's sides. On some of the lower courses, the gap between steps was three feet and more, and only the energy of youth allowed the boys to take them at a run.

Mr. Perez and the rest of the class were still walking up the wide avenue from the Pyramid of the Moon, the teacher pointing out the carved stone jaguars and serpents that adorned the walls, the boys pretending to listen as they jostled each other and laughed. No one had noticed the Torres brothers stride on ahead.

Tony and Xuasus ignored the metal guide rail and the fifty or so people who were using it to haul themselves up the punishing climb. His early start had given Xuasus a slight lead, but over the sound of his own labored breathing he could hear his brother's footsteps catching up.

A plump, middle-aged woman shouted as they went racing by her, but neither could tell if it was admonishment or encouragement. They didn't slow down to find out.

Xuasus's lungs felt as if they were burning, and his

aching leg muscles threatened to quit at any moment. He forced himself on, no longer able to leap from step to step, but using his hands to help him vault up.

Tony was just about to pass his brother when he slipped, slamming his shin against the rough stone. He stopped and clutched his leg, half cursing, half crying.

Xuasus seized his chance and clambered on.

Seconds later, panting and gasping, Xuasus stood alone and victorious at the top. Tony was about twenty feet below, the race forgotten as he rolled up his trouser leg to inspect his injury. Xuasus's grin was so broad, his cheeks were beginning to hurt.

He turned himself to the four directions, looking out over the tree-covered mounds that Mr. Perez said were ancient buildings waiting to be discovered. According to the teacher, their ancestors had lived here for many centuries. Beyond the plain, the smog from the city all but blotted out the panorama of surrounding volcanic hills.

On a sudden impulse, Xuasus knelt down on the flattened summit. He stared hard at the square stone in the center, its face worn smooth by centuries of human contact. For this was where mothers brought their children, to touch their heads against the warm rock and allow the pyramid's mystical energies to flow through them. A lot of the younger people laughed at the custom, but all the women said it brought good luck.

Xuasus's own mother had brought him here as a baby—not that touching his head to the stone seemed to have done him much good. He was hopeless at school, and though he was good enough at sports, Tony always beat him. Until today, of course.

Perhaps the energies are like the battery in my radio, he thought, stooping lower, his forehead only inches from the stone. *They have to be recharged sometimes.*

Before he knew what happened, a jet of erupting piezoelectricity took his head clean off.

"That man—the one skulking in the alley mouth. Tell me about him, Cassandra."

They were sitting in the window seat, and Cassandra craned her neck to see where Grandma was pointing. A trolley clattered by, blocking off her view, but the man was still there when it passed.

She couldn't see him distinctly. He appeared to be dressed all in black, and stood so that his face was concealed by shadows.

Cassandra looked at his feet. *Strange. He's not wearing any shoes.*

A sudden, unpleasant odor drifted in through the open window. The stench of decaying meat mingled with the old lady's lavender. Cassandra felt a terrible sense of foreboding. Something evil was coming her way.

The man was stepping out of the shadows. Cassandra tried to turn her head away, but it refused to move. Paralyzed, she could only watch, her heart pounding faster and louder in her chest as the figure looked directly up at her.

He had the face of a bull, and golden horns grew from the scalp above his ears.

With a strength of will she didn't know she possessed, Cassandra tore her gaze away. Then she started to shiver uncontrollably, and cowered, whimpering, against her grandmother.

A few time zones to the east of Gotham City, in the Republic of Ireland, Seamus Milligan gunned the engine of his Honda Big Red and sent it hurtling down the narrow, hedge-lined lane.

The cattle were in for the afternoon milking, but a tube had ruptured on the milking machine. No chance of making it to town before the ironmonger closed. Indeed, if old O'Bannion was running true to form, the shop would be closed already and the first pint of stout balanced in the old man's hand.

Milligan decelerated fiercely as the little four-wheel-drive car roared toward a right-angled corner. He swung the car around, the left-hand wheels briefly losing contact with the road. Then all four tires gripped again and he hit the accelerator hard. A couple of late-season tourists scrambled up onto the verge as the 4X4 shot by, and Seamus waved regally.

Visitors to the tomb, he thought, *disappointed to find the season's over and it's closed until spring.*

He threw a glance over his left shoulder toward the stubby green mound that was the Newgrange burial chamber, the largest Neolithic structure in all Ireland. Milligan had lived here all his life, farming dairy cattle in this fertile bend of the River Boyne, yet he'd never set foot inside the vast grave.

At least, he reflected, *some think it's a grave. Others claim it's the place where the living could speak to the dead, and the future was revealed to the witches. When I was a child, they whispered it was where the demons had gone to live when men stole their world.*

Milligan had seen it from the outside, huge white stones laid along its perimeter, their surfaces scrolled with ancient, mystifying symbols.

Once each year, at the winter solstice, a single beam of light entered a receptacle above the doorway. It streamed down the long, narrow passage to the center of the mound and lit it up like summer. For three hundred sixty-five days of the year, the interior lay dark and silent, guarding its secrets well. But for a few brief minutes the sun illumined the intricately carved lining stones, before they returned to darkness for another year.

Milligan was past the turf-covered mound now, onto a long, straight road hedged with hawthorn, elder, and the odd rowan tree. He heard a sound behind him, like the engine of a car impatient to overtake. He risked a glance back, and his jaw dropped at what he saw.

A thin fountain of viscous red liquid was jetting from the center of the mound into the overcast sky.

Lava, Milligan thought. *Only it can't be lava—not here!*

Where it fell to the ground, flames sparked up as vegetation caught fire and blazed fiercely.

At the last moment, Milligan noticed that his 4X4 was veering sharply. He tried to correct the steering, but he was going too fast. A front wheel caught the edge of the verge, and the vehicle somersaulted off the road and through the air.

There was a ripping of metal and splintering of wood as it smashed into the trunk of a rowan tree. The old folk called it the witches' tree, and claimed no evil spirit could stand in its presence.

Seamus Milligan lay on the verge, his head twisted unnaturally, his neck broken in the fall. He wouldn't see the fires converge into one huge conflagration that would soon sweep over his farm and spread out until half the valley was in flames.

Sunset in Cairo, a riot of purple, red, and gold gleaming off ten thousand mosques and minarets. The streets resounded with the roar of traffic, mingled with singsong chants calling the faithful to prayer.

Outside the city, up on the Giza Plateau, the Sphinx and the Great Pyramids stood in sand-strewn silence, as they had for at least four thousand five hundred years. The only sound was the occasional grunts of camels as they were led home to their quarters for the night. The tourists would be back tomorrow.

Professor Simon Ferzal, Director of Research at Giza, led his party along the side of the old canal, long empty and dry, knowing they'd get the best view of the Great Pyramid silhouetted against an awesome sky.

"When it was built, of course," the professor said,

"the pyramid had a golden capstone. It would have reflected light like this for hundreds of miles, marking Giza as a truly magical place."

"Magical?" Cindy Barnes queried. She and a delegation of American investors were visiting Giza, with a view to sinking money into a noninvasive expedition that would produce the very first sonar mapping of the entire plateau. Rumors of hidden chambers, buried secrets, and hoards of gold that made the treasure of Tutankhamen's tomb pale in comparison, had abounded for years. The American mystic Edgar Cayce had predicted that a chamber would be found containing the written works of fabled Atlantis.

Previous sonar surveys had located several unknown tunnels, caves, and chambers running through the plateau's limestone bedrock. Barnes and her team were willing to bet that there were more.

Of course, they'd receive no payment if they struck lucky—not directly, anyway. The Egyptian government would own whatever was found, and it would be made publicly available as soon as the experts had finished their analysis. But Cindy's husband, Don, was already working on the book; TV and movie rights were secured, and a little professional marketing would help them and the government share equally in the photographic rights.

Now, Cindy Barnes frowned. "I thought the ancient Egyptians were the apex of technology for their times, Professor. Why would they bother with magic?"

Ferzal waited a moment before replying. They'd reached a flight of steps, and he signaled to his aide to light the way with a powerful spotlight. Graciously, the research director took Cindy's elbow and assisted her up the stairs.

"My ancestors were technocrats indeed," he said in his impeccable English, lifting his gaze to the massive bulk of the pyramid. "They were able to quarry, move, and lift an estimated six million tons of stone to produce the Great Pyramid alone. Yet at the same time, they lived mired in a world of ritual and superstition. There was a god or goddess for everything, from domestic cats to the universe. All had to be propitiated, or disaster might follow."

The spotlight marking their path, Ferzal led them over toward the rough-hewn rock enclosure that housed the mighty Sphinx, the most enigmatic of all ancient monuments. Its red sandstone blocks almost glowed in the fast-fading sunlight, changing to purple as the shadows deepened.

Ferzal was about to drop a few pearls of wisdom regarding its age and pedigree when he heard a startled shout from one of the others: Cindy's husband, Don, the lanky bookworm. Ferzal hoped he hadn't tripped and hurt himself.

But Don was looking back at the Great Pyramid. Cobalt blue flames poured from its top and ran down the limestone casing like dry ice, rushing down to the ground below.

Ferzal and the others turned to run, but an avalanche of swirling cold fire engulfed them before they'd gone twenty yards.

* * *

All over the world, the sacred sites of the ancients began to reenergize.

At Carnac in northern France, location of the world's largest collection of menhirs, blue light blasted from more than a thousand standing stones.

In Spain, Czechoslovakia, and Bulgaria, hidden caves that knew the dreams and spells of sorcerers before the Ice Age were bathed in violet waves. Those few people in the caves—spelunkers and a University of Vienna anthropology team—suffocated within seconds.

The once-holy Mediterranean island of Malta was engulfed in a green mist that seeped from the ancient, subterranean Goddess sanctuaries.

Lhasa, Tibet's holiest city, lit up in the biggest "fireworks" display ever seen.

In Russia and China, throughout Japan and Southeast Asia, forces that had slumbered for millennia awakened and threatened to bring disaster in their wake.

Fear is the messenger, not the message.

Cassandra heard the words as clearly and distinctly as if Batman was in Grandma's apartment.

Like empathy, she thought, *fear is a gift. An early warning system. But it's not meant to paralyze. It's supposed to spur you to action. Fight or flight. Your choice. But do something. If you fail to act, your fear will claim you.*

Slowly, fearfully, determinedly, Cassandra opened her eyes. Grandma had disappeared. Cassandra looked out the window, her heart pumping with terror at what she would see, but knowing that she had to see it.

The bull-headed man had grown to colossal size, until he bestrode the planet. The shrieking of a billion people filled the air. The mountains split open and rolled over everything below, while new peaks burst up from the sea.

"No!" Cassandra screamed. "Never, never, never!"

Far away, she heard a voice. "Dr. Valerian! She's awake!"

CHAPTER 13

Battle Lines

The teleporter disgorged Batman and J'onn J'onzz within fifty yards of where the base of the Gotham pyramid had been.

It was a beautiful autumn evening, the air crisp and fresh, the sky painted with stars. An almost full moon was rising in the east, its bright light shrouded by a mass of dark clouds low on the horizon. Somewhere in the distance, a fox was barking.

Batman stood staring for a full minute, as if determination alone would enable him to tell if the pyramid was really there or not. Finally, he shook his head.

"If it's there," he admitted, "I'm not seeing it."

"You're not alone," Manhunter replied. He had scanned the site with his peculiar Martian vision, which allowed him to see through virtually any object. "None of my senses is picking up anything out of the ordinary."

"I guess there's only one way to find out."

Batman walked ahead in a straight line, stepping over the barrier erected by the police when they closed off the site. His penlight picked out a path through the low scrub bushes and rough grass. Even with the aid of the infrared lenses in his mask, he could see little except the ground beneath his feet and the steep-sided riverbank ahead.

J'onn watched his companion, his eyes never leaving him. Suddenly, there was a flash of color, as if the air itself had rippled and moved aside.

Batman disappeared from view.

"It's here all right, J'onn," Manhunter heard the vigilante call.

The Martian moved forward, a tingle of static electricity caressing his green skin as he walked through the unseen barrier and joined Batman on the other side.

The pyramid rose before them, its massive bulk blotting out half the night sky.

"Refracted light waves," Batman said quietly. "The thing's invisible until you're in front of it."

J'onn's feet left the ground, and he hovered in the air above the grass. He was able to fly using his telekinetic abilities, the power of his mind alone carrying him through the air.

"Going up?" he asked.

Batman shook his head. "I'll climb, thanks."

Like Cassandra, who had been taught by her grandmother, Batman had an incredible eye for detail. On the previous trip to the pyramid, he had committed as much of its layout and setting to memory as he could. He wanted to confirm that knowledge now and get his bearings, before rushing into confrontation with their dangerous foe.

"The hidden chamber was on the fifth course," he told J'onn as he began to clamber up the pyramid's side, the Martian hovering close to him. Here and there tufts of parched grass grew between the stones. "We should check it out before we do anything else."

"I can use my telepathy," J'onn suggested, "to probe the Stone King's mind. If he's here, that is. It might give us an insight into how to tackle him."

"Too risky." Batman clambered onto the third course, springing over the flat-packed stone to reach the next part of the upward climb. "If he realizes what's going on, it'll alert him to our presence. Judging by what happened last time, he's likely to come out on top in any confrontation. Best if we keep the element of surprise on our side."

The words were hardly out of Batman's mouth when he realized that the element of surprise had already been lost. Even as he reached out for a handhold to haul himself up onto the pyramid's next ledge, something was forming in the air above him. A patch of what he'd taken to be night mist began to swirl and take on solid shape.

Batman caught a glimpse of scaly, lizardlike skin, a pair of eyes glowing like fiery coals, and a long, thick tail surmounted by a spiked knob.

Then the thing was diving at him, and he was falling back in an attempt to cushion its assault. He heard Manhunter's exclamation of surprise and guessed that he, too, had come under attack.

Before they had time to react, the world became a madhouse of flashing claws and jagged, ripping teeth.

The shaman stood in the hidden chamber, his head thrown back and his arms outstretched as a symphony of colored lights flashed from his fingertips. They danced in the air like living things, red and blue and gold swooping and swirling, coalescing and breaking up again into individual patterns. They played around the heads of the captured heroes, lighting them up in grotesque caricature, draining them of their incredible powers.

Peter Glaston felt unaccountably stronger. He'd made several tentative attempts to approach his possessor's mind, to get inside it and learn its strengths and weaknesses. What he found there was the history of an evil man.

Five thousand years ago, the Stone King reigned supreme over a sprawling empire in what is now considered North America. He had been brought up as one of the elite astronomer-priests, an interpreter of cosmic omens, the human link between the gods above and the people below. It was his sacred duty to maintain the balance between what his human subjects needed and what the earth could provide for them.

The Stone King was well-versed in the paths of power. He'd been taught how to control the potent energies that swept through the earth and lay hidden in the secret depths of the stones. He knew secrets it had taken his ancestors tens of thousands of years to accumulate.

When his training was done, he should have taken

his place as the people's champion, the bridge between the stones and the stars. His was the task of
guiding his far-flung tribes, of ensuring that the rituals
and practices they had kept for millennia would continue unchanged.

But the Stone King had other plans. The power he
wielded had seduced him, corrupting the ideals im-
planted in him by his priestly teachers. Instead of
being his people's servant, he would be their master
through power and pain and torture.

As if in a vision, Peter saw a horde of warriors
swarming like worker ants to construct the Stone
King's Pyramid of Power. He saw the shaman stand
atop it, surrounded by a blazing aura as the earth energies coursed around and through his body. The people bowed their heads and made obeisance. Lacking
rational consciousness, their impressionable minds accepted everything at face value.

This man in the bull mask was their master; they
had no choice but to serve him, to follow his every
command.

Power corrupts, and absolute power corrupts
absolutely.

The Stone King's demands increased. He took the
tribe's healthiest, most fertile women and locked them
in a hidden compound to which only he had access.
He executed the tribal elders to prevent any action
they might take against him. He sent his warrior
bands to raid rival tribes, slaughtering the men and
stealing their women for himself and their children for
grisly human sacrifice.

Then came the drought. The rains ceased and the
sun grew hotter, until the rivers themselves dried up.
It was the shaman's age-old task to help his people, to
ease their suffering, to tell them why the gods were
angry and make the appropriate sacrifice to propitiate
them.

But the Stone King's tyranny knew no bounds. He
began to demand the tribe's own children, intending
to sacrifice them in appeasement.

It was a step too far.

Peter saw a group of warriors creeping up the pyramid on a moonless night. Stone axes rose and fell. A
poison-tipped spear impaled the shaman's chest even
as he struggled and showered them with vile curses.
He died with vengeance on his lips and a burning
black hatred in his heart.

They burned his body on the altar in the secret
chamber. They buried the ax head—the symbol of the
Stone King's power—in the chamber floor. Then they
closed up the entrance with heavy stone slabs and
turned their backs on the pyramid and the traditions
of ten thousand years. Then the whole tribe aban-
doned the area to seek water elsewhere.

So . . . at least he can be beaten, Peter thought, contem-
plating all he had gleaned.

The knowledge gave him fresh heart. He knew it
was now or never. The Stone King intended to annihilate every man, woman, and child on earth . . . and
somehow, he seemed to have the power to do it.

"Screw your courage to the sticking-place."

The line from a Shakespeare play he'd read in first-year English Literature came back to him. But Peter's courage was already screwed to the sticking-place . . . and he felt as if it was indeed *stuck*. He couldn't go any further.

No! his mind protested. *You have to do it! Just don't be beaten by your own fear.*

He wavered, his mind running through all the options, dreading what might happen to him. If he failed, the Stone King might torture him forever. Or wipe him out as if he never existed. Or drive him mad, an insane captive in a mind that was no longer his own. Or . . .

If he succeeded, perhaps everything would be restored to the way it had been.

But how to do it? This was Peter's mind; surely he could choose the arena of battle? Or, the thought occurred to him, maybe even create it!

Peter had been a member of the university fencing team for a couple of semesters, until archaeology claimed his interest full-time. He hadn't been very good at it, but at least he knew how to hold a blade, how to wield it and avoid getting hurt by his opponent.

He imagined himself a hero, like Superman or Batman, tall and proud and strong. As if in answer, somehow, a burnished sword of justice appeared, flaming, in his hand. There was a bright metal shield strapped to his left forearm.

He saw his foe clad in skins, his bull's head and horns held high. Peter no longer saw him as a fiend rom hell, only a man, an evil man whose power was wesome but not total.

Peter took a deep, metaphorical breath . . . and harged.

"You don't really expect me to drop everything and drive out of town with someone I don't even know?"

There was incredulity in Jenny Ayles's voice. She tood in the half-open doorway of the apartment she hared with two other young women, staring at the tranger whose windswept platinum hair tangled around her pretty face.

Cassandra had expected to be greeted this way. She herself would have reacted no differently. She sought or the words to convince Jenny of the rightness of her cause.

Within an hour of emerging from her coma, Cassandra had walked out of the hospital, Dr. Clay Valerian's dire warnings ringing in her ears.

"We haven't finished your tests," he protested. "There could be something serious!"

But Cassandra felt fine, at least physically. Inside, she was deeply afraid of what she knew she had to do. But she forced herself to sign the treatment waiver the nurse held in front of her, reclaimed her own clothing, and hurried out into the street.

She had just enough money in her pocketbook to cover the cab fare to her apartment. Her thoughts raced urgently as the taxi driver sped through the streets. People were already starting to gather for the street party; it wasn't dark yet, and their masquerade costumes made them stand out like sore thumbs.

Halloween, she thought, feeling a stab of pity for the would-be partygoers, *the day the Stone King will destroy the world! And I might be the only person who can stop him. . . .*

The solution had come to her in those confused minutes that followed her awakening. The Stone King was really Peter Glaston, possessed by a spirit stronger than himself. But if Glaston's mind still survived, it should be possible to make contact and urge him to throw off the mental shackles that bound him.

And what better person to do it than the girl Peter loved?

Batman had told her and the commissioner about Jenny Ayles, the possessed man's girlfriend. Cassandra had no idea where Batman might be. And no doubt Commissioner Gordon would have his hands full with policing the street party. This was something Cassandra would have to do alone.

She had found Jenny's address in the telephone directory and decided to have a quick shower and change of clothing before heading over there. She'd switched on her radio and stood soaping herself in the shower's stinging jets as she listened to the news of the mayhem that had befallen the world.

From Ohio's Serpent Mound to Uluru, Ayers Rock, in the middle of the Australian outback, the same horrifying picture was presented. Strange energies had erupted from every sacred site, bringing death and destruction to the immediate vicinity. Emergency and

ilitary teams had been despatched to back up the
vo dozen or so Justice League heroes who, thanks to
atman's warning, were already directing rescue and
amage control exercises.

After the first violent outpourings, the energy levels
emed to have stabilized.

At least it's not getting any worse, Cassandra thought,
en added, *Yet.*

She'd called another cab, then barely had time to
wel-dry her hair before she heard the driver honk-
g his horn down on the street.

Her driver was a young eastern European immi-
ant who seemed to speak little English but who kept
a deprecatory commentary on the journey in his
vn language. Cassandra was surprised to see the
owing crowds, many in fancy dress or scary Hal-
ween masks. Didn't they listen to the news? Didn't
ey know the world was facing a crisis and the Justice
ague's most powerful members were missing in ac-
on? How could they even think of partying when
ey, and the planet itself, were skirting so close to
om?

Perhaps it was because the thought of impending
saster was so hard to accept. The street party filled
me psychological need—as if it was easier for peo-
e to bury their heads in the sand, to pretend that if
ey acted normally, then everything would soon re-
rn to normal.

Cassandra was one of the few who knew that wasn't
e case. She breathed a heartfelt sigh of relief when
e discovered Jenny at home.

A sea mist had poured into Marlbuck Poin
overnight, and failed to lift in the morning. Jenny an
Jamie Stewart had sat around for hours twiddling
their thumbs before Hamish had sent them hom
rather than muddy up the dig. Besides, it would sav
him the expense of an afternoon's wages.

Jenny started to close the door—she'd had enoug
from the press, from strangers badgering her. The las
thing she needed was to head off who knows wher
with a woman she didn't know, someone who wasn
even making any sense.

"It's Peter," Cassandra said with grim finality.

It was the last thing she'd wanted to say. She knew
exactly how Jenny would react: shock, grief, a blad
cutting at an open wound. Cassandra could literall
feel the chill that swept through the girl.

"Peter?" Jenny whispered.

Cassandra apologized for her bluntness, but ther
really had been no other way to make Jenny listen. Sh
started to give a hurried explanation of what had hap
pened, but Jenny stopped her almost at once.

"You're saying Peter didn't kill Professor Mills?
The relief in the girl's voice was unmistakeable. "I
was this . . . spirit that's possessed him?"

"That's what the Batman told me. And as far as I ca
judge, he's right." Cassandra glanced at her wrist, a
the elegant, old-fashioned watch that had once be
longed to her grandmother. "We don't have muc
time. Do you think we can talk while we travel? I hav
a cab waiting."

Jenny pulled a leather jacket from the hall-stand in

side the door. "My car's not very passenger friendly," she confessed, "but it gets me to Marlbuck and back each day. I'd rather drive myself."

Cassandra paid off her driver, and minutes later Jenny's fifteen-year-old Nissan compact was heading for the city limits. The springs in the passenger seat had worn out years ago, and Cassandra squirmed uncomfortably as they raced toward the freeway on-ramp at almost double the speed limit.

The flaming sword arced downward, with all of Peter's strength behind it.

Taken unaware, his bull-headed foe had no time to react. The gleaming blade sliced through the animal skins, biting deep into the shaman's flesh, sending him toppling to the sandy floor of Peter's imagined arena.

The monster rose on one elbow, its other hand swinging the razor-sharp stone ax it held. Peter's sword arced again, and the weapon went careening from the shaman's hand.

This is too easy!

Peter almost laughed as a flood of elation surged through him. To think he'd crouched, cowering and quivering as he tried to conceal himself in his own mind, terrified of this entity! And now he had it at his mercy.

The flaming sword rose and fell, time and again, splashing gouts of blood in the air. But Peter gave no quarter, and continued to hack frenziedly at the shaman's body long after there was any need.

* * *

Batman was beginning to wonder if he was fighting some mirror image version of himself.

Every attack he launched was effectively parried. Karate, kick-boxing, jujitsu—his opponent seemed to know them all, and defended itself accordingly.

A brutal chop was deflected by a scaly elbow. A stunning chest kick was stopped by a cross-wristed block. Even aikido—a martial arts system that uses the attacker's strength against him—proved of no value. Only the occasional blow landed home, and then more by luck than by judgment. When it did, the creature made no sound and gave no sign that it felt pain.

By the same token, Batman managed to repel the lizardlike humanoid every time it became the aggressor. Booted feet and gauntleted hands warded off a succession of blows flung at him from every conceivable angle. When one of the beast's blows struck home, Batman grunted and rolled with the impact.

The confrontation was more like a ballet than a battle. *Almost as if we're perfectly suited to each other,* Batman thought, failing to connect with a wild, swinging kick. He ducked under the inevitable counterattack, deflecting a punch with an upraised forearm. *As if whoever controls this creature is providing only so much energy, and no more. As if he's conserving his power for something else.*

It could only be the Stone King.

Batman ducked a flurry of punches, slipping open a pouch in his Utility Belt. He had something here that ought to give him the edge. His hand closed around a vial inside the pouch. Scarecrow's special fear gas might turn the fight in his favor.

But as Batman prepared to lob the vial, his foe struck. Its tail lashed out like a whip, the spiked knob at the end ripping painfully into Batman's arm. The vial went flying from his numbed fingers, landing on a patch of grass growing between the stones.

The Dark Knight didn't waste time cursing his ill fortune. He aimed a series of rapid kicks at his misshapen opponent, using the time they bought him to slide his bola from its pouch. Holding it firmly by the center, where the three thongs met, he started it spinning with a flick of his wrist.

Each thong was tipped with a small lead weight, the weighted ends singing as they quickly whipped up speed.

Extending his hand with the whirling bola in front of him, Batman lunged at his foe.

The weights thudded into the side of the beast's scaly head, one after the other in quick succession, with enough power to knock out a horse. The lizardman fell back, momentarily stunned, and Batman tried to press home his advantage.

Again the three whirling balls powered into the creature's head. But this time, it didn't react. Instead, with greatly increased strength, it delivered a savage backhand blow that sent Batman smashing against the pyramid's rock face.

Looks like there's something in my theory, he mused, wiping a trace of blood from the corner of his mouth. *It came back at me like a powerhouse when it needed to.*

Using the pyramid wall as a springboard, Batman backflipped to evade another smashing blow. A clawed fist slammed into the stonework with an impact that sent fragments of granite flying. Batman's hand snapped to his Utility Belt, trying to decide whether it had really been such a good idea to test his theory, after all.

J'onn J'onzz was faring little better against the creature that had gone for him. When he flew, it flew. When he landed a blow with Martian superstrength, the beast reeled, but recovered to strike back immediately. Similarly, when its slashing claws struck him, his near-invulnerability shrugged off the attack.

As if it's only trying to delay me, he thought.

The moon had come out from behind the clouds. The huge white disk cast an almost surreal light on the scene.

J'onn! Manhunter heard Batman's telepathic call.

They'd been aware of each other during their individual fights, but only peripherally, with all their attention focused on their opponents.

Manhunter risked a glance along the course, and paid immediately for his indiscretion as the lizardman struck him in the thigh. But he'd had time to see Batman retreating before the other creature's maniacal onslaught, its claws raking, jaws slavering, spiked tail twitching as it sought an opening for the kill.

This one's power seems to be wavering, Batman thought. *Might be a good time to switch dancing partners.* Batman used his wrist to block a chopping blow. *Now!*

J'onn had also felt a slump in his own foe's power levels, as if whoever was controlling it had more pressing business to attend to. Immediately, J'onn used one of the unusual Martian powers that were his birthright. He thought hard, and the light waves striking him responded somehow to his conscious will, bending themselves around him. Turning him invisible.

It was a talent he could employ only for short periods. But it should be long enough.

J'onn soared a dozen feet into the air, turned on a dime, and sent himself crashing at speed into the lizard-man Batman had been fighting.

The impact crushed the creature against the course's retaining wall, and the beast slumped like a sack of sand.

Batman had turned to run at Manhunter's foe, which hovered with uncertainty a few feet out from the side of the pyramid. A bat-line shot from the Dark Knight's hand, its grapple biting home around the lizard-man's neck. Batman yanked hard on the line with both hands, pulling the surprised beast toward him.

As it loomed closer, it seemed to recover somewhat. Its eyes glittered dangerously, and its maw opened to reveal jagged yellow teeth. Its drooling jaws opened wider—

And Batman tossed two percussion grenades down its throat.

The resulting explosion blew the creature apart.

Batman stood for a moment to recover his breath, and J'onn materialized beside him.

"I believe you lost this." J'onn held out his hand. Nestling in his upturned palm was the vial of fear gas Batman had dropped.

"Thanks." Batman took the vial and slipped i
back into his Utility Belt. "My guess is the Stone
King was distracted," he went on thoughtfully. "He
was trying to save his energy, presumably because
it's needed elsewhere. But something took his mind
off the job."

J'onn gestured upward with his head, his craggy
eyebrows looking more like a carapace under the
moon's light.

Two stories above them, plasmoid light was flicker
ing from the burial chamber.

"That's where we'll get our answers," the Martian
said grimly.

Finally, Peter's strength gave out.

Soaked in perspiration, panting with effort, he le
the flaming sword slip from his fingers. His rage and
terror had exhausted themselves, and he felt a curious
detachment from any emotion. He could hardly believe it had been so simple.

This being, this shaman of unimaginable power, had
crumpled like paper under Peter's frenzied attack.

I guess I've got my body back. I'm in charge again.

He looked down at the bloody, torn remains of his
possessor, and a sudden chill froze him to the spot.

The eyes in its disembodied head blinked open, and
fixed Peter with a look so malign it might have been
Medusa, the Gorgon who turned men to stone with
her malevolent glare.

Pain stabbed in Peter's temple. Something warm

was trickling down the side of his face. Curiously, he touched it with his finger. Blood. His blood.

His temples were throbbing now, the tempo quickening. He felt faint. He tried to marshal his thoughts, but everything was turning red.

Peter's scream lasted only for an instant, then his mind exploded.

CHAPTER 14

Preliminary Skirmish

Jenny Ayles sent the old Nissan bombing over Canyon Bridge, with the raging waters of the Gotham River a hundred feet below.

When the road forked, she branched right, taking them through deep pine forest for several miles. There were no other vehicles around, no roadside lights marking the position of farms and houses.

Jenny felt strangely detached, the way she often did when she was traveling. She'd left her own problems behind her. Their destination, and the problems she had to face there, still lay in the future, where she didn't have to worry about them. Yet.

Beside her, Cassandra traveled in silence. More than once, the empath asked herself if she was doing the right thing. Each time, her answer was the same: *What alternative do I have?*

A mile before they reached the site of the dam itself, Jenny turned the car off the paved highway. The Nissan bounced down an old farm track, Cassandra's self-examination all but forgotten as she struggled to avoid injuring herself on the passenger seat's broken springs.

"I don't understand," Jenny exclaimed as they rounded a corner that brought them in plain view of the riverbank. "The pyramid . . . it's not there!"

"Perhaps we've come to the wrong location," Cassandra suggested. "You're upset. It would be an easy mistake to make."

Jenny slowed the car to a walking pace and wound down her window. Clouds covered the moon, but there was enough light for her to know she was right. After all, she'd worked here every day for weeks.

"There's no mistake," Jenny insisted. "Look— here's the stand of cottonwood trees growing out of the riverbank. The dam's less than a mile upstream. This is where we used to park the university SUV."

She stopped the Nissan and switched off the engine.

Jenny felt a chill of foreboding as she opened the car door and slid out. This place had already taken from her the man she loved . . . and Robert Mills, a man she didn't love. But if there was a chance of getting Peter back, no matter how slim, she was willing to take it.

"Perhaps we just can't make it out in the darkness," Jenny told Cassandra, as she too got out of the car. "I'm going to walk up the path we used."

Cassandra's mind was working overtime. If they couldn't find the pyramid, they couldn't confront the monster. Peter Glaston wouldn't be freed. And the world would end.

Long grass whipped their ankles and bushes tugge at their clothing as they sidestepped the police barrie and made their way along the narrow path of fla tened vegetation.

Jenny kept looking around her, shaking her heac How could something so big simply disappear?

There was a sudden rippling of the air around then and both women came to an abrupt halt.

The stepped pyramid rose in front of them, its dar bulk limned against the moon that was now rising be hind it. About halfway up the steep sides, intermitter flashes of strange light were being emitted.

"But . . ." Jenny said feebly. "How?"

Cassandra shook her head, at a loss for words.

In silence, they made their way to the foot of th pyramid. Terrified of what might await them, Jenn clutched Cassandra's arm and kept her eyes fixe straight ahead.

Batman and the Martian Manhunter crept quietl along the wide ledge of the fifth course. Just ahea several large rock slabs had been moved aside, revea ing the entry to the hidden chamber.

Motioning Batman to fall back a little, J'onn move toward the doorway. If they were met with violence better for J'onn's near-invulnerable body to be in th vanguard. Manhunter edged closer, then leaned in t peek around the stone lintel.

Quickly, he beckoned Batman to join him.

Be ready for anything, J'onn cautioned. *There's n telling what's going to happen in there.*

Batman nodded his assent.

Inside the chamber, the Stone King was on his knees, his head lowered until it was almost touching the floor. His hands grasped his bull's skull headpiece, and his eyes were screwed shut, as if he was in terrible pain.

He didn't open his eyes as they approached, nor did he acknowledge their presence, as the two heroes silently entered the Stone King's domain.

He seems to be in some sort of distress, Manhunter opined. *If his guard is down, this could be our optimum moment for attack.*

Batman wrinkled his nose. The smell of stale blood and putrefying flesh was sickening. Quickly, he inserted a pair of nose plugs under his mask.

Beyond, he could see that the chamber's recess was filled with chaotically flickering light.

You may well be right, Batman agreed. *But wait just one moment.*

The Dark Knight pointed to the chamber floor. The rotting shreds of flesh that lay everywhere had attracted a significant amount of insect life. Beetles and maggots scurried from one scrap of meat to another. A chunky, black beetle's path took it directly toward the motionless Stone King.

About six inches from the Stone King, the beetle paused momentarily. Its antennae brushed the air, as if it sensed that something was not quite right. Then the insect jerked forward again, and was instantly disintegrated in a soundless blue flash.

He's protected himself with a force field. J'onn groaned

inwardly. *And short of direct attack, we've no way of knowing how powerful it is.*

Keep an eye on him, Batman responded. *I'll find out what else is in here.*

Noiselessly, the vigilante moved deeper into the rock-lined chamber, his every nerve alert, every muscle tensed for action. But what he saw made him expel his breath in a low, sibilant hiss.

Superman, Wonder Woman, Green Lantern, and the Flash were trapped there, imprisoned in the living stone. Only their hands and faces were visible; the rest of their bodies were buried in the dense rock.

They're here, J'onn! Manhunter felt a surge of pleasure as Batman broadcast the thought. *They're trapped. I'm going to try to release them.*

A high-powered laser from his Utility Belt was already in Batman's hand. He snapped it on, guiding the deadly beam up and down the mass of stone that surrounded Superman. It bubbled under the intense heat where the beam struck it, tiny fracture lines branching out from the main central cut.

Batman worked with the beam for several minutes. Finally satisfied, he laid the laser aside and took several small compressed-air pellets from a pouch. He crammed them into the deep split in the rock, wedging them between the rock and Superman's body. He turned away as he waited for the five-second delayed fuses to ignite. Superman's invulnerable body would suffer no harm.

The pellets detonated simultaneously with a soft pop, sending up a puff of dust as several large chunks of stone broke off. Batman seized a loosened section and pulled with all his strength.

The rock imprisoning Superman shattered in a dozen places, falling away to reveal his costumed body. But the liberated hero didn't move. His eyes remained closed, and he showed no sign that he was aware of Batman's presence.

What's the situation, J'onn?

Manhunter's gaze had never left the stricken Stone King. He was motionless now, as if cemented to the spot where he remained kneeling on the hard-packed floor.

No change. He still seems unaware of our presence. Whatever he's doing, it's absorbing all his attention.

I could use you here. Superman's free, but he doesn't seem to know it.

J'onn threw one last, lingering look at the Stone King, then crept past him and joined Batman in the depths of the cavern.

Gods of Mars! J'onn was shocked to see his companions, three of them still entombed in the rock, and Superman lying sprawled on the floor. *What's happened to them?*

I'm hoping your telepathy can discover that, Batman rejoined.

J'onn hesitated. Back in the days when he had first perfected the telepathic link to keep his fellow Justice League members in contact during times of crisis, there had been a certain amount of concern. Most heroes had a secret identity, a disguise they wore that allowed them to live some semblance of a normal life.

And every hero had secrets he or she preferred not to share. Those identities and secrets could easily be compromised if anyone—even one of their own number—discovered what they were.

J'onn had promised that he would never probe any of their minds without prior permission, and he'd kept that promise. But now, it seemed he had no other choice.

Batman watched as Manhunter consciously narrowed the focus of his thoughts. He directed his mind toward Superman's, waiting for the strange, alien feeling that would tell him he'd achieved contact. But contact never came—

A flash behind them alerted them to the danger.

They turned, but it was already too late.

A pulsating ball of plasma slammed into them with the force of a locomotive. The Kevlar lining in Batman's costume absorbed and redistributed the blow, but even so, the impact was so great that the vigilante was thrown face-first against the cavern wall. He was out cold instantly.

J'onn J'onzz managed to get both arms out in front of him to break the impact as he was hurled against the wall. His hands, however, sank up to the wrists in the solid rock.

Before he could wrench them free, the rock closed around them like granite handcuffs. J'onn tugged frantically, but the rock wouldn't budge. He heard a groan as Batman started to recover, pulling himself to his knees.

"The cycle will be complete."

The Stone King's words hung in the air, at once a promise and a threat.

He stood behind them, fully recovered now from his mental war with Peter Glaston. The unexpected attack had taken him off balance, fouled up his carefully constructed ritual, and blemished the purity of his thought processes.

It had taken a lot out of him, but he had eventually managed to repel Glaston's manic assault. And now he could concentrate again on the task at hand.

The pupils of his eyes began to enlarge, and he stared hard at the duo who had dared to invade the sanctity of his lair.

Batman and Manhunter were in no position to resist the shaman's mental bombardment. Pictures leaped into their minds, vivid visions of horror and death that would linger for a long time.

They saw the sacred sites of the world ablaze with energy.

Machu Picchu, the Incas' mysterious mountaintop sanctuary, belched sulphur and lava from a yawning crater that opened in its summit.

A violent electrical storm raged around the giant rocks of Stonehenge, lightning bolts of unstoppable power streaking destructively into the surrounding countryside.

Sections of Black Mesa, in the Hopi heartlands of the Four Corners, burned uncontrollably as the coal buried in the mountainside spontaneously combusted.

Vision followed awful vision with startling speed. Gotham City crumbling and collapsing as conflagration raged. New York shuddering with seismic shock as the bedrock beneath Manhattan turned to a jelloid mass. Kilimanjaro, Africa's highest mountain, disintegrating in an explosion that could be heard all around the world. The Orkney Islands, scene of Europe's first Neolithic settlers, sinking beneath the Atlantic waves.

Still dazed, unable to shut the visions out, Batman's heart filled with growing despair. To have come so close, only to see victory snatched away! The whole world was burning. Billions of innocent people had perished. The Apocalypse prophesied by almost every religion was upon them.

And there was nothing Batman could do about it. Fear of failure raged within him, until his very soul felt crushed.

Manhunter felt physically ill under the mental onslaught. The death of his family and friends—his whole planet!—had left him scarred inside forever. To see the same thing happen on Earth was more than he could bear.

Yet he was helpless, as his adopted world faced its own wholesale destruction at the hands of this maniacal monster.

Still the visions persisted.

Tokyo in ruins, the world's most modern city reduced to a barren wasteland by earthquake and volcanic eruption. Russia brought to its knees by plague and pestilence, corpses piled as high as the Kremlin itself. An America they didn't recognize, the land ripped and torn, the people fleeing in panic from a foe no army could fight.

Time and again, history had presided over the rise
and fall of mighty civilizations. The Persians, the As-
syrians, the Greeks, and the Romans; the Etruscans,
Minoans, Aztecs, Maya, Toltecs, and Olmecs; the
crazed hordes of the Mongols and Huns, charging
through the cities of the world, baying for blood.

Every one of these civilizations had reached its
apex, then plunged to its doom. But there had always
been other cultures, ready to expand and take the
place of those that failed.

This time, the collapse would be total, and planetwide.

Batman and Martian Manhunter saw the few survivors come crawling out of the holes and caves where
they'd hidden. The cycle would start again.

The Stone King would lead them into a new life,
cleansed and pure. The electromagnetic fields he controlled would be their lodestone, their guiding star. All
would be well—as long as everyone did what the
Stone King commanded.

Paralyzed by the Stone King's will, wracked with
hopelessness, it was all the Dark Knight could do to
remain conscious as the horrific visions never faltered
for a moment. For once, the message that his fear carried could not be acted upon.

"Peter? Peter, are you there?"

From far away, Batman recognized the female voice.
Jenny Ayles!

Jenny and Cassandra stood in the chamber doorway, Jenny's fingers tightly gripping her companion's

arm. Both were filled with terror, made queas
by the disgusting stench that seeped out from th
interior.

But they stood their ground, even as the Stone Kin
turned toward them. Peter Glaston's consciousnes
had been destroyed; the bull's skull still hid his fac
and greasy animal hide covered his body. The smell h
gave off was almost unendurable.

Repulsed by the foul image, Jenny had to fight to r
mind herself that this had been the man she cared fo
above all else.

"I . . . I love you, Peter," she faltered, heart poundin
in her breast.

She wanted to turn and flee, to run as far as sh
could from the nightmare figure who stood before he
She felt nauseated by its monstrous presence, dese
crated by the evil possessing her lover.

She pulled herself together, her knuckles white a
her grip on Cassandra's arm tightened even more.

Cassandra could feel every nuance of the younge
girl's cartwheeling emotions, but she steeled he
self. Jenny needed support, and whatever misgiv
ings Cassandra felt, she was the only one who coul
offer it.

When Jenny spoke again, her voice was loude
firmer. "I've always loved you, Peter," she declare
"since the first day we met. But you know how I hat
argument and confrontation. That's why what hap
pened in Peru, with Robert, poisoned everything w
meant to each other."

Jenny's eyes filled with tears that began to slid

down her cheeks. "I made a mistake, Peter," she went on. "I want you to forgive me."

The Stone King stood like a statue, making no sound or motion that betrayed whether he had even heard the words, let alone understood them. He seemed to be involved in some inner struggle that diverted his attention from his self-ordained task. The eyes beneath the bull skull blinked shut.

When they opened again Jenny's heart raced.

Those are Peter's eyes!

She hardly dared breathe, her gaze riveted to the Stone King's face. His words came falteringly, as if operating the facial muscles required a tremendous effort. Peter Glaston's eyes held hers, and it was Peter Glaston, and not the Stone King, who said in a thin, strangled voice:

"I . . . love . . . you . . . too . . . Jenny."

Peter Glaston had thought he was finished when the Stone King struck back.

For what seemed like an aeon he had experienced nothing, not even the cognizance of his own thoughts. There was no pain, no regrets, no flashback memories of his all-too-brief life. No heaven, no hell.

Just nothing.

And then, after an eternity of darkness, he thought he heard Jenny's voice.

"I . . . love you, Peter."

It was as if a dam had burst in his mind. He remembered everything: the first time he saw Jenny, hurrying across the campus lawn, late for a class. He remem-

bered asking her for a date, silently cursing hi
tongue-tied shyness. The elation he'd felt when sh
said "yes." Their first kiss, long and sweet and tende
on a warm summer night.

Peter had never been in love before. He embrace
the emotion the way he embraced Jenny herself—as i
he never wanted to let go.

Her brief affair with Professor Mills had shocke
him to his core, hurt him in a way he'd never experi
enced before. It was soon over, but the damage wa
done. Jenny said she was sorry; Peter said he forgav
her. But there was a shadow between them that hadn'
existed before, and the more they avoided discussing
the issue, the deeper the shadow became.

From somewhere, the scattered remnants of Peter'
personality found the strength to reemerge. He wasn'
fighting for himself anymore. He was fighting for th
woman he loved.

This was his body. The Stone King had no right to i
no right to steal his life, no right to part him from th
only girl he had ever loved.

So he fought back as hard as he could, and taste
victory as his lips parted to say:

"I love you, too, Jenny."

When the Stone King first diverted his attention t
Jenny and Cassandra, both Batman and Manhunte
had felt the power that held them wane slightly.

He's preoccupied again. Manhunter flashed the messag

His mind still reeling from the Stone King's menta
assault, Batman struggled to gather his thoughts.

think I know how he's holding the others captive, but it's
going to take your psionic powers to free them.

The key was electromagnetism. Batman was certain
of it. He recalled a scientific journal he'd once scanned,
one of the hundreds of items he committed to memory
every month.

Volunteers had lain on a gurney, which was rotated
at different speeds within a potent electromagnetic
field. A surprising number of them, well over eighty
percent, had reported undergoing almost exactly the
same experience: they hallucinated that they'd been
abducted by aliens.

Not just any aliens. There were no postexperiment
reports of cosmic octopi with dozens of wriggling ten-
acles, no little green men with funny ray guns de-
manding, "Take me to your leader." Every volunteer
claimed to have met with the same race, the ones
known as "the grays," small beings with dispropor-
tionately large heads and black, almond-shaped eyes.

And not just ordinary hallucinations, either: the ex-
perimentees claimed the experience was real, as real to
them as their everyday lives.

For Batman, the important revelation was that
finely tuned EM fields could interact with the subtle
fields produced by electrochemical activity in the
brain. If it could be done with ordinary humans, it
could be done with super heroes.

Now, as the Stone King stood transfixed, his mind
overwhelmed by the intensity of Peter Glaston's emotion, his power over Batman and Manhunter decreased.

On my count, Batman thought. *Three, two, one . . . go!*

A snarl rose deep in J'onn J'onzz's throat. The anger aroused by that succession of hellish visions poured out of him. He flexed his arms, bringing all of his fantastic extraterrestrial strength to bear on the rock that held him.

It gave with a loud crack, and his arms pulled suddenly free.

Batman gestured toward their teammates. *I think the Stone King's using electromagnetism to hold them.*

I'll let them know what's going on, J'onn told him. *Green Lantern first. He'll be able to will his ring to alter the EM patterns in his brain.*

Manhunter converted his thoughts into a pulse, explanation nested within explanation like a set of carved Russian dolls. He sent the pulse hurtling directly into Green Lantern's mind.

There was no response.

Again, J'onn sent the thought, shrinking it to the tiniest quantum of information he could manage. Was that a flicker? A neuron in Lantern's mind firing briefly?

Desperately, he sent the thought a third time, already beginning to feel the strain. Unless it was with the voluntary cooperation of the recipient, telepathy on this scale could be debilitating to him.

For the briefest of moments, nothing. Then Green Lantern's eyes opened, blinking in the cavern's flickering light.

J'onn's thought package had told him everything from the possession of Peter Glaston to the present sit uation in the burial chamber. Shrugging off the memory of the agony that had consumed him for so long, Green Lantern grinned and gave a thumbs-up sign to his relieved rescuers.

Thanks, guys! That creep was really giving me a hard time!

Lantern's eyes narrowed in concentration, and a thin, intense beam of emerald energy lanced from his ring. Silently, it sliced into the granite that was solidified around the Flash and Wonder Woman. In a silent puff of thick green smoke, the rock dissipated.

Free now, the duo lay unmoving next to Superman on the chamber floor. The emerald beam briefly reached out to touch their foreheads, subtly negating the electromagnetic waves that held them in thrall.

Consciousness returned at once.

Peter Glaston wasn't so lucky.

Even as Jenny watched, her vision misted by tears, Peter's voice tailed away and died. The recognition in his eyes faded abruptly, to be replaced by a look that begged for help.

"Peter!" Forgetting her horror, Jenny gave a sob and started forward, but Cassandra's arm tightened around her waist and held her back.

There was nothing they could do as the Stone King regained control. Somewhere deep inside his own mind, Peter Glaston's consciousness began to break apart. Stray thoughts and memories seemed to explode into oblivion as Peter Glaston was finally obliterated.

Forever.

The Stone King regarded the women as if they were laboratory animals. His eyes burned deep into them, seeming to strip away all the layers of civilization until their souls were laid bare before him.

Then he turned away. They no longer mattered. They were insignificant specks, not worth killing.

Waiting to face him was the Justice League.

CHAPTER 15

Puzzle Pieces

Don't look into his eyes!

Batman shot the urgent warning into the minds of his comrades, followed closely by: *The women!*

Green Lantern received the message and acted a nanosecond later. The beam from his ring formed itself into a gruesome emerald figure, with stumpy, jagged wings on its back. It swooped down and swept up Cassandra and Jenny, one under each arm.

Batman and J'onn J'onzz exchanged a puzzled look, but neither spoke.

Almost instantaneously, Lantern's demonic green figure deposited the two women back where they'd parked Jenny's car, leaving them standing confused and bewildered.

Outside the Stone King's sphere of influence, the pyramid and everything it contained had become invisible to them again. They were alone with the moon and the windswept grass, backed by the rushing waters of the nearby Gotham River.

Sorry about the demonic imagery, Lantern apologized to no one in particular, as his creation disappeared again. *Didn't have time to think of a more suitable alternative.*

The others were standing in a loose semicircle, almost filling the chamber with their presence.

The Stone King faced them, immobile but alert, jagged balls of plasmoid lightning darting around his fingertips. Every now and again his entire body pulsed slightly, as if he was receiving an unseen electric shock.

He's sizing us up, Superman thought.

The Man of Steel did a little sizing up of his own as he scrutinized the motionless shaman. *My heat vision could take him down. Or I could use my speed and strength to capture him before he's aware of what's happening.*

We have already tried, Martian Manhunter pointed out. *He's protected by a force field. We don't know the full extent of his powers, only that he can somehow tap into the energies of the planet itself.*

Superman, Wonder Woman, the Flash, and Green Lantern all broadcast the same thought. *How could he possibly siphon off Earth's energies?*

Believe it, Batman informed them. *Since the Stone King captured you four, there have been major incidents at dozens of sites across the globe. A lot of deaths, a lot of damage. I've called up all of the League's reserve members to handle the crisis, but unless we can figure out how to defeat the Stone King, it'll all be to no avail. As far as J'onn and I can tell,* he finished grimly, *his aim is to destroy the world.*

in precisely—Batman depressed a stud on the wrist of his gauntlet, and the HUD display inside his cowl lit up briefly—*Twenty-three minutes. Midnight, local time.*

And that's what he's waiting for? The Flash was outraged. *More to the point, what are we waiting for? I could create an instant vacuum at super speed, deny him all oxygen—*

Your idea might work, Batman admitted. *So might Superman's. Our problem is: what happens if they don't?*

He waited, but no one answered him.

The Stone King is obviously preparing himself now, J'onn J'onzz thought. *Even though the pieces of this puzzle have yet to fall together, we must act before it is too late.*

Galvanized by Manhunter's solemn finality, Batman turned to Green Lantern. *Is there anything more your ring can tell us?*

The Emerald Warrior shook his head. *No. I tried, but I just can't make sense of it at all.*

Batman frowned. He hadn't seen Green Lantern use the power ring. But, keeping the rest of his thoughts to himself, Batman came to a sudden decision. *Flash, try to penetrate his force field. If you can negate it, we'll attack en masse.*

Instantly, the Flash's body began to vibrate, disappearing from the others' vision. Every molecule acted in unison as the Scarlet Speedster swiftly ranged through the spectrum, from subsonic to ultrahigh frequency, seeking the exact wavelength of the Stone King's protection.

Suddenly he saw it—a shifting, sinuous pattern of energy that danced around the shaman.

Got it! he announced triumphantly. *It's in the electro-magnetic band. I'm going in!*

The Flash fine-tuned the speed of his vibration, until it perfectly matched the force field's energy configuration. He stretched out a hand, which should have moved through the barrier like water running through a sieve.

Instead, there was an explosion of blinding light that blasted the Flash back into normal mode. He stared in astonishment.

The Stone King remained standing immobile. But now, surrounding him like guardian demons, another five Stone Kings had appeared.

Before any of the super heroes could react, the dop-pelgängers rushed to the attack.

"C'mon, everybody. It's party night!"

The man in the Dracula mask and blood-red cloak capered among the crowd on Finger Avenue, urging them to join in his alcohol-fueled dance.

The mood of the partygoers in downtown Gotham was relatively subdued. Pumpkin lanterns adorned every streetlight, but the flotilla of colorful floats that drove slowly through the city center in the famous Night Parade was only half the size of previous years. On the floats, people dressed in a dazzling array of Halloween costumes sang and cavorted. Despite the grim events of recent days, thousands of spectators had turned out to line the route.

Several street bands filled the night with music, and the smell of a hundred different fast foods mingled in the air.

"Look, Mommy!" A laughing child in a wizard's costume pointed up between the walls of the concrete canyons. "The Man in the Moon has come to our party!"

His mother gazed up at the almost-full moon that hung over the city, its pale light given a faint orange tinge by the pollutants in the air. A huge face had appeared on its surface—a gigantic head of a man-bull, complete with horns.

The mother smiled. "It must be an advertising stunt, dear."

A ragged cheer went up as more people noticed the impressive face. A group of students masquerading as zombies performed an impromptu dance in the middle of Main Street. Children out to trick-or-treat clapped their hands in delight.

Several concession holders, camped out in their booths along the procession route, made a mental note to complain to City Hall about their lack of advance information. What a great mask that face would have made!

In his office high in Police Headquarters, Jim Gordon stood at his window, looking down on the city below. His men were out in force tonight, but so far, so good. There had been virtually no arrests.

The disasters throughout the world had dampened everyone's spirits. Gordon found himself comparing the partygoers to ostriches burying their heads in the sand rather than facing up to danger. But maybe that was unfair. When people were afraid, they needed something out of the ordinary to help them forget their worries.

Gordon's mind, however, kept straying to Cassandra's vision. She said the city would be destroyed at midnight on Halloween, and Batman seemed to have taken her very seriously indeed. Gordon hadn't heard from Batman since, but that wasn't unusual. They had no regular contact. When one of them needed the other, he was always found.

The commissioner took a last look at the moon, wondering how on earth the sponsors had managed to project a hologram onto the lunar surface, then turned away from the window.

He glanced at his pipe, which lay on his paper-strewn desk beside a pouch of tobacco and a box of matches. The evening had been largely stress-free, and Jim had been able to comply with his decision not to smoke again.

I'll give it till midnight, he thought. Gordon pulled out the old pocket watch that had belonged to his father and his father's father, from his waistcoat pocket. *Twenty minutes to go. All quiet so far. Has to be a good omen.*

Then the face in the moon spoke.

Every man, woman, and child in the city heard it, yet no microphone would have picked it up, no tape recorder could have translated it to audio. The voice spoke directly inside their heads, coming from a location that seemed to be at the heart of their being, their very center of existence.

And the voice prophesied doom.

"Your foulness will be cleansed, as the foulness of the world is cleansed. The cycle is ending. Make peace with your gods. Tonight, every last one of you will die."

Jim Gordon's stomach lurched. With sinking heart and shaking hand, he reached for his pipe.

Meanwhile, at the pyramid, lightning flashed from the eyes of the five duplicate Stone Kings as they launched themselves at their foes.

The Flash was first to react. In the blink of an eye he accelerated to superspeed from a standing start, spinning around like a top, his arms outstretched and fists balled. The centrifugal force was tremendous as his fists slammed into the Stone Kings with devastating effect, knocking the creatures off their feet. One was sent careening into the chamber wall, sparks flying from its point of impact.

But even as the Flash slowed to a halt, the Stone Kings were recovering, springing to their feet to renew their assault.

Superman dived headlong, his arms taking two of the figures around the waist. The momentum sent all three crashing through the outer wall in an explosion of stone and chalk.

J'onn J'onzz pinned a third Stone King to the hard earth floor, increasing the density of his molecules in an effort to crush the creature into submission.

Wonder Woman's golden lasso snaked out to loop over the fourth Stone King's body and slip down over his arms. Wonder Woman pulled the lasso taut, jerking the beast off its feet again.

Batman took a couple of steps to the side, moving behind the altar stone with its covering of dried blood and rotting animal entrails. The original Stone King still stood in the center of the chamber, the intense pulsations that affected his body coming more frequently now. Batman glanced toward Manhunter and saw the duplicate he was fighting suddenly heave the Martian away as if he were made of feathers.

Green Lantern! Batman thought urgently. *J'onn's in trouble!*

For the briefest moment Green Lantern looked flustered, as if unsure what to do. Then a solid green beam sprang from the power ring, its end shaped like a medieval battering ram. The beam took J'onn's foe in the chest, blasting the creature off its feet and hurling it into the wall with brutal impact.

Time's running out, Batman informed his teammates *Only seventeen minutes left!*

Most of the Western Hemisphere was in darkness. Almost midnight in Gotham meant almost nine P.M. on the West Coast. In Europe, it was five in the morning, with dawn still more than an hour away. Across the globe, more than a billion people were sleeping.

And every one of them had heard the Stone King's warning. It came to them in their dreams, or they wakened with a start . . . to his physical manifestation.

A Navajo medicine wheel laid out in the New Mexico desert started spinning like a top, spitting out cobalt-blue sparks. The Ohio Serpent Mound began to undulate as if it were a living thing. In California's Death Valley, a thick, sulfurous smoke began to spew forth from the old bauxite mines, suffocating everything it came in contact with.

A British army patrol on night maneuvers reported thirteen giant figures dancing around the sacred stones of Avebury in a slow shuffle. Each one wore a bull's-head mask.

An ominous plume of smoke spewed out of volcanic Mount Etna in the Mediterranean. Grimacing in its swirls and roils were the faces of a thousand demons.

After a silence that had lasted two thousand years, the cave-dwelling Oracle at Delphi in Greece began to speak again. But where once the air was perfumed with burning laurel leaves, now it was dank, and heavy toxic fumes spewed up from the cavern's depths.

The voice the Oracle spoke in was the voice of the Stone King. And the message it delivered never changed.

Your time has come. Prepare to die.

Outside the chamber, on the slopes of the pyramid, Superman struggled to hold the two duplicate Stone Kings. Their strength seemed almost as great as his, and each time he tried to use a superpower against them, they countered with powers of their own.

Inside, Batman's gaze was fixed on the real Stone King. What could be seen of his skin under the animal hides he wore was glowing with fluorescent light. Dark flashes danced from his brooding eyes. His muscles rippled continuously, as if raw physical power were coursing through his body.

Almost imperceptibly, the Stone King seemed to be growing.

These clones are merely decoys! Batman shot suddenl·
at the others. *Their only purpose is to delay us!*

The Flash was grappling with one of the creatures
trying to stun it with rapid-fire blows from his fist
that landed with the power of a triphammer. When h·
received Batman's message, the Scarlet Speedster im·
mediately switched tactics.

He began to run at speed in a small, tight circl·
around the floor, accelerating until he was little mor·
than a red blur. Around him, a spiraling tornado of ai·
formed, whirling at high speed in the confines of th·
chamber.

Suddenly, the Flash shifted his trajectory, and th·
roaring cyclone dipped to envelop the duplicate Ston·
King. The vacuum created at its center sucked th·
creature in, imprisoning it in the near-solid column o·
rotating air.

Still struggling with their own adversaries, J'on·
J'onzz and Wonder Woman didn't need telepathy t·
tell them what the Flash was up to. Unexpectedly de·
creasing his molecular density, Manhunter grabbe·
his foe's arm and used superstrength to hurl the crea·
ture into the center of the vortex. The Amazo·
Princess followed suit, using a judo throw to toss he·
own opponent over her shoulder. It disappeared int·
the Flash's tornado.

Giving the Stone Kings no time to fight free, th·
Flash shot out of the chamber and down the side o·
the pyramid.

Below, Superman was engaged in a titanic struggl·
with the two duplicates he'd carried from the cham·

ber. The Flash sent an urgent warning to Superman as the cyclone veered toward the battle. The Man of Steel dived aside as the supersonic whirlwind enveloped the startled Stone Kings before speeding away across the countryside.

Superman flew up to the chamber. He had barely reentered before the Flash was back.

I dumped them halfway across the Atlantic, the Scarlet Speedster informed his waiting comrades. His speed was so great, he could run on water as if it were dry land.

Only one Stone King left. Wonder Woman gestured to the pulsating figure in the center of the chamber. He seemed to have grown by a foot or more, his body expanding in proportion. *Do we launch a full scale assault?*

We do, Batman replied, taking a step closer to Green Lantern. The vigilante glanced over at J'onn J'onzz, who gave a slight nod.

Right after this—Batman went on.

There was a sudden, searing pain deep inside their minds as J'onn J'onzz sent out the strongest telepathic jolt he'd ever mustered. As one, Green Lantern, the Flash, Superman, and Wonder Woman clutched their heads at the bone-jarring agony. Only Batman and Manhunter himself remained unaffected.

Batman clenched his fist and swung it with the whole power of his body behind it. The punch exploded against the point of Green Lantern's chin, and the Emerald Warrior slumped to the ground, unconscious.

CHAPTER 16

Man Versus Planet

Goliath himself couldn't have withstood Batman's blow. His protective force field switched off by Manhunter's mental assault, Green Lantern fell poleaxed to the floor.

Superman and the others stared aghast at the unconscious Emerald Warrior, hardly registering Batman's urgent message in their shock. *Explanations will have to wait. Trust us. It was necessary.*

You can't just—Wonder Woman began, but Batman ignored her protest and plunged on.

The key to defeating the Stone King has to be earth energies, the vigilante explained. *He's drawing his power from the planet itself—and that's where we can hurt him. If Superman and Wonder Woman can disrupt the flow of Earth's energy currents, we may just spoil his schemes completely.*

Batman flicked on his cowl's digital display. *But we need to be quick. It's thirteen minutes to midnight.*

The Stone King reacted as if he'd understood every word. He whirled suddenly, emitting a roar that reverberated through the pyramid. Bolts of cobalt fire shot out from his extended fingers, aimed at the heroes. Batman ducked under a bolt and saw several others ricochet off the bodies of his two invulnerable teammates, while yet more beams were deflected by Wonder Woman's silver bracelets.

Where the bolts hit the walls and ceiling, they rebounded at a tangent, crisscrossing the chamber in a mesh of crackling energy.

Seeing the danger, Batman dived full-length, wedging himself in the cramped space between the altar stone and the wall behind it. The Flash wasn't so fortunate.

Even moving at superspeed, the Fastest Man Alive was unable to avoid all of the streaking bolts that came at him from every angle. One caught him in the small of the back, knocking him off balance. As he staggered, a tracery of other beams struck his legs and sent him tumbling to the floor. His head caught on the front of the altar, and he slumped unconscious.

Fighting his way through the network of ricocheting energy, J'onn J'onzz threw himself forward and grabbed the shaman's wrist, exerting all his Martian strength to hold it. Superman seized the Stone King's other arm, and together the duo tried to wrestle both arms behind the creature's back.

As the storm of energy faded, Batman leaped to his feet. "Hold him," he urged. "I have something in my Utility Belt we can use against him."

Wonder Woman uncoiled her golden lasso and sen
it looping toward the Stone King's head.

She was a microsecond too late.

The Stone King tore one arm free with a wrench tha
sent Manhunter sailing over his head. Wonder Woma
had no space to avoid him, and they both went dow
in a crumpled heap.

The other arm lifted Superman off the ground
slamming him into the chamber's corbeled ceilin
with brutal force.

Lunging at Batman, the Stone King tore through th
vigilante's martial arts defense like paper. Clutchin
fingers raked his costume's Kevlar lining in a trail o
blue sparks, slashing clean through it and ripping hi
cape in half.

As the hand clawed through the air again, Batma
back-flipped to avoid it. His heel struck the low ceil
ing, throwing him off balance.

He recovered to land acrobatically on the chambe
floor, relieved that his comrades were already prepar
ing to renew their attack.

Deep within the Earth, tectonic plates ground to
gether, unstoppable force meeting immoveable object
Piezoelectricity shot upward in tiny plasmoid spheres
passing through the bedrock, flowing toward th
pyramid.

In the burial chamber, the Stone King felt the shoc
and welcomed it.

Deeper still, molten rock at a temperature of thou
sands of degrees swirled and eddied, creating forces a

yet unknown to science. As they surged through the ground in massive low-frequency waves, the pyramid absorbed their power and channeled it to the Stone King.

And deeper yet, deeper than any man had gone or ever could, at the very center of the earth, electromagnetic forces pulsed and twisted. The gravity-compressed, near-solid iron core broadcast on a wide range of frequencies, weaving webs of unbelievable force as it spun on its orbit around the sun.

In the chamber, planetary energies caressed the Stone King's skin, pulsing through it, man and planet merging.

With a wild shriek of triumph that shook the entire pyramid and sent boulders cascading down its slopes, the Stone King began to grow.

Clinging to him, Superman, Wonder Woman, and Manhunter were dragged along as he shot up at colossal speed, smashing through the slabbed ceiling in an explosion of stone.

Half the pyramid was demolished as his body expanded and swelled, thrusting hundreds of tons of rock and soil aside as if they were marbles. The plateau on top was already half destroyed, from the last time the power manifested here. The Stone King grew past it, sending avalanches racing down its sides.

Almost deafened by the initial roar, Batman collected his thoughts and sent a desperate message to Superman and Wonder Woman. *You must go underground! Disrupt his power at its source!*

Batman saw two beings peel away from the monstrous, pulsating figure. They looped once in the air then dived groundward like twin missiles.

Rocks and debris rained around him as Batman grabbed Green Lantern's arm and tried to haul his teammate to some kind of safety. He raised an arm toward off a falling chunk of rock, and grunted as another thudded into his shoulder.

The Flash needed help, too, but there was no way Batman could carry both heroes at once. Batman saw that the altar stone had been half torn out of its foundations; he hoped it would provide the Flash with sufficient protection until Batman could return for him.

Typically, his first thoughts weren't for himself. It was at Batman's instruction that Manhunter had negated Green Lantern's force field. If the Emerald Warrior died, crushed by one of the multiton boulders that were crashing around them, Batman would bear the responsibility.

He backed up just in time. A massive lintel beam plunged to the floor just ahead of him. The air was full of choking dust. Batman's respirator would protect him, but what about Lantern?

Desperation lent him strength. He dragged Green Lantern under a huge rectangular block that had fallen at an angle, leaving a crawlspace beneath. Batman pushed the Emerald Warrior in. Hardly satisfactory, but he had no other option.

He moved away again, intent on rescuing the Flash, and was surprised to find the Scarlet Speedster had already recovered.

Stay in cover, the Flash warned him. *I'll handle this.*

Moving so fast that the plummeting granite blocks seemed to be falling in slow motion, the Scarlet Speedster was able to shove them aside with ease. For the tiny fraction of a second that he touched them, they seemed weightless to him, easy to direct away from his teammates.

Outside, the Stone King reached a height of a hundred feet before his size stabilized. The energy that had kept the pyramid invisible was siphoned back to him, and now a bright glow lit up the sky for miles around.

Towering over the countryside, surrounded by an aura of swirling fluorescence, the Neolithic shaman raised both arms in a gesture of victory. Flashes of blue fire flickered from the bull's skull that covered his head, running down the animal hides that clothed his body in a sparkling, fiery waterfall.

Clinging to the giant's shoulder, J'onn Jonzz dodged the rivers of flame that fell past him. The Martian's only weakness was a vulnerability to fire, which could reduce one of the Justice League's mighty members to abject helplessness. This was why he hadn't accompanied Superman and Wonder Woman on their subterranean mission—the risk of encountering lava and pockets of fire was too great.

Then the Stone King began to chant. The low, oscillating mantra was so far down the tonal scale that Manhunter felt it rather than heard it. Great, slow waves of painful nausea writhed through his internal organs.

Ultralow frequency sound, Manhunter thought. *Immensely destructive to all physical material. I have to stop him before it shakes my body apart—from the inside!*

Manhunter soared away from the massive figure, circling in a broad loop to increase his speed and momentum. He set his teeth grimly against the waves of pain that continued to assail him and dived headlong toward the Stone King's chest.

Streaking in like a bullet, at the last moment Manhunter increased the density of his molecules to the maximum.

He cannoned into the Stone King's chest with the force of a nuclear explosion.

Superman's heat vision seared through the solid bedrock of the earth's crust, tunneling a path that he and Wonder Woman could follow.

They were ten miles down when they came upon the first anomaly.

A thick seam of granite was grinding against a similar but heavier seam. Piezoelectricity sparked like a billion fireflies. Tiny globes of plasma darted through the boundary between the granite layers, rising upward, joining together until they became a wide, fast-flowing river of energy.

Any ideas? Superman asked, thankful that J'onn J'onzz's telepathic link was still functioning at this depth.

We can try to fuse the seams together, Wonder Woman suggested.

Both brought their strength into maximum use

straining against the face of the thick, dense seam. Even while he pushed, Superman used heat vision to melt and soften the rock, making it more pliable.

The myriad pinpoints of light began to fade, and finally died away.

In little over a minute, the two super heroes were diving deeper.

The Stone King staggered as Martian Manhunter slammed into his chest. A bellow of frustration and rage echoed for miles around.

The chanting stopped.

That certainly attracted his attention, Manhunter thought approvingly. Returning his molecules to normal, he streaked away at high speed, intending to repeat the maneuver.

This time, though, the Stone King was ready for him. He gestured with one hand. The heavy boulders strewn across the pyramid top levitated instantly, shooting up at incredible speed. Manhunter rocked as a granite slab that must have weighed five tons slammed into his legs. He spun to the side, out of control.

The Stone King opened his massive mouth wide, exhaling a gusher of white-hot lava that engulfed the falling Martian.

Where it touched J'onn, the lava cooled instantly, forming into a rapidly hardening shell. Although vulnerable to flame, J'onn's body was impervious to great heat. But as fast as he battered his way out of the lava cocoon, the shell reformed around him.

It's impossible to keep flying, J'onn broadcast. *I'm going down.*

He hit the ground with a force that disintegrated the lava cage, but left Manhunter himself unconscious.

Down on the fifth course, Batman and the Flash had pulled Green Lantern out of the ruins of the chamber.

Pity you knocked him out, the Scarlet Speedster flashed at Batman. *We could sure use his power ring now!*

Batman made no reply as the Flash picked up the still unconscious hero and ran and leaped down the pyramid's buckled side. It was ironic that this integral member of the Justice League would take no part in their final battle.

The Flash was several hundred yards away before he stopped and set Green Lantern down on the grass. He glanced up at the mighty figure of the Stone King atop the pyramid in triumph. The flickering aurora that surrounded him was spreading, sending tentacles miles long into the sky.

A heartbeat later, he stood beside Batman in the rubble of the pyramid.

"The telepathic link is broken," Batman told him. "J'onn is either unconscious, or . . ." He didn't finish the sentence. "We have no way of knowing how Superman and Wonder Woman are faring."

"Just you and me now, buddy." The Flash nodded. He tilted his head to stare up at the Stone King. "And that is one awesome dude!"

* * *

Sixty miles beneath the surface, Superman and Wonder Woman reached the Moho discontinuity. Here, at the bottom of a deep layer of basalt, the earth's crust met the more solid, rigid mantle. Crustal slip, as the layers slid over each other, was a major source of seismic energy.

A massive finger of denser mantle projected upward, impaling the layer of basalt, preventing it from moving. Already kinetic force was building up, a slow, unstoppable pressure that would be released as a massive shock wave when the mantle finally broke.

Wonder Woman tried to send a telepathic message reporting on their progress, and realized that the link was down.

"I hope everything's all right on the surface," she said.

"J'onn's the ultimate survivor," Superman replied. "He'll be okay."

They couldn't allow themselves to think any other way. They had a task to accomplish, and worrying about their comrades would only impede them.

Superman used heat vision to excavate a spherical chamber in the outcrop of mantle. Wonder Woman took up a position in the center. She inhaled deeply, then suddenly brought both arms swinging up above her head. The silver bracelets crashed together, and there was a blinding white light as the power of the gods themselves was released.

The dense outcrop of mantle disintegrated completely, allowing the layer of basalt to slide smoothly onward.

But already, Superman and Wonder Woman were heading deeper: four hundred fifty miles through the mantle, to the planet's outer core.

"We may have one last chance, though it's a slim one." Batman motioned toward his Utility Belt. "My fear gas was tailored to affect the Stone King when he was still human-sized. It's concentrated, but chances are it won't affect him now."

"Only one way to find out." The Flash scooped Batman up in his arms. "Let's go deliver it."

Consciously controlling the molecules of his body, Flash went from standstill to superspeed in less than the blink of an eye. His momentum was so great, he was able to run straight up the behemoth's leg as if it were a level track.

But with his increase in power, the Stone King's sensitivity had also been magnified. He looked down at the red blur, and his massive hand shot out at blinding speed.

The Flash had no time to brace himself for impact. The Stone King's hand swatted him like a fly, sending him soaring high in the air, unconscious from the impact.

As Batman tumbled from the Flash's grip, a grapnel went shooting from his hand. It snared on a tangle of animal hairs, made massive by the Stone King's increase in size. Batman grabbed the Flash's wrist, while his other hand held tight to his line.

Batman extended his feet to break the impact as they swung into the giant's body just above his waistline. Batman scrabbled for a hold on the pelt, quickly lashing the dazed Flash with a length of line so he didn't fall.

"Think I've broken a rib," the Flash muttered through clenched teeth. "Leave me."

"But—"

"Move, man. By my count, there's only three minutes left!"

CHAPTER 17

One Minute to Midnight

Across the world, lights flickered and died.

Orbiting 350 miles up, the crew of the space shuttle *Lincoln* saw the cities of Earth plunged into total darkness. Communication with Houston ceased.

All electrical supply lines had been disrupted by the massive energies the Stone King had brought into play. Every generator, every junction box, every circuit burned itself out.

Television broadcasts ceased immediately. The screens that fed civilization its news went dead. The comforting, friendly celebrity faces vanished, to be replaced in a billion homes by blank screens.

Every computer in the world crashed. The Internet went down. All radio transmission ceased.

The disaster movies had suddenly become real.

Tonight, every last one of you will die.

On its own, the Stone King's sinister voice had been frightening enough. Coupled with the total loss of

lectricity, there was a sudden realization that the
prophecy of doom was starting to come true.

Children huddled in frightened silence, seeking re-
ssurances that their parents couldn't give. Men and
women in their nightclothes swarmed onto the dark-
ned, alien streets, looking for someone who could
ell them what was going on. Was this some mass
hallucination? LSD in the water supply? An enemy
rick, to be followed by military invasion? An act of
errorism? Some crazed dictator getting back at the
world?

Many just pulled blankets over their heads and
prayed it would all go away.

In tens of thousands of hospitals, the respirators and
dialysis machines and life-support systems crashed.
Emergency generators were hastily brought into play,
only to die in their turn.

The missile bases and the nuclear submarines, and
the aerial reconnaissance planes that never landed,
found their weapons could not be fired, their bombs
could not be dropped.

In cities, towns, villages, and isolated homesteads,
people stood outside and looked at a sky alive with
dancing waves of energy, like the aurora borealis on a
global scale.

And all across the world, animals howled and people cried.

Batman's foot slithered as he struggled to gain purchase on the Stone King's pelt.

He clutched desperately at one of the pelt's massive

hairs. It was slick with dried blood, and his hand started to slip. He swung himself around in order to get a better grip, and a wave of dizzying pain swept through his back and right shoulder.

Where the boulder had struck its glancing blow, his skin was swelling in a huge bruise. He wouldn't be surprised if a bone had broken. Every time he flexed the arm, his vision swam red and he felt like passing out.

He closed his eyes for a moment, centering himself, calling up all of his hidden reserves. If ever he needed them, it was now.

Yet it seemed so unreal: in just a few minutes' time, this creature from a bygone age intended to destroy the world. And here was Batman, halfway up a giant's body, in danger of falling off and plunging to his death on the pyramid below. At any moment, the gargantuan Stone King might notice this irritating insect clinging to him and squash him like an unwanted bug.

All who choose the Way of the Warrior know that Death follows at their shoulder, patiently waiting for the right time, the right place, the right circumstance. One slip, one single mistake, and Death always claims its own.

Only a fool doesn't fear death. And such a fool does not live long.

But as well as a messenger, fear can be a springboard.

If it's going to end, Batman thought, *I go out the way I came in . . . fighting!*

Holding back his nausea, doing his best to ignore the pain that was spreading to make his whole torso one huge, throbbing wound, Batman moved. He leaped upward, reaching as far as he could with his left hand, grabbing onto whatever he could.

This time luck was with him. His grip held, and he was able to defy the pain and swing himself another six feet higher.

Around him, the night air felt alive, expanding and contracting with multicolored lights as the Stone King amassed his power, ready for the climax of his ritual. A hundred yards off to the side, a localized electrical storm was raging; a scene that was playing out in a thousand locations around the world.

Batman's right arm felt like it was being torn off. He shifted his weight, taking as much of the strain as he could on his other arm. He'd been running a mental countdown since the last mention Flash had made of time. It was something he'd trained himself to do as a teenager, and it had come in useful dozens of times in his crimefighting career. All he had to do was start the count, and his unconscious mind would keep it going.

Approximately two minutes left.

Kicking away from the pelt's slimy surface, Batman took all of his weight on his left hand, and swung. His body arced slightly away from the giant, to hang suspended for a moment with that sixty-foot drop below. Then his right hand caught around some matted hair.

Batman's arm felt like it had been torn from its shoulder socket. But he didn't pause. Summoning every last ounce of resolve, he swung again, nearly passing out under the pressure exerted on his injured arm.

Perspiration ran down his face under the mask,

trickling behind the nightsights and into his eyes. The pain from his shoulder was like a living thing, gnawing at every nerve ending in his upper body. But he had no time to stop for recovery.

The seconds were ticking away on the countdown to the end of the world.

Bone weary, his right side on fire, Batman valiantly hauled himself another few feet upward.

There's no way I'm going to make it in time, he realized.

His luck had run out—and with it, the luck of the whole world. A black wave of despair swept through him. After everything, that it should all end like this. . . .

I have to try, Batman thought bleakly. *I have to make one last effort.*

But at last the Stone King had noticed the gnatlike super hero intruding on his territory. His hand swept up, gigantic fingers trying clumsily to pinion Batman. The super hero twisted away from them, and the Stone King's finger and thumb snapped shut on the remains of his tattered cape.

Five hundred miles down, Superman and Wonder Woman crashed through a thin shell of solidified sulfides and arrived at the earth's outer core. More than a thousand miles thick, it consisted mainly of a semisolid mix of nickel and iron.

The temperature was more than two thousand degrees, and the pressure was almost incomprehensible. Despite their powers, neither super hero wanted to spend more time in these surroundings than was absolutely necessary.

Huge currents swirled and eddied in the magma. The kinetic energy they produced was siphoned off upward, to be metamorphosed by the pyramid into raw power for the Stone King.

Superman and Wonder Woman set their sights on what was perhaps the single most difficult task they'd ever faced: to slow these planetary tides, to disrupt their motion, even to reverse them if they could.

Together they plunged into the maelstrom and began to swim against the currents with as much speed as they could manage.

The Stone King yanked Batman violently upward, the giant hand dangling him by his cape until he was on a level with the creature's face.

The stench of its breath was like a charnel house. Batman kept his gaze averted for fear of being hypnotized, but he could literally feel the Stone King's power burn from its eyes as the creature scrutinized him at close quarters.

He could understand why it had once been worshiped as a god.

In the nickel-iron outer core, new currents churned, formed by the super heroes' motion.

Whirlpools swirled in the semimolten mass, cutting across the regular flow. Massive eddies and swirls churned up the metal magma, each one sending out its own concentric ripples.

Incredibly, the tides began to turn.

* * *

The Stone King felt the energy that was feeding him flicker and wane.

He lurched unsteadily and almost stumbled forward.

The monster's cavernous nostrils loomed beside Batman, and sudden hope flared from the depths of despair. *This is my last chance!*

Batman's left hand pulled the vial of fear gas from its pouch. He kicked back with both feet, then forward, the way an acrobat starts a trapeze swinging. The resulting pendulum motion was all he needed to bring him close enough.

Forget the pain . . . it's now or never!

His left hand extended to its full reach, and he hurled the vial of concentrated gas with all his strength. It shattered inside the nostril, on the sensitive lining inside what once—it seemed aeons ago—had been Peter Glaston's nose.

Nothing happened.

The sickness in the pit of Batman's stomach was a palpable thing. *It's over!* he thought with dreadful finality. *For all of us. For everything.*

Then the gas, absorbed into the Stone King's bloodstream, hit the monster's brain.

He stared at Batman, transfixed with horror. Electric bolts of cobalt blue sparked around his face, and his flashing eyes rolled back in his head.

For a second, the giant seemed to recover. The huge eyes opened again, their gaze zeroing in on the dangling vigilante, drinking in every detail. The horned ears. The cape with its scalloped edges. The batsymbol on his chest.

The Stone King trembled with fear. His mouth opened in a scream of terror, a deafening shriek that was heard all around the world. He hurled Batman away from him, the way one might brush off a scorpion, in fear and disgust.

The cape ripped from Batman's shoulders, and the pain he had held at bay for so long overwhelmed him.

Everything faded to black.

The Stone King threw back his head, extending his arms out and up, as if trying to regain control of himself and his tremendous powers. But the damage was done. His careful buildup of power had gone awry. The energies he was controlling had slipped their leash.

Lightning bolts seared out of nowhere, raining down on the Stone King himself. They impacted explosively, crackling streaks running like water down his body to disappear into the pyramid.

Fountains of lava erupted at the monstrous figure's feet, spattering his legs, bubbling up over his ankles.

Beams of energy sizzled out of nowhere, beating a grim tattoo against the Stone King's shuddering body.

Something had to give.

When the Stone King hurled Batman from him, the Flash saw his teammate spin away through the air.

Forcing himself to forget his own pain, the molecules of the Flash's body began to vibrate. He slipped off the line that held him to the Stone King's shaking, shuddering body. Vibrating at the same frequency as the air itself, he was able to race along it like a road.

The pain in his side was intense, but he forced himself on. It was a full mile from the pyramid before he managed to overtake the hurtling body and scoop it to safety in his arms.

Seconds later, the Flash landed on the small treed ridge on the riverbank where he had left Green Lantern. Now, Batman lay unconscious beside the Emerald Warrior. The Flash crouched down and ripped the Utility Belt from Batman's waist, searching through its pouches for something that might help.

As he held a small vial of smelling salts under Batman's nose, trying to revive him, the Flash glanced up.

On the summit of the pyramid, the Stone King was now falling victim to the very forces he had released and tried to control.

The body of the behemoth filled with cobalt-blue light, pulsing to twice its already massive size. Streams of white energy spiraled from the Stone King's eyes, exploding savagely in the air around his head. Lightning bolts streaked from out of nowhere, blasting against his body.

Desperately, the Stone King turned this way and that, trying to avoid the energies building up inside him. He writhed and shuddered, silhouetted against a sky that was swirling with every color in the rainbow.

Abruptly, his efforts ceased, as if he had accepted the futility of further resistance. The powers that he had awakened were ready to claim their own.

The Stone King's whole body began to pulse, expanding and contracting in rhythm with his heartbeat. He swayed back and forth for several seconds, blood and sparks gushing in fountains from every orifice. His fingers clawed blindly at the air.

Then, as a final bombardment of lightning bolts burned into it, the body began to disintegrate. Blood and limbs and organs seemed to unravel, as if some unseen hand was pulling them. They spiraled away wildly, spinning with a life of their own, before they faded into a blood-mottled mist that dispersed on the night breeze.

The lightning ceased and the seething skies returned to normal, as if nothing had ever happened.

The silence that followed was louder than any cry of triumph.

CHAPTER 18

Fear Is a Bat

"Were . . . were we in time?"

Batman's eyes flickered open. The pain in his shoulder throbbed as if he were being struck by a hammer and his voice was hoarse and cracked. Every muscle in his battered body begged for relief.

But he was alive. He would recover.

Superman, Wonder Woman, Manhunter, and the Flash were grouped around him.

"We were," Superman informed him. "Wonder Woman and I churned up the planet's core. And whatever you did to the Stone King, it worked. Look—"

Batman was still lying on the grass of the ridge, propped up against the smooth trunk of a century-old beech tree. He breathed carefully, deliberately, trying to ease the pressure on his aching limbs, as his eyes followed Superman's pointing finger.

The pyramid looked as if it had been hit by a bomb. It was little more than a disordered heap of stones

blackened and burned by the incredible energies the
Stone King had released. Magma still oozed slowly
from several craters, fiery red turning to gray as it ran
down the jumbled stones, cooling and hardening.

Otherwise, there was nothing to mark the titanic
battle they had all taken part in.

"Green Lantern?" Batman murmured.

The Emerald Warrior stepped forward into Batman's view. His eyes were still a little glazed, and he
held one hand to his face, nursing his badly swollen
jaw.

"Well, dude, you saved the world." Green Lantern's
eyes twinkled behind his mask, until he winced at the
pain in his mouth. "And all it cost me was a sock on
the jaw!" He looked down at Batman with mock seri-
ousness. "Let me guess, was it something I said?"

"Explanations can wait," Superman insisted. "The
Stone King may be beaten, but we still need to deal
with the chaos he created!"

Without another word, the Man of Steel soared into
the air and powered away at maximum speed. Wonder Woman, Green Lantern, and Martian Manhunter
followed at once, while the Flash raced off into the
distance.

Batman took a final look at the collapsed pyramid,
then reached for his communicator to call Alfred.

Cassandra had taken Jenny Ayles to the empath's
own apartment, driving through the empty Gotham
streets. The partygoers had dispersed when the Stone
King spoke, scattering panic-stricken for their homes.

If this really was to be the end, they wanted to be with those they loved.

The women sat together on the sofa in Cassandra's living room, holding each other for comfort as they counted down the minutes to midnight.

Seconds before the Stone King's deadline was due to expire, a terrible, unearthly scream echoed around the city. A blinding flash lit up the night sky, brighter than a thousand moons, pouring through the apartment windows, throwing everything inside into stark relief.

Then it disappeared, leaving Cassandra and Jenny blinking at its intensity. There followed a long, deep silence.

"Wh-what was that?" Jenny whispered at last, her voice fearful.

Cassandra didn't answer at once. Her eyes were closed as she allowed her mind to roam free. She felt suddenly lighter, as if a vast burden had been lifted from her shoulders. For the first time since Raymond Marcus came to see her, Cassandra felt like her normal self.

"I think the Stone King is . . . dead," she said slowly, hardly daring to hope she was right. "I can't feel any trace of his presence."

"And Peter?" Jenny asked sharply. "What's happened to Peter?"

But Jenny already knew the answer. She'd known since she saw the light die in Peter's eyes, back at the pyramid, as the Stone King regained its mastery over him. Peter Glaston had made the ultimate sacrifice. He had given his life, for love.

Jenny's eyes filled with tears, and sobs shook her body as she cried for everything she'd lost.

The Earth had escaped destruction, but a high price had been paid. Millions of people had been killed, and millions more injured.

During the following two weeks, the world witnessed a frenzy of super hero activity unmatched in history, as the Justice League and its many allies strove to make good the massive destruction caused by the Stone King.

As soon as Superman managed to restore power to Gotham, Oracle used her expertise to set up a computerized databank of all reported disaster areas. Responding to computer analysis of every location, she was able to assign teams or individual heroes as the different situations required.

Green Lantern's will was tested to the limit, as he used his power ring to rebuild shattered cities in a dozen different countries. Earthquakes had struck hardest in Central and South America, destroying large expanses of land and creating millions of human refugees. The ring brought in countless tons of food and uncontaminated water before its bearer turned to the task of rebuilding what the Stone King had smashed.

Aquaman, King of the Seas, despatched legions of dolphins to assist people who'd been shipwrecked or swept out to sea when tsunamis struck the islands of Japan and Indonesia. Oracle sent the Flash, whose speed enabled him to run on water as if it were dry land, to assist. Later, the Scarlet Speedster would use friction generated by moving his hands at superspeed to seal the holes and cracks in scores of ancient temples.

Using Justice League technology, Plastic Man and the Atom teleported from city to city. The former's flexibility, coupled with the latter's ability to change his size, made them ideal for rescuing survivors trapped underground.

Wonder Woman used her vast powers to tunnel deep into the planet's mantle, where she labored tirelessly for days on end to repair destabilized seismic fault lines.

Superman seemed to be everywhere at once. His super breath cooled and extinguished hundreds of raging fires. He used his strength to hold up sagging buildings, while his heat vision fused and sealed the damaged structures. And his X-ray vision found survivor after survivor who would otherwise have been missed.

Gotham City had escaped with relatively little damage, for which the battle-weary Batman was grateful. He devoted his time to helping Oracle, acting as anchorman for the unprecedented relief efforts she was so brilliantly coordinating.

Global recovery would be long and slow, and would take every ounce of aid the super heroes could give. But, in time, humanity would come to terms with its shock and grief.

It was almost three weeks after the catastrophe when the Justice League met up again in the Watchtower.

They teleported in from wherever they were in the
world, replying to a summons broadcast by Green
Lantern. The Emerald Warrior was already waiting,
seated at the large, circular conference table in the op-
rations room.

Wonder Woman and Superman arrived simultaneously, followed instants later by the Flash and J'onn
'onzz.

"What's the problem?" Superman demanded.
"Not . . . the Stone King again?"

"No problem at all," Green Lantern assured them
as they took their places around the table. He broke
off as Batman appeared, then waited for the vigilante
to seat himself before announcing, "I figure it's time I
got my explanation. Or am I fated never to learn why
you and Manhunter ganged up on me that night at
the pyramid?"

"It's simple," Batman told him. "You were still
hypnotized."

Green Lantern frowned. "But you and Manhunter
freed us from the Stone King's influence," he
protested. "I snapped out of it, just like the others."

"The others snapped out of it," Batman corrected
him. "Not you. I quickly realized that. Although you
seemed to be fine, you were in fact still under the spell
of a deeper hypnosis."

"I was?" Green Lantern was skeptical. He looked to
the other team members, hoping for corroboration.

Wonder Woman shrugged. "We're as much in the
dark as you are," she said to Lantern.

The Emerald Warrior glanced back at Batman.

"Okay," he nodded, "lay it on me. How could you tell I was still under the Stone King's influence?"

J'onn J'onzz took up the story.

"Our first indication was the demonic figure you conjured up to carry Cassandra and Jenny Ayles to safety," the Martian began. "It was too out of character—as if it wasn't your will that was powering your ring. That demon was something the Stone King might produce."

"I think we all noticed that," Wonder Woman admitted. "But we merely accepted Lantern's explanation that he didn't have time to think of anything else."

"When Batman asked you to probe the energies with your ring," Manhunter continued, his gaze fixed on Green Lantern, "you claimed you had already done so. But you were imprisoned in the rock, not in control of your own thoughts. You couldn't have used the ring."

Puzzled, Lantern shook his head. "I guess not. But I had this overwhelming impression that I actually *had* used it."

"The final clue"—Batman took up the story again—"was when the Stone King created those bodyguards. He only made five, yet there were six of us present. He must have figured that he didn't need one for you. You were his ace in the hole, his secret weapon to use against us if all else failed."

"You could have been wrong about Lantern," the Flash pointed out. "I noticed these things, too, but it didn't occur to me that there was anything out of the ordinary."

He paused, then added wryly, "Guess that's why Batman's a detective, and I'm not."

"So the Stone King hit me with a double whammy?" Green Lantern shook his head in wonderment. "Incredible!"

"I couldn't tackle you on my own," Batman resumed. "I had to wait till J'onn figured it out, too, and used his telepathic power to negate your personal force field. With the threat you posed negated, we were free to attack."

"So where did the fear gas come from?" Flash wondered. "Or is that something you carry around as a matter of course?"

Batman told them how his early suspicions had led him to visit Scarecrow at Arkham Asylum. "The Stone King tried to use fear against me," the vigilante concluded. "I figured, if I ever got the chance I'd reverse roles. I almost used it when we were attacked after J'onn realized the secret of the pyramid's disappearance. In retrospect, it's a good thing I didn't."

"You mean"—A slow smile spread over Superman's face—"You made the Stone King afraid of—"

"Bats."

Superman and the others laughed out loud.

"Combined with your actions underground, the fear was enough to upset the balance of the forces he was absorbing," Batman concluded. "When the energy escaped from his control, it turned against him . . . and destroyed him."

The Flash shook his head in admiration. "So the world is saved, thanks to a fear of bats."

"Hey, I know what that feels like." Green Lantern rubbed his jaw ruefully. "But it only needed a punch on the chin for me to learn!"

Batman rose to his feet, and the others followed as he walked to the observation balcony.

Stars spattered the inky blackness, shining steadily, without the twinkle caused by an atmosphere. As one, the Justice League gazed toward distant Earth, a view that humbled even the mightiest of heroes.

From here it looked as it always did, serene and blue and beautiful, with no trace of the scars left by the Stone King's evil.

Epilogue

Nepal, January 1

The snow-capped Himalayas reflected the light of the dawn like a mirror.

Pale pink fingers of sunlight probed the darkness of a hidden valley. They stole among the houses, casting a rosy glow, then crept up a wooden wall and in through a bedroom window.

Fourteen-year-old Tenzen Wyung came instantly awake as the light swept across the floor and rested on the pillow by his cheek. He threw off the heavy yak-skin hides that kept him warm on the coldest Nepalese nights, and shivered in the chill air.

Quickly, Tenzen pulled on his heavy cotton shirt and trousers, ignoring the metal basin and jug of water that stood next to the bed. He'd wash later; now, the noise might wake his parents.

He picked up his multicolored yak-hide boots and

sneaked across the room. He pushed aside the thick blanket that hung as a divider between his bedroom and the hallway, and gently lifted the heavy wooden latch on the door.

The old latch creaked. To Tenzen's ears it sounded as loud as a gunshot. His heart pounding in his chest, he held his breath, waiting a brief moment.

No sound of movement from his parents' room. Good. They wouldn't wake for another hour, until the sun itself, not its reflected light, was shining in the sky over the valley. Plenty of time for Tenzen to reconnoiter his find.

He moved through the pink-tinged half-light, breathing deeply, savoring the taste of the crisp, fresh air. Somewhere up the valley a yak lowed, the echo rolling gently over the tiny village that Tenzen called home.

Once away from the turf-roofed stone huts, he stopped to pull on his knee boots. Then he began to walk steadily down the rock-strewn mountain road with deceptive speed. Here in the Mitakula Valley, almost twelve thousand feet above the level of the distant sea, it was wise not to run. Even the locals could suffer altitude sickness if their lungs couldn't extract enough oxygen from the thin air.

The high peaks surrounded the valley like a dome, shades of pink beginning to shift to orange as they focused the unseen sun's light on the tiny green scar on the mountainside.

After a few hundred yards the road narrowed, hugging the face of a precipitous cliff. Tenzen adjusted his pace to a slow walk, pressing his back against the sheer rock that rose a thousand feet above him and a thousand feet below into a ravine where mountain torrents roared.

There had been a landslide the previous week, after a winter of heavy rains. A massive section of cliff face had collapsed, dragging tens of thousands of tons of rock into the deep gash below.

Tenzen had gone with his father when the men of the village inspected the damage. Fortunately, this was the village's secondary road, a ribbon of gravel that tortuously followed the contours of the rock face for nearly a dozen miles before it rejoined the main highway. The road was too narrow and dangerous for vehicles of any type. The landslide would mean an added ten-mile hike for any villager heading for the nearest bus stop to find transport to the Low Valleys.

In the wisdom of adulthood, it was decided by the village council that the road could never be repaired. The children were told to steer clear of it, and the matter was forgotten.

But Tenzen had seen something the others hadn't.

In the fractured rock face a dozen feet above the road, he'd seen a small oblong opening. Like a window. He hadn't said anything to his father, because he knew he'd never be permitted to climb up and explore.

The memory of that tiny opening had stayed with him. He'd heard tales of the old Buddhist temples, carved directly into living rock, furnished with paintings and tapestries and golden meditating statues.

He lay in bed each night, dreaming of the hidden vaults and caverns that might lie beyond.

Perhaps . . . Tenzen hardly dared admit the thought.

Perhaps it was even older, a fabulous shrine or royal treasure trove from the ancient days, when long-forgotten warriors roamed these inaccessible valleys.

When Tenzen was a child, his father had told him of a stone ax a neighbor had dug up in his tiny field. A spiral had been incised into one side of the ax blade. On the other a strange beast was carved, like a cross between a man and a bull.

Unable to bear the tension any longer, Tenzen had come back this morning, determined to find out one way or the other what was on the far side of that window.

He rested his hand lightly against a massive boulder that completely filled the road, projecting out over the chasm by a good ten feet, and looked up.

Yes, it was a window. What else could it be, cut so carefully in the rock?

His heartbeat quickened as his eyes scanned up the cliff, searching for handholds. It wasn't going to be easy, but Tenzen had always excelled at climbing. He could do this.

He vaulted up onto the fallen boulder, careful not to snag his boots in the wide vein of rough quartz that ran through it. From this improved angle, he could see that the opening was definitely not natural. As far as Tenzen could tell, the corners were perfect right angles.

Tenzen's hand reached up to grasp the almost invisible

spur of rock that would serve as his first handhold. He'd never felt so excited. He was going to be the first to discover a long-lost secret. What kind of treasure would a man-bull hide away from the world?

"Stop where you are, boy!"

The voice cut sharply through the air and echoed away into the mountains. Tenzen's heart sank. His father.

The boy leaped back down from the boulder, his eyes downcast. His father waited until Tenzen drew near to him, then turned on his heel and stalked back toward the village without saying a word.

Tenzen followed drearily. He had disobeyed his father. He would be punished—extra chores, probably, carrying wooden buckets of water from the stream almost half a mile away.

If only I was a man! he thought fiercely.

He walked into the house under his father's stern glare, careful not to betray the secret smile that had started to play around the corners of his mouth.

It wouldn't be that many years before he *was* a man. Then he'd be able to do whatever he wanted, and no one could stop him.

And on that day Tenzen Wyung would climb the cliff, and scramble through the window, and show the whole world the treasures of the man-bull.

About the Author

ALAN GRANT has been a comic book writer for more than twenty years, handling most major characters from Batman and Lobo to Judge Dredd. He is also the creator of MacAlien. In recent years Alan has worked mainly on computer games and on film and television scripts. His comics work currently encompasses creator-owned material with Simon Bisley, Greg Staples, and Rafa Garres. Alan Grant works in a Gothic mansion in the Scottish border country with his wife and guardian angel, Sue.